A Passion for Consumption

A Passion for Consumption:
The Gothic Novel in America

Anna Sonser

Bowling Green State University Popular Press
Bowling Green, OH 43403

Copyright 2001 © Bowling Green State University Popular Press

        Library of Congress Cataloging-in-Publication Data
Sonser, Anna.
    A passion for consumption : the gothic novel in America / Anna Sonser.
        p.   cm.
    Includes bibliographical references and index.
    ISBN 0-87972-843-4 -- ISBN 0-87972-844-2 (pbk.)
    1. Horror tales, American--History and criticism. 2. Gothic revival
(Literature)--United States. 3. Economics and literature--United States--
History--20th century. 4. American fiction--20th century--History and criti-
cism. 5. Consumption (Economics) in literature. I. Title.

PS374.G68 S66 2001
813'.087209355--dc21

                                                        2001018420

Cover design by Dumm Art

ACKNOWLEDGMENTS

Many thanks to Rick Asals for his patient, pragmatic guidance and to Joseph Adamson who pointed me in the right direction in the first place. For their encouragement and enthusiasm from the outset to the end of this journey, I would like to thank Linda Hutcheon, always generous in her comments, and Magdalene Redekop, always an inspiration.

My heartfelt appreciation goes to Kim Matthew Bryson for his customary steadfast and unstinting support and to the late Dr. Joseph Meszaros whose influence remains with me still.

CONTENTS

INTRODUCTION

I Consume, Therefore I Am

It has become all but aphoristic to declare that America is, in its essence, a consumer culture. A society whose roots reach deeply into a past laden with stories of material consumption, the metanarrative that defines American identity always comes back to social relations that are simultaneously economic and cultural, and where value is objectified, symptomatic of a relentless push "towards the commodification of everything" (Wallerstein 107). Whether we are talking about fleeing the old world for the new, lighting out for the territories, conquering nature, or conjuring dynastic ambitions, the flow, circulation, and expansion of value form the foundation from which social meaning and in turn the "self" is produced.

Yet it is paradoxical that the romance genre, a subset of which is the American gothic novel, provides the skeleton upon which this materialization as social sign hangs. The American romance, as Hawthorne wrote, takes place somewhere between "the Actual and the Imaginary" (*Scarlet Letter* 2197) or in the words of Poe in "Dreamland," "out of space—out of time" (*Collected* 23), in effect a world elsewhere, seemingly disengaged from politics, ideology, and market forces. As Richard Chase was first to argue, nineteenth-century American fiction, which he called romance as distinct from the novel, was characterized by its antimimetic, allegorical, and symbolic structure, an effective strategy for eliding sociopolitical issues. Yet, as Leslie Fiedler argues, "Until the gothic had been discovered, the serious American novel could not begin; as long as that novel lasts, the gothic cannot die" (143). It would seem, conflating both viewpoints, that to write gothic was not mere escapism but escapism of a significant sort from the cultural, economic, and political American landscape. What were these issues that required elision, and were these issues so frightening that their avoidance was masked in gothic terms?

In revisiting the American gothic, the work of Toni Morrison, Joyce Carol Oates, and Anne Rice directly engages the underlying currents that define American culture as one of consumption, a history of social experience that is conducted at the level of the commodity-form. For my purposes their texts, which are both allusive and subversive, serve as a conduit, a way of rereading canonical works to reveal the persistent symptoms of a socio-economic referent for the American gothic. Their

1

novels operate as a palimpsest, revealing the traces of a narrative of commodification and consumption in the American gothic/romance. By commodity, to borrow from John Frow, I mean "any object produced for use or exchange. . . . A generalized abstraction, it loses all its historicity and its social particularity" (132). As Frow elaborates, the relentless pursuit of commodification destroys all activities which are not themselves commodified; production is the indifferent medium for capital valorization (138). The loss of historical and social particularity exacts a price and, therefore, the byproducts of commodification are two-fold. Subjectivity is unstable, transient, fluid, and always contingent on commodity signs and, as such, encourages deviation from social constraint and the responsibilities of morality, ethics, conscience, and other forms of social affiliation. As social relations are transformed into a progressive extension of the commodity-form, there emerges a subtext of violence and horror that materializes as a hallmark of gothic fiction, a violence that is brought to the surface in Morrison's, Oates's, and Rice's revisioning of seminal gothic works. Violence in the American gothic is predicated on the operations of subjectivity defined by commodity signs, a sense of identity that is conferred by the historical ownership of plantation and slaves, a sense of selfhood that is withheld by dispossession as a consequence of race and gender, a subversion of relationships into an economics of reproduction, and finally, a subversion of ontological certainty that destabilizes the concept of subjectivity itself. Morrison, Oates, and Rice cast a light on that which has always lurked, albeit allegorically or symbolically, in earlier gothic texts. Consequently, I would suggest that their project is subversive, simultaneously engaging and disrupting a literary legacy that is anything but "out of space . . . out of time."

A component of this subversion grows from a preoccupation with the erotic and the seductive, a predilection that, according to critics such as Fiedler and Chase, is little in evidence in American gothic fiction. "[T]here is no real sexuality in American life and therefore there cannot very well be any in American art," proposes Fiedler (30), citing Hawthorne's, Poe's, and Faulkner's "chary treatment of woman and of sex" (31). If we choose to accept Georges Bataille's definition of the erotic as nonproductive, excessive, polymorphous, and uncategorizable, then it would stand to reason that the erotic would best stay repressed in a world where the productive, the rational, and the quantifiable—within the context of a frontier psyche—are the guarantors of survival and success. Contrasted with the British gothic tradition, with its bonanza of horrors specifically sexual in nature, the American version is positively tame. Beginning with "Monk" Lewis's experiment, a crude plot rife with enforced seduction, perversion, incest, and multiple rape, the British gothic tradition trades in what Robert Druce refers to as a "continual inter-traffic between pornography, Gothic horror, and anti-Papism, each feeding the other" (238). Further, there is no Lewis, certainly no continental De Sade, and not even a Richardson to be found in American letters, a situation which is not surprising given the political and economic climate in the new world of the eighteenth and nineteenth century. Whereas in England the gothic might be perceived as a vehicle for attack on established moral belief and political/social hierarchy (Druce 235), in America fomenting anti-Catholicism or revolutionary fervor had no place or productive purpose. Freedom of religion prevailed, the revolution was won, and the order of the day was to subdue nature in order to carve out either a fortune or a simple living. In short, anything excessive was necessarily disruptive and best repressed so as to sublimate or redirect energies toward the productive. This tendency is reflected in the literature of the era. The latent eroticism in *The Scarlet Letter* is held in check; we are not privy to the seduction scene that arguably is the catalyst for the entire story. Similarly, we never get too close to the triangle that drives *Absalom, Absalom!,* nor to the sexual escapades that produced the dilemma in the first place. "The Turn of the Screw" revolves around the question of seduction and yet coyly avoids answering the question as to the "secret at Bly" (James, "Turn" 137). Simply stated, and at least on one level, the erotic is disruptive to the process of commodity production and the flow, circulation, and expansion of value. The continuity and productivity of Salem could only be maintained if the Hesters and Dimmesdales adhered to the rules; Sutpen's dynasty was undermined by his own carnal digression, and the veiled and sinister accusations swirling around the children at Bly could only result in disaster, that is, the disruptive and the nonproductive.

Significantly, by the close of the twentieth century, capitalism has discovered a mechanism for the co-optation of the erotic by aligning it with the seductive, the instinctive gratification that marks material consumption. No longer necessarily disruptive, the erotic can be pressed into service, translated into a longing for submission that has been institutionalized by commodity culture. It is no coincidence that the most powerful and lucrative American product and export is culture and entertainment. Potentially transgressive forces (from rock music and hip hop to sexuality) are effectively pulled into the process of exchange-value and commodification. Sex sells cars; rock concerts sell beer; and the black ghetto sells music. The true terror of existence is manifested in the touchstones of commodification, represented by a fragmented subjectivity that only can find recompense in a culture of consumption. The seductive in contemporary gothic narrative underscores the uncertainty and dislocation of the self. Rice's vampires can survive only by consumption of both blood and material goods, and emerge as commodified objective correlatives of late-twentieth-century America. Correspondingly, "the lust for acquisitions" propels the Bellefleur family in a multigenerational quest that is driven by *"insatiable* interest" (Oates 117), a conflation of frenzied desire and material consumption. It is also Beloved's seduction of her mother that crystallizes the connection between taking control of capital (in this case children) and self-definition. In essence, then, my argument situates the American gothic within a market economic mythology.

My preoccupation with the American gothic and material consumption first arose from basic observations about the popularity of gothic fiction in the United States. To some degree, its essential popularity makes it a commodity, an issue that critics have acknowledged only peripherally. As Louis S. Gross has noted in his seminal work *Redefining the American Gothic,* gothic fiction in America, unlike the English gothic, has always been an aspect of mainstream culture. "There is a more central position for the Gothic in American fiction than in any other national literature" (2), he writes, citing a literary pantheon that includes Poe, Hawthorne, Melville, and Faulkner. The definition of "popular" is problematic and itself contingent upon variables as wide-ranging as gender and historical context. Pierre Bourdieu has argued persuasively that popular culture has been aligned with feminine consumption and corrupted femininity. (Only picture Madame Bovary devouring her romances, or young Victorian women being warned against the debasing influence of novel reading.) Further, the allure of the popular can also be perceived as seductive. The texts of Morrison, Oates, and Rice indeed play with the trope of seduction, but they are also seductive in their accessibility, a characteristic which, coming full circle, renders them "popular." Theoretically, the texts of Morrison, Oates, and Rice could be interpreted as a representation of popular gothic literary production in the contemporary United States, moving from high (Morrison), to middle (Oates), and finally, low (Rice). Particularly in an academic arena where the first impulse remains to categorize, qualify, and canonize texts, these distinctions seem rather convenient. Critics with the appropriate cultural capital may weigh in with their pronouncements, their principles of vision and division. Morrison's texts have been deemed complex and important, all the more worthy having survived the unseemly interest of book clubs and television talk-show hosts. Oates's text is more difficult to categorize; densely allusive, yet disturbing in its plunder of violence and the contemporary idiom of celebrity, her work probably should be more popular than it is, both among critics and the general reading public. Finally Rice (the author and her work) is a readily, unmistakably recognizable commodity that happens to be wildly popular if sales figures are to be believed.

Interesting though these distinctions may seem, my project does not intend to furnish a thorough discussion of popular literature via the gothic texts of Morrison, Oates, and Rice. I proceed on the assumption that the novel has always been a solidly bourgeois cultural product, its success due in most part to the rise of Thorstein Veblen's leisured middle class, whose predilections ran more toward entertainment than strict edification. However, rather than mining that particular vein, my focus on Morrison, Oates, and Rice hinges upon the juxtapositions their texts suggest. In essence, their seemingly "popular" gothic novels interrogate a male tradition—from Brockden Brown, Hawthorne, and Poe to Melville, James, and Faulkner—that has been thoroughly canonized. Their interrogation invites James's governess into the same room as Rice's Rowan Mayfair, Faulkner's Sutpens into the company of Oates's Bellefleurs, and Morrison's Sethe into the shadow of Hawthorne's Hester Prynne.

Such mixed company makes for some interesting conversations. As women writers playing with a male tradition, Morrison, Oates, and Rice are critiquing a tradition of exploitation, colonialization, and commodification within the American capitalist experiment. While an aesthetic mode of investigation, their texts serve as a conduit, a way of rereading canonical works to reveal the persistent symptoms of a socio-economic referent for the American gothic. Critics of American gothic move closest to such a socio-historical analysis in their appraisal of the role of women both reading and writing the genre. Ellen Moers's (*Literary Women*) and Juliann Fleenor's (*The Female Gothic*) groundbreaking work in the area proposes that the gothic is schizophrenic in nature, "a fictional rendering of social reality . . . borne of self-fear and self-disgust directed toward the female role, female sexuality, female physiology, and procreation. . . . It reflects a patriarchal paradigm that women are motherless yet fathered and that women are defective because they are not males" (Fleenor 15). Moers's and Fleenor's investigations, which interestingly enough make few distinctions between the American and British gothic tradition, emphasize "social reality" as a contributing factor to the rise of the female gothic. Moreover, they open the door to an evaluation of the contemporary gothic, a segment of the genre largely ignored, or, perhaps worse, relegated to the territory of popular culture, a tendency driven largely by the genre's association with women. Both Kay J. Mussel and Elizabeth Janeway suggest that the contemporary gothic simultaneously gives "the fantasy of adventure but . . . reinforces the validity of the social myths which cause the tensions that lead women to read them in the first place" (Fleenor 66).

I would argue that Morrison, Rice, and Oates depart from this tradition of the sentimental gothic primarily because the heritage they are subverting was generated principally by male writers, such as Brockden Brown, Poe, Hawthorne, and Faulkner as opposed to the British legacy of female writers such as Ann Radcliffe and the Brontë sisters. The exception that I make concerns Mary Shelley's *Frankenstein,* which has particular resonance for the American version of the gothic in its preoccupation with commodification, in terms of reproduction and colonial expansion. The text departs from the Radcliffean, or sentimental, gothic tradition, pushing aside the fleeing woman trope in favor of "masculine figures occupy[ing] its center" (Wolstenholme 37). These masculine figures concentrate the text on disclosing power structures as well as resistance to those structures. Likewise, Morrison's, Oates's, and Rice's revisioning of the texts of Hawthorne and Faulkner, rather than the noncanonical works of Louisa May Alcott or Harriet Jacobs, is playing a far more dangerous game, one that unsettles a national literature by unashamedly emphasizing its gothic, rather than its more acceptable "romantic," nature. Teresa Goddu notes the gothic's mainstream positioning and the critical fervor to provide the American literary canon with a more respectable foundation. Beginning with Fiedler's statement that American literature might be "embarrassingly, a gothic fiction" (6), critics have located the origins of the American novel in the romance genre. Critics such as Richard Chase have safely followed Hawthorne's use of the term in order to define a respectable canon, burying the gothic beneath the headstone of melodrama.

The term has taken on a general meaning beyond the Mrs. Radcliffe kind of thing and is often used rather more loosely to suggest violence, mysteries, improbabilities, morbid passion. . . . It is a useful word but since, in its general reference, it becomes confused with "melodrama," it seems sensible to use "melodrama." (37)

Further, as Nina Baym has noted, before 1860 the term romance suggested qualities usually associated with the gothic, including supernatural or marvelous events (437). Following in this tradition, David Reynolds in *Beneath the American Renaissance* uses the term "Dark Adventure" to describe gothic texts by substituting "dark" for "gothic" as the modifier of romance. This darkness, according to Goddu, has come to signify the profound in American literary criticism, and is carefully stripped bare of any racial connotations. Darkness relates to the mystical and metaphysical, as in the "deep far-away things" in Hawthorne (7). Similarly, Harry Levin also reads this darkness as a vision of evil representing the introspective mind in a manner similar to Fiedler's emphasis on the symbolism of psychological and moral blackness (28).

At one level, Morrison, Rice, and Oates are upending the old critical argument that the "high" or serious form of romance/gothic is written by men while the subliterary, sentimental, and popular gothic is purveyed by women. Their texts question these interpretive habits, and consequently, by essentially rewriting canonical texts, Morrison, Rice, and Oates recuperate and validate the gothic genre by blurring the boundaries of the marginal and the mainstream. In doing so they take the recuperation one step further by engaging directly the underlying currents that define American culture as a culture of consumption, currents that are reflected within the gothic genre as a history of social experience conducted at the level of the commodity-form.

Morrison, Rice, and Oates also play with another critical tradition, one that has marginalized the gothic as a regional genre, a substratum that allegedly belongs to the South in all its racially transgressive infamy and ignores the contributions of such Northerners as Brockden Brown, Hawthorne, Melville, and James. According to Goddu, Joan Dayan, and Harry Levin, the oppositional identity of the South operates as the "dark" Other, the repository of corrupt impulses in which the bright new world of America wanted no part. Consequently, it is not surprising that in *The Power of Blackness*, Levin suggests that the appropriate subject for the southern writer is southern gothic and slavery (233). Later, Fiedler equated the images of the gothic's blackness with the South when he wrote about Poe that "it is, indeed, to be expected that our first eminent southern author discover that the proper subject for American gothic is the black man, from whose shadow we have not yet emerged" (397). Thirty years later in her critical work *Playing in the Dark*, Toni Morrison confirms this viewpoint with one essential difference, insisting on the restoration of race to the whole of American literature, suggesting that the term for this haunting is "gothic" (35, 36). The connection between the African American experience and gothic iconography is clear: possession, entrapment, imprisonment, and familial transgressions (Goddu 73). Morrison's argument that the specter of slavery, and along with it the gothic, cannot be contained within the South is a contention that has particular resonance for the genre as a whole, allowing it to escape from its regionalized and marginalized status as idiosyncratic cousin to romance. Indeed, Morrison, Rice, and Oates cannot be called regional in any respect and their texts are an amalgam of both northern and southern sensibilities, allusive in a way that is eclectic and parodic, that is, postmodern.

Indeed, it is the postmodern element that most defines their version of the contemporary gothic, and which, I would argue, makes the connection between the gothic impulse and commodity culture clear. At a basic level, as Theo D'haen has written, the gothic is characterized by a common set of techniques and conventions that could as easily apply to a description of the postmodern: self-reflexivity, metafiction, eclecticism, multiplicity, intertextuality, parody, pastiche, dissolution of character and narrative, erasure of boundaries, and the destabilization of the reader (283). However, as D'haen notes, "only fantastic postmodernism can speak of what its postmodern counterparts must needs be silent: of what it means to be the dominant culture's, or late capitalism's 'other'" (294). He maintains that in the original gothic novel, the dominant cultural order is ultimately reconfirmed, that is, the supernatural is explained away whereas the postmodern gothic does not allow for such rational resolution. Instead of being reduced to the dominant culture's version of "reality," the postmodern gothic creates alternate realities that challenge the dominant cultural order. D'haen picks up threads of Rosemary Jackson's and Linda Hutcheon's arguments that the fantastic in literature has both a subversive effect while often and contradictorily upholding the status quo. For Jackson, "fantasy characteristically attempts to compensate for a lack resulting from cultural constraints: it is a literature of desire, which seeks that which is experienced as absence and loss" (3). Alternatively, Hutcheon categorizes fantasy as the other side of realism representing a parallel literary tradition, in a vein similar to Goddu and Baym. I prefer to amalgamate several of these perspectives in my reading of Morrison, Rice, and Oates and draw upon the postmodern as introducing the "'unreal' as a meaningful category" (D'haen 289), a claim both to representation and to meaning(s).

The title of my investigation refers to three aspects of the contemporary gothic that fall variably under the rubric of postmodernism: subversion, seduction, and commodification. The texts of Morrison, Rice, and Oates are simultaneously allusive and subversive, drawing attention not only to the gothic as a historical and political construct but also to the historical and political construct of the self. By repositioning certain canonical texts, their novels reveal the gothic landscape of subjectivity as defined by socio-economic and political imperatives. An aspect of this subversion emerges from a preoccupation with the seductive, an eroticism that is simultaneously subversive and complicit. From Hawthorne and Poe to James, the concept of seduction is implicated in what Jean Baudrillard would refer to as the semiological code of capitalism, on the one hand challenging the principles of production and consumption, that is, the expansionist, materialist impulses predicated on commodification. On the other hand, the erotic is also implicated in preserving the principles of production by satisfying desire within a culture of consumption.

This particular reading of the contemporary American gothic is informed by critics such as Lacan, Bataille, and Baudrillard, whose theories straddle both the poststructural and the postmodern in such a way as to illuminate social and cultural phenomena pivotal to a reappraisal of the gothic genre. Jacques Lacan's ideas about language as a manifestation of structures in the unconscious have, dare I say it, a practical application, shedding light upon subjectivity as defined by socio-economic and political imperatives. More concretely, Lacanian theories outline the relationship between discursive practices and power (economic) in society, tracing that nexus to reveal the language of ownership, the agency of interpretation and control. His phallocentrist perspective conveniently suggests alternative critical perspectives precisely because it articulates presumptions that are socially dominant but which have largely remained unarticulated.

The concept of subjectivity, and hence Lacan's applicability to this project, is critical to an understanding of how the "self" in American gothic literary production is produced. Baudrillard adds to that understanding with the thesis that the entire history of consciousness and ethics *is* the history of the political economy of the subject. While Lacan focuses on the production of the subject through language, Baudrillard pursues the idea of an ever-proliferating world of objects and its hegemony over the subject. Hence, subjects and objects reverse roles. Influenced by the work of Georges Bataille, Baudrillard interprets pre-capitalist societies as being governed by a logic of symbolic exchange wherein objects are exchanged in rituals that value waste and expenditure and are indifferent to production. Conversely, capitalist societies, according to Baudrillard, reduce symbolic practices to the quantitative nexus of use- and exchange-value. Consequently, in the Baudrillardian sense, the gothic genre can be interpreted as transgressive as it privileges expenditure, sacrifice, and destruction as fundamental principles antithetical to a materialist process of production.

However, the evolution to a more mature market economy has resulted in the means to co-opt these counterproductive tendencies by absorbing them into the logic of the system. For example, the initial primacy of seduction over production (endlessly deferring the goals of production) is overturned in the postmodern, heralded by the collapse of the subject into seduction itself. This "cool seduction," according to Baudrillard, is characteristic of the postmodern age, in which the subject is

merely a point on a network, unmoored in a world of proliferating
objects that threatens to destabilize or even subsume it. Explained more
directly by Wolfgang Haug, "the essence of the commodity-body as a
use-value, is shifting away from being simply 'an external object, a thing
which through its [physical] qualities satisfies human needs of whatever
kind' [Marx, *Capital*, vol. i] towards an increasing emphasis on representation and symbolism in the commodity." According to Haug, the balance shifts from an unmediated, materially purposeful use-value to
thoughts and associations, "which one links to the commodity or
assumes that others must associate with it" (97). Ultimately, seduction is
no longer disruptive but pressed into service, a symptom of which is the
instant gratification that marks material consumption and maintains the
cycle of productivity.

Lacan and Baudrillard have proved useful in this inquiry, directly
and indirectly helping to raise questions about the mechanisms behind
the gothic genre in America. How and why is subjectivity determined by
and contingent upon commodity signs? Why the reluctance to historicize
the genre? What of the socio-economic implications dressed in the form
of gothic décor? How do contemporary gothic texts rewrite, or perhaps
even redress, the past? My objective is to look again at certain canonical
texts and resituate them in a context that cracks open old ways of reading them. I then proceed to review more recent texts that seem to be
located in the space made by those breaks, enriching the response to
novels that might otherwise be regarded as one dimensional within a
contemporary popular culture context.

The first section of this book takes up the theme of subversion. On
the most basic level, Morrison's, Oates's, and Rice's texts are subversive
in that they play with canonical texts, the result of which is a repositioning, or at least a reevaluation, both of traditional and contemporary
gothic novels. This reorientation reveals how subjectivity is produced
through socioeconomic and political contexts, the self as contingent
upon commodity signs. The juxtaposition of *Beloved* and *The Scarlet
Letter* in the first chapter highlights the discursive practices that produced the categories of race, gender, and motherhood. In a further elaboration of the categories of gender and motherhood, and their
socio-economic implications, the discussion of *Beloved* and *Frankenstein* in chapter 2 addresses the rift of "motherlessness" in the gothic by
empowering the maternal trope, constituting it as a figure of agency in a
genre traditionally interpreted as hostile to such a role. It also discloses
the gothic's preoccupation with commodification, in terms of reproduction and colonial expansion wherein the social construct of womanhood,
black or white, was predicated on a reproductive function largely con-

trolled and manipulated by the perceived exigencies of colonialization and economic expansion. And what are the ramifications of such a monstrously constructed subjectivity?

In its evaluation of *The Witching Hour, Frankenstein, Wieland,* "Ligeia," and "The Turn of the Screw," chapter 3 addresses that question, reworking the mix to reveal how the subversion of ontological certainty destabilizes the concept of subjectivity. Rice's text invigorates the symbolism and allegories of the gothic tradition by stripping away the distortions informing our own readings of the genre, accentuating epistemological conflicts underlying attempts to constitute subjectivity and, in turn, confer and validate meaning. The final chapter in this section, juxtaposing *Bellefleur* and *Absalom, Absalom!,* similarly exposes the false hierarchical links through which the "real" is read. Oates's text is a critique of America, a parodic recasting of Faulkner, revealing the mythology and distortions that not only inform our own readings of that culture but also define economic and social relations in America. What begins ostensibly as a Faulknerian story of patriarchs, dynasties, and grand designs covertly ends with single women, multiple voices, and alternative plots.

A corollary of subversion, in the hands of Morrison, Oates, and Rice, is the concept of seduction which, I suggest in the second section of this book, has always haunted the American gothic novel, albeit indirectly, as an influence that is disruptive to the process of commodity production and the circulation of value. More concretely, seduction challenges the principles of production and consumption, reducing that which is gendered masculine, that is, the expansionist, materialist impulses predicated upon commodification. The texts of Morrison, Oates, and Rice continue their subversive trek by retracing the patterns of repression of the erotic in canonical works. The first chapter in this section deliberately focuses on two canonical texts, *The Scarlet Letter* and "The Turn of the Screw," to foreground this pattern of repression. If as, according to Baudrillard, seduction is the mastery of the world of symbolic exchanges and a transgression of the productivist code, then the texts of Hawthorne and James allow for a tentative acknowledgment of the erotic as nonproductive and therefore dangerous.

What arises from the subtexts of Hawthorne and James carries over into Morrison's, Oates's, and Rice's revisioning of the gothic novel, highlighting an eroticism that is at once latent and manifest, simultaneously subversive and complicit. The second chapter of this section takes up the patterns of dominance and submission, subject and object, established in the texts of Hawthorne and James and sees them reconfigured in *Interview with the Vampire* and "The Jolly Corner." It is seduction, specular seduction, that is the guarantor of subjectivity in both texts, symptomatic of a long line of vampiric seductions (consumptions) that are socially, economically, and historically inscribed in American culture. The seductive element in gothic narrative underscores the uncertainty and dislocation of the self which can only find temporary surcease in a conflation of desire and material consumption. The consumption of blood, metaphorically and figuratively, is implicated in the construction of subjectivity. In the final chapter of this section, the texts of Poe, Oates, and Morrison reveal how seduction is closely allied to a violence that is predicated on the operations of subjectivity as defined by commodity signs—conferred by the ownership of slaves and withheld as a consequence of race and gender.

What is the overarching premise to which the themes of subversion and seduction correspond? The last section of this project explores subversion as it concerns itself with seduction on two levels, one which marks it as disruptive of the process of commodity production and circulation of value and the other that implicates it within the semiological code of capitalism. The result is a continuum that reveals a cultural process increasingly dominated by the consumption of signs themselves. The erotic/seductive has come full circle, from being dangerous to productivity, and therefore repressed, to being co-opted and assimilated within capitalism in the form of instant gratification that is consumption. The first chapter in this section pairs *Bellefleur* and *The House of the Seven Gables,* revealing a tropic structure that conflates the images of consumption and eroticism. To borrow from Baudrillard, we are what we consume, and American gothic can be read as a continuum of feeding desire within a culture of consumption. The subsequent chapter, drawing on the concepts of appropriation and value in *Beloved* and "Benito Cereno," depicts a world delineated by the arbitrary and dangerous constituents of ownership, an arena in which the dangers and the violence of possession are played out both in gothic and realist terms. The logical extreme of this continuum, the collusion between seduction and consumption, is disclosed in the apotheosis that is the logic of late capitalism—desire institutionalized by commodity culture. In the last chapter of this book, an analysis of Rice's *The Vampire Lestat* traces the current evolution of the gothic genre which began its career as depicting the patently unreal only to emerge in *Lestat* as a close approximation of reality, the reality as simulacrum that pervades postmodernity—where the artificial is produced as an effect from the models and codes that precede it.

In the end, the essential horror of the gothic is not its goblins and vampires but its latent power to address the disenchanted world of production and the commodification of the social. At the conclusion of this past century, this disenchantment is reflected in the proliferation of cultural images and signs that dissolve individuals and social groups into a hyperreality dominated by an indeterminate play of simulations (or simulacrum). The power of Morrison's, Oates's, and Rice's texts lies not with any abstract considerations of aesthetic assessments but with their ability to disclose a terrain of social and cultural experience of material consumption, the metanarrative that defines American identity.

Perhaps the unconscious recognition of that metanarrative is the key to the American gothic's continuing appeal. In other words, it is popular precisely because it speaks to the commodification/consumption paradigm that has formed American cultural experience. From its first glimmers in the eighteenth century, gothic has always commanded the interest and attention of mainstream, mainly middle-class readers. Within that context, little has changed, as gothic novels from Stephen King and Anne Rice to Toni Morrison catapult to the top of the bestseller lists and movie listings. Literature, after all, paradoxically reproduces and often resists the ideology in which it is inscribed. In that regard, the gothic genre has come full circle, reflecting a commodification that is self-reflexively complete.

I. SUBVERSION

"Let the black flower blossom as it may!"
—Hawthorne, *The Scarlet Letter*

To be subversive is to turn upside down, to delve into corners that have remained undisturbed for too long. To some degree, the texts of Toni Morrison, Joyce Carol Oates, and Anne Rice borrow such trouble, interrogating the cultural framework that defines the traditional gothic novel by offering their own variations on the gothic theme. Their version of the "black flower," their interpretation of the gothic, is more than just a revisioning; it is also a repositioning of both the traditional and contemporary gothic text.

This repositioning or reorientation focuses primarily on how subjectivity is produced through socio-economic and political contexts. As William Patrick Day has argued, the traditional gothic has been obsessed with the "fable of identity fragmented and destroyed beyond repair, a fable of the impossibility of identity" (6). This disintegration of self, according to Day, is manifested in an absorption with doubled and divided characters as well as with altered states of consciousness. It is this preoccupation with subject formation in the traditional gothic context that finds renewed treatment in the work of Morrison, Oates, and Rice; it is a manipulation, however, that both appropriates and subverts certain of the genre's discursive practices. Theirs is an intertextuality that draws attention not only to the gothic as a historical and political construct but also to the historical and political construct of the self.

What we have, then, is a revealing interanimation of texts that underscores the process of subjectivity as unstable, transient, and contingent on commodity signs. Thus, through *The Scarlet Letter, Frankenstein,* "The Turn of the Screw," and *Absalom, Absalom!,* the texts of Morrison, Oates, and Rice invigorate the symbolism and allegories of the gothic tradition by stripping away the distortions that inform our own readings of the genre. *Beloved*'s juxtaposition with *The Scarlet Letter* and *Frankenstein* allows for a rewriting of the discursive practices that produced the categories of race, gender, and motherhood. Rice's *Witching Hour* and James's "Turn of the Screw" together resonate with the epistemological conflicts underlying attempts to constitute subjectivity and, in turn, validate meaning. Finally, *Bellefleur*'s parodic echoes of

14

Absalom, Absalom! are a self-reflexive amplification of the gothic genre's tropes which allows for an alternative literary legacy, that is, subjectivity not as monologic but reflected in "a tale still being told—in many voices—and nowhere near its conclusion" (Bellefleur 562). These are also stories reflecting mother-daughter relationships, drawing on the ambivalence that Juliann Fleenor has isolated as the drama of procreation, which leads to "constriction not freedom, madness not sanity, and monsters not symmetry" (16). However, I would suggest that a rereading of both canonical and contemporary gothic texts reveals that the maternal figure has the power to break through these constrictions when the assault is contextualized as rebellion against a society of commodification.

In effect, these texts explore the gothic landscape of subjectivity as defined by socio-economic and political imperatives: identity that is conferred by the ownership of slaves; subjectivity withheld by dispossession as a consequence of race and gender; the subversion of relationships into an economics of reproduction; and the subversion of ontological certainty that destabilizes the idea of subjectivity and the self.

1

THE GHOST IN THE MACHINE:
BELOVED AND *THE SCARLET LETTER*

In *Black Literature and Literary Theory,* Henry Louis Gates, Jr. contends that the black critical essay necessarily refers to two contexts and two traditions, the Western and the black (8). As a critical mode, this supposition proves important in examining the gothic genre and its potential for the destabilization of traditional readings of the literary canon. *Beloved* reveals the intertextual practices which offer both "a matrix of literary discontinuities" (Spillers 3) and an alternative literary legacy. Rewriting or revisioning the American canon through inscriptions of race involves a radical redefinition of the subjectivity and experience of "blackness" traditionally positioned opposite, outside, or next to the social dominant of whiteness in modes of cultural expression. Why else begin here with a reappraisal of the gothic? As Toni Morrison has argued in her critical work *Playing in the Dark: Whiteness and the Literary Imagination,* realities, rather than simply fantasies, of race influence American literature as a whole and, more particularly, the gothic strain that runs through it. Disagreeing with Herman Melville's contention that American literature does "derive its force from its appeals to that Calvinistic sense of Innate Depravity and Original sin," ("Hawthorne and His Mosses" 243), and instead arguing its derivation from social exigencies, Morrison suggests that issues of race be reinstated in American literature. The dynamic in her novel *Beloved* is located in such an act of revision, comprising simultaneously the canonical and the subversive by invoking "the ghost in the machine . . . those active but unsummoned presences" of blackness in canonical American literature that can "distort the workings of the machine and can also make it work" (*Playing* 11).

In the case of *Beloved,* Morrison's summons invokes more than the ghost of a young black woman, conjuring as well the specter of Hawthorne's *The Scarlet Letter,* traditionally considered the earliest fictional representation of the subject in American society. Initially, the rationale behind this intertextual revision remains at best obscure and at worst contradictory. Why position *Beloved* alongside Hawthorne's "classic" when the surfaces of the two narratives are chasms apart in terms of ideology, genre structure, voice, and plot? Yet what appears as incongruity may also serve to disturb traditional interpretations of the gothic and its place in the canon. As one of America's foundational narratives, *The Scarlet Letter* can be re-read through Morrison's text as a site of cultural contradiction, one that yields "a narrative incoherence" and "the instabilities of America's self-representations" (Goddu 10). To begin quite rudimentarily, both novels examine the lives of women who have broken a law or taboo, who have been "marked" and ostracized by their respective societies. Hawthorne's and Morrison's texts are also historical novels, dealing in the idiom of romance formerly and the gothic latterly, involving mothers and daughters, ghosts and witches, oppression and judgment, communities and exorcisms. Most significantly, both novels trace the intersection of subjectivity and social power, with *Beloved* a paradigmatic shift removed from *The Scarlet Letter*'s privileging of the consciously elaborated idea of Western and, needless to say, white, individualism.

Socially and historically produced representations of subjectivity emerge in both Hawthorne's and Morrison's texts through the territory of genre. As it is, defining American gothic presents considerable difficulties given that it is "so shadowy and nebulous a genre, as difficult to define as any gothic ghost. . . . it cannot be seen in abstraction from the other literary forms from whose graves it arises . . . assembled out of the bits and pieces of the past" (Kilgour, *Rise* 3-4). Worse still, it is associated with the popular, the formulaic, and the feminine, masquerading as a cruder version of the romance, which traditionally serves as the bulwark of the American literary canon. As Morris Dickstein notes, "gothic novels . . . are among the bastard children of literature" (60), while David Reynolds reveals in *Beneath the American Renaissance* how the gothic and the popular are often conflated. Given the genre's unsavory reputation, it stands to reason that the romantic and the gothic remain in their separate corners. As Teresa A. Goddu has argued, critics are anxious to provide the literary canon with a respectable foundation by choosing to have the category of romance dominate critical discourse "while the term *gothic* is almost fully repressed" (6). There must be no miscegenation, as the goal remains "a clean canon" (6). This fear of contamination might also mask a fear of defamiliarization, a strategy that could conceivably yield alternative histories and an alternative canon. In other words, re-reading *The Scarlet Letter* as a gothic rather than a romantic text, or reading it through *Beloved*, challenges literary conventions and critical perspectives governing not only genre but also ideas about the construction of subjectivity. In the romance tradition, for example, Hester is anointed as the first American heroine, given that she symbolizes the concept of the individual in pursuit of an idealized quest. However, she can also be read through the prism of the gothic, as an alienated, solitary individual isolated from a social context and threatened by unseen and possibly malevolent forces. When she emerges from the prison door in the marketplace scene, she is "marked," that is, separate and distinguished from the mass of Puritans, by the "A" emblazoned on her breast. She is both subject and aberration, in effect, heroically challenging authority for the better in a way that champions traditional American utopic rhetoric while simultaneously reflecting a cultural dissidence dangerously disruptive both to herself and to the established order of the Puritan community.

The conflation of subjectivity and aberration is a persistent theme in the canon of American literature, constituted in the interrelationship between subject and object, or more precisely, subject and Other. As Tony Tanner and Jerry Bryant have documented, American canonical literature is essentially anti-authoritarian, concerned with the contest between the idealistic hero and the corrupt society surrounding him. The idealistic hero is, in effect, a misfit or outcast. Conversely, alienation is an aspect of the "normal state" of the African American in Western society, a condition manifested in Morrison's text as a complex stream of impressions, recollections, shifting pronouns, and fragmented identities. In introducing a haunted house "packed to its rafters with some dead Negro's grief" (5), Morrison claims a derivative of the traditional gothic with an imagined historical novel in which the supernatural functions as history (Ferguson 113). The genre offers the idiom to express what has remained inexpressible through a ghost story while simultaneously dismantling hegemonic narrative processes. The rhetorical and symbolic processes integral to the gothic, the disregard for "natural" and physical laws, serve both as a challenge to the realist aesthetic and as an alternate interpretive space for the interrogation of racial identity. Unlike *The Scarlet Letter*, in which the construct for subjectivity emerges from a rift in society, *Beloved* explores the difficulties of racial subject formation in an environment denied social cohesion or continuity through the institution of slavery, that is, through the commodification of human beings. Sethe's transgression, infanticide, results in banishment from her own nascent, racially defined black community. While as outcast Hester represents the particularity necessary to self-definition within a white, patriarchal system, Sethe, as a trespasser among the human race, is denied the fragile African-American social and cultural framework without which already unstable boundaries of subjectivity further disintegrate. As Linda Anderson has written, *Beloved* is an "attempt to imagine a different relationship between subjectivity and history" (137).

A gothic reading of *The Scarlet Letter* and *Beloved* allows for the "hauntings" which propel Hawthorne's and Morrison's texts into controversial territory, intensifying the painful histories which mark the illusory boundaries between self and society. Hawthorne's "Custom-House" preface establishes the narrator's desire to expiate familial guilt, to exorcise "the figure of that first ancestor. . . . It still haunts me . . . a bitter persecutor" (2181). As the narrator is soon to remark, "the past was not dead" (2192), "the ghostly hand" and "the ghostly voice" (2195) exhort him to tell the story of Mistress Prynne in an act of remembering through the "tarnished mirror" (2196) of the imagination. All but invoking specters, the narrator declares, "Ghosts might enter here, without affrighting us" (2197).

The haze of memory, a brooding mist (2202), indeed the spectral, is integral to the novel in its representation of subjectivity as a social construct, as the following passage concerning Hester's banishment discloses:

Every gesture, every word, and even the silence of those with whom she came in contact, implied, and often expressed, that she was banished, and as much alone as if she inhabited another sphere. . . . She stood apart from mortal interests, yet close beside them, like a ghost that revisits the familiar fireside, and can no longer make itself seen or felt; no more smile with the household joy, nor mourn with the kindred sorrow; or, should it succeed in manifesting its forbidden sympathy, awakening only terror and horrible repugnance. (2222)

Hawthorne's narrator's "haunting" by a Puritan ancestor has led to the story of the "ghost-like" (2219) outsider, a remembering that is intended to redress the injustice of a repressive society whose national rhetoric has promised freedom from oppression. Similarly, Morrison has acknowledged that she based *Beloved* on a historical event, that the novel is an imaginative reworking of the life of Margaret Garner,. who escaped Kentucky "with four children. . . . she tried to kill the children when she was caught. She killed one of them just as in the novel" (Anderson 137). As many critics have elaborated, *Beloved* concerns itself with "rememory" (36), the 60 million and more disremembered and the unaccounted for grafted upon the ghost of a murdered baby girl. Analogous to Hester Prynne's position vis-à-vis the Puritan community, Beloved's haunting of the house on 124 Bluestone underscores her mother's alienation from both a racist society and her own community, her crime awakening "terror and horrible repugnance" and the "condemnation Negroes heaped on them; the assumption that the haunting was done by an evil thing looking for more" (37).

The "evil thing" in both *Beloved* and *The Scarlet Letter* is predicated on Sethe and Hester's hard-won decisions to live outside social codes in an attempt at self-definition. Pearl is the child purchased at great price (2224), as is Beloved, her name, "the one word that mattered" (5), purchased with Sethe's body. Both women assert a power that is terrifying in its ability to undermine patriarchal structures, the ability to name, to destroy, and to legitimize. By breaking the taboo associated with the construct of motherhood, Sethe and Hester confront and challenge the patriarchal and racist frameworks of their respective societies. The concept of naming is important here on several levels in terms of the Lacanian socio-symbolic contract. According to Jacques Lacan, the Name-of-the-Father is both the source of authority, the signifier of that authority, and the gateway to the symbolic, a governing law in the dual function of restricting and prescribing. It is a substitute for the power of language and culture to rule through the threat of foreclosure and, thereby, establish boundaries for law, desire, gender, and difference. By refusing to reveal, quite literally, the name of Pearl's father, Hester denies the Name-of-the-Father and inclusion in the symbolic order; she lives outside the Puritan community on the outskirts of civilization. Similarly, by refusing to allow her children to be repossessed as slaves by schoolteacher and his sons, Sethe gains not only physical freedom but also the power to possess and name her own dead Beloved. However, as with Hester, her act consigns her to the margins of her community.

Beloved's name inscribed upon a headstone and Hester's "ignominious letter [to] be engraved upon her tombstone" (2211) signify a space outside the symbolic, a pre-Oedipal imaginary expanse characterized by a "concentrated language of elision . . . in which a fluid sense of 'identity', 'self' and 'body' . . . cannot be pressed into language" (Ferguson 117). As several critics have demonstrated, Morrison's representation of women's interior voices, through the use of images, shifting pronouns, and fragmented syntax, indicates a semiotic space through which unspeakable thoughts are left unspoken and yet, paradoxically, are proclaimed. This discourse is most closely distilled through the haunting device that governs *Beloved*, through the voice or voices filtered through the supernatural. In *The Scarlet Letter* Pearl is also perceived as a supernatural creature, "the living hieroglyphic" (2286), embodiment of the scarlet letter on her mother's breast and, by extension, on her mother's tombstone (2315). Dancing upon a grave, "perhaps of Isaac Johnson himself" (2248), and fashioning a letter from the burrs surrounding the tomb, Pearl mocks a representative of the Puritan patriarchy, setting herself apart and outside the symbolic order. Accordingly, she is alternately described as an elf child, a demon offspring (2229), unearthly (2227), in essence "a creature that had nothing in common with a bygone and buried generation, nor owned herself akin to it. It was as if she had been made afresh, out of new elements . . . a law unto herself" (2249). Pearl is denied an earthly father while vigorously declaring that she has "no Heavenly Father" (2229). Similarly, Beloved's father and brothers are as ineffectual as Dimmesdale but, more important, Beloved has evaded enslavement by escaping appropriation and naming by schoolteacher. Paul D asks Beloved whether she uses a last name: "'Last?' She seemed puzzled. Then 'No,' and she spelled it for them, slowly as though the letters were being formed as she spoke them" (52). Outside the symbolic order, the women at 124 Bluestone communicate with a "code they used among themselves," one that Paul D "could not break. . . . They were a family somehow and he was not the head of it" (132). The code reinforces the idea of semiotic discourse, a fluctuating sense of separation and connection manifested by Sethe and Beloved's symbiotic relationship. Paul D's presence is threatening precisely because he represents a paternal figure and the possibility of Sethe's reintegration into the symbolic order. "Make him go away" (133), Beloved tells Denver as she endeavors to maintain an illusory sense of self:

Pieces of her would drop maybe one at a time, maybe all at once. Or on one of those mornings before Denver woke and after Sethe left she would fly apart. It is difficult keeping her head on her neck, her legs attached to her hips when she is by herself. (133)

Beloved must seduce Paul D in order to circumvent the possibility of his assuming a paternal position in the household and to forestall the possibility of Sethe's return to her community. Consequently, without Paul D and alone with Beloved and Denver, Sethe's sense of dissolution grows, her identity merging with her daughter's as her distance from the symbolic increases: "Paul D convinced me there was a world out there and that I could live in it. Should have known better. . . . Whatever is going on outside my door ain't for me. The world is in this room. This here's all there is and all there needs to be" (182-83).

Paul D, representative of a social order where authentic identity is an impossibility, constituted by competing and often contradictory meanings imposed by a sexist and racist system, poses both an opportunity and a threat to Sethe. Beloved, however, remains the precarious foundation upon which the delusory hope of pre-Oedipal, primary wholeness is based, and through which subjectivity as process rather than fixed identity must progress. She is the touchstone, the reminder of all that which Sethe and her ancestors have lost in terms of maternal, familial, and cultural continuity. Yet ironically, she is the story that cannot be passed on precisely because she connotes alienation and disconnection from the fragile fabric of the African American community, a dissociation which is born of resistance to sexist and racist definitions or constructs of selfhood.

This resistance is also manifested in *The Scarlet Letter* in the form of Pearl as the embodiment of the scarlet letter and, therefore, lawlessness. Outside the symbolic living with her mother in a "lonesome dwelling" over which was cast "a mystic shadow of suspicion" (2220), her role is similar to Beloved's, serving as a constant reminder of her mother's transgression. She allows Hester neither to forget, to remove the letter, nor to reconnect with the Puritan community. Her strange remoteness and intangibility, her "preternatural activity," and her "shrill, incoherent exclamations . . . so much the sound of a witch's anathemas in some unknown tongue" signify a pre-Oedipal semiotic toward which Hester is drawn as "mother and daughter stood together in the same circle of seclusion from human society" (2227). Pearl is almost as much a specter as Beloved "hovering in the air and might vanish, like a glimmering light that comes we know not whence, and goes we know not whither" (2226). Hester feels compelled to "snatch her to her bosom . . . not so much from overflowing love, as to assure herself that Pearl was flesh and blood, and not utterly delusive" (2226). Both Pearl and Beloved prove to be necessary, though illusory figures in terms of the genesis of subjectivity, their metaphorical exorcisms reestablishing, albeit in different ways, the boundaries for law, desire, gender, and difference.

In terms of the Lacanian symbolic contract, the laws of language are governed by the Name-of-the-Father as the signifier of authority which simultaneously sustains desire and its prohibition; in essence, it is the linguistic phenomenon which operates to socialize the subject. Dimmesdale's acknowledgment of paternity (and Pearl's exorcism, as it were) takes place upon the scaffold in the marketplace in the presence of the Puritan community, a scene of shared recognition sealed with a kiss at which "a spell was broken" (2311). Pearl is transformed from a "wild infant" into a child destined to live her life among humanity, her errand as messenger of anguish to her mother, and society, fulfilled. As emissary of anguish and embodiment of the scarlet letter, Pearl represents the problematics of the production of meaning in relation to the linguistic subject. In other words, through the dialectical struggle between the semiotic and the symbolic, the meaning of the letter "A" is transformed in Hawthorne's text, reflected and duplicated almost endlessly and ultimately evading the fixed meaning—adulteress—intended by the Puritan patriarchy.

Moreover, Beloved's exorcism also involves the crucible of the symbolic law involving, indirectly, Paul D, who initially banishes the baby ghost, and ultimately a community of women and a white man, Edward Bodwin, whose intercessions disclose the structures of meaning and subject formation in the symbolic. In the interim, however, Sethe and Hester have challenged the unidimensional, patriarchal model of language and self, their transitional subject positions the product of a dialectical process, a sliding between the semiotic and symbolic poles. It is important to note that after their exorcisms, Beloved and Pearl do not simply vanish but rather fragment into traces, the mark of the absence of an anterior presence, a reminder that nothing is ever fully present in the language of the symbolic. Pearl's fate is a matter of conjecture, her subjectivity a series of traces that mediate between presence and absence: a shapeless piece of driftwood, letters bearing an armorial seal, "trifles, too, little ornaments, beautiful tokens of a continual remembrance" (2314).

Correspondingly, Beloved dissolves into a succession of impressions: the rustle of a skirt, the photograph of a close friend, footprints that "come and go, come and go" (275). The footprint as trace mediates between presence and absence, the idea that no sign is complete in itself but leads to another indefinitely. In other words, subjectivity is a fragmented construct existing only through repeated displacements. Hester is neither Puritan nor adulteress, but rather a subject in process whose own meanings and self-definitions emerge through disruptions to the symbolic or paternal order. As a consequence, the meanings for the scarlet letter multiply, moving from "adulteress" to "able," "admirable," "angel," "artist," and so on, suggesting that the "A," that is, the subject, is the source for an indefinite and boundless array of interpretations. Similarly, Sethe refuses the sexist and racist definitions or interpretations set out for her by the institution of slavery, by the obscene measurements of schoolteacher, by orthodox conceptions of family, woman, and motherhood. By reconnecting with the traces of disremembered history through Beloved, she begins to deal with the profound fragmentation of black female identity and experience by uniting the severed bonds of a matrilineal line. However, as a divided speaking subject, marginalized as a woman and dispossessed as a consequence of race, Sethe's place in the framework of a white, patriarchal society (symbolic) leaves her with a shifting and self-contradictory sense of self. "You your best thing, Sethe. You are," Paul D tells her, to which she can only question, "Me? Me?" (273).

While language comprises both the semiotic and the symbolic, Western patriarchal society has always privileged the latter, positing a unitary model of language through which the self must be constituted. The pre- or trans-linguistic modality of inscription undermines the idea of fixed meanings or stable identity, and, more concretely, it challenges hegemonic social and cultural practices. In effect, Morrison's and Hawthorne's texts concern the intersection of subjectivity and social power at which junction occurs the ability to interpret and to control. Consequently, the mark—the scarlet letter in the case of Hawthorne and the scar in the case of Morrison—concentrates the debate over meaning as a matter of arbitrary convention and social negotiation. Who has, in other words, the power to interpret the scarlet letter, the Puritan magistrates, Pearl, Dimmesdale, the community, or Hester herself? Mirrored and distorted in the reflection of the armor at Governor Bellingham's hall, the scarlet letter represents the viewpoint of the magistrates who see Hester Prynne simply as sinner and threat. Represented again in Pearl, in her lavishly embroidered garments as well as in the child herself, the letter connotes passion and rebellion. Hester's extravagant embroidery of the symbol allows her to appropriate another meaning as well, at once aesthetic and political. Through imagery rather than words, Hester subverts the magistrate's intentions by asserting her own artistic talents in order to transform the letter into a proud symbol of beauty. In a similar sleight of hand, she embroiders the magistrates' ceremonial garments, insinuating herself into the public forum by co-opting the signs of the Puritan patriarchy. Hester's alienation from the community, ironically, gives her the opportunity to appropriate and manipulate meaning, to influence and render multivalent meaning, to control what the letter "A" stands for, and by extrapolation, to control the language which shapes her as a subject.

The marks in *Beloved*, the literal and figurative scars of slavery, undergo a transformation, a re-reading and reinterpretation that qualifies, much like Hawthorne's scarlet letter, the relationship of language to self-definition. The brand is the language of slavery denoting the ownership of "property that reproduced itself without cost" (228), the sign of inclusion in an economics of bondage. The slave owner and white society have the power first to inscribe and then to interpret the mark, the prerogative to disrupt the systems—language and culture—that construct subjectivity. Sethe's mother has no name or identity other than a brand which she tries, in an act of self-definition, to teach her daughter to recognize, that is, to read. The mark is the only sign which links her to her daughter, the one child she chose to acknowledge and allow to survive but also the one who misreads the symbol. Little girl Sethe wants the same mark, a connection that would reinforce the tenuous bonds linking her to the faceless woman in a straw hat seen only from a distance in a field but would also, ironically, link her more closely to a system which commodifies human beings. After her mother's brutal hanging, she looks for the symbol of connection on her mother's corpse but is unable to find it. Importantly, decades later, it is Beloved who allows Sethe to pick the "meaning out of a code she no longer understood" (62), by giving her the power of memory to interpret the fragmented discourse, the language she shared so briefly with her mother and Nan as a child.

The "circle and a cross burnt right in the skin" (61) speaks the language of ownership, as does, provisionally at least, the tree on Sethe's back. However, the letter is also resonant of crucifixion and resurrection. Beloved comes back to life first emerging from a stream to lean against a mulberry tree (50). Sethe comes back from the brink of death to see Amy leaning against a "young ash" (82); her blistered and bleeding feet have been revived by Amy and then wrapped in leaves. She then gives birth to Denver in a boat (a hollowed-out tree) filled with two bird nests. The chokecherry tree on her back bleeds roses (93), the stigmata signaling her twenty-eight days of freedom at Bluestone Road; Paul D follows the "tree flowers" (112) north to freedom. The sign of the tree is dependent on interpretation for its meaning: slavery or resurrection. In other words, the relation between the whole sign and what it refers to is arbitrary, with no "natural" connection between the sign and the thing to which it refers. Consequently, Amy interprets Sethe's scar not as a mark of bondage but rather as a chokecherry tree:

It's a tree, Lu. A chokecherry tree. See, here's the trunk—it's red and split wide open, full of sap, and this here's the parting for the branches. You got a mighty lot of branches. Leaves, too, look like, and dern if these ain't blossoms. Tiny little cherry blossoms, just as white. Your back got a whole tree on it. In bloom. What God have in mind, I wonder. (79)

Amy's reading of the sign also underscores the connection of "the family tree 'branching' outwards, generation to generation" (Biedermann 404). Sethe after all imagines her children "in beautiful trees, their little legs barely visible in the leaves" (39, 86) and for her twenty-eight days of liberation, she envisions herself as the great mother of all. Yet Paul D's interpretation of her scar is a projection of his own interrogation of racial identity. His kissing the tree causes the house at 124 Bluestone to shake, yet unable to accept both its legacy and implications in terms of his own subjectivity, he is compelled to hold its meaning at bay: "And the wrought-iron maze he had explored in the kitchen like a gold miner pawing through pay dirt was in fact a revolting clump of scars. Not a tree, as she said" (21). Similarly, Sethe's emerging sense of self is profoundly dependent upon the "reading" of her scar, emblematic of the correlation between subject and discourse formation. Does she accept the definition of escaped slave and murderess or can she begin to reach outside those categories to a yet unarticulated linguistic and symbolic process of representation?

The answer comes at a great price, symbolized by Beloved's scar, "the little curved shadow of a smile in the kootchy-kootchy-coo place under her chin" (239). It is Sethe's inscription, her act of self-definition, the mark which, at last, undermines the power of slavery to determine, distort, and fragment the social constructs significant to subject formation. By killing her daughter and leaving her own mark, Sethe figuratively reappropriates the ink which she had made and which was used for schoolteacher's loathsome purpose of categorization and commodification. Her radical inscription is at once an act of revision, appropriation, and subversion, a rewriting of the discursive processes that produced the category of "race."

It is also an act that summons a ghost in the machine of canonical American literature, the textual representation of another woman incarcerated with an infant, whose brand served to establish her priority as a subject and whose story was, perhaps, one of the first to be passed on—a text passed on and rewritten by Morrison to reflect a radical redefinition of the identity and experience of "blackness." In terms of the gothic, it is also a text that offers a radical reinterpretation of the genre, linking horror, not with some vaguely allegorical and inconceivable terror, but with the very real economics of possession. Re-reading *The Scarlet Letter* through *Beloved,* as gothic rather than romance, throws into sharp relief the power relations underlying the phantasmagoria of the stigmata both Hester and Sethe carry. It also questions Leslie Fiedler's assessment that American fiction is "a flight from the physical data of the actual world" (29). Morrison's appropriation of traditional, discursive processes opens the door to new readings of other gothic texts, to invocations of other ghosts still in the machine.

2

THE MONSTER AND THE MOTHER:
FRANKENSTEIN AND *BELOVED*

As we have already seen, Toni Morrison's intertextual revisioning in *Beloved* conjures the ghost of Hawthorne's *The Scarlet Letter* but only to appropriate and subvert its traditional discursive processes by highlighting the implications of commodification in subject formation. The juxtaposition of the two novels reveals the discursive practices that produced the categories of race, gender, and motherhood. In a further elaboration of the categories of gender and motherhood, and their socio-economic ramifications, this chapter will disclose the gothic's preoccupation with commodification in terms of reproduction and colonial expansion wherein the social construct of womanhood, black or white, was predicated on a reproductive function largely controlled and manipulated by the perceived exigencies of colonialization and economic expansion.

An evaluation of *Beloved* and *Frankenstein* offers a reappraisal of the maternal trope, which, in these two texts, is constituted as a figure of agency in a genre traditionally interpreted as hostile to such a role. The reappraisal begins with echoes that can be heard in Morrison's text, reverberations that more than hint at what Sandra M. Gilbert and Susan Gubar have called the "conscious or unconscious awareness of the monster woman implicit in the angel woman" (240), a gothic tradition with its own particular twist.

It is exactly this twist, this duality of female monstrousness and domestic angelicness, that exists in both Mary Shelley's *Frankenstein* and Morrison's *Beloved*. I would argue that Shelley's text has particular resonance for the American version of the gothic in its preoccupation with commodification, in terms of reproduction and colonial exploitation. *Frankenstein* departs from the Radcliffean, or sentimental gothic tradition, pushing aside the fleeing woman trope in favor of "masculine figures occupy[ing] its center" (Wolstenholme 37). These masculine figures, in contrast to the alleged absence of female figures, concentrate the text on disclosing power structures as well as resistance to those structures. Mary Shelley's novel expresses in a necessarily metaphorical way what is made complete by *Beloved* a century and a half later. Morrison finishes the sentences begun by Shelley, who, not unlike the authors of nineteenth-century slave narratives, was unable fully, or openly, to represent the exigencies of a world in which birth, life, and death were outside a woman's control, experiences she rewrote not as realism but as gothic fantasy (Moers, "Female Gothic"). In a similar vein, nineteenth-century slave narratives were unable to "communicate slavery's personal dimension as human tragedy" (Waxman 58), functioning instead, as Henry Louis Gates, Jr. has outlined, as plantation novels, moral exempla, and spiritual biographies (129). It is Morrison who completes the picture, fleshing out the horror of slavery and the commodification of reproduction, that only a century of distance can allow.

The response to the commodification of reproduction is extreme, culminating in the representation of two socially constructed roles for women: the nurturing mother and the murderous monster. To borrow from Nina Auerbach, "'So like, and yet so unlike' are the female angel and the demon. It requires only the fire of an altered palette to bring out the contours of the one latent in the face of the other" (*Woman and Demon* 107). Even Mary Shelley, in her 1831 introduction to her novel, reflects on the question posed to her so frequently concerning her monstrous creation: "How I, then a young girl, came to think of, and to dilate upon, so very hideous an idea?" (7).

How indeed, in a world where the social construct of womanhood, black or white, was predicated on a reproductive function largely controlled and manipulated by men? In Sethe's world, relationships are subverted into an economics of reproduction where the value of humanity is calculated in financial terms. The seemingly pastoral life she enjoyed at Sweet Home was hers only because she served as "property that reproduced itself without cost" (228). In *Frankenstein* the role of reproduction is also exploited at great potential cost to humanity. Just as white men control and direct their slaves' reproduction, so does Victor Frankenstein go about his own "filthy business" as he dabbles "among the unhallowed damps of the grave, or tortured the living animal to animate the lifeless clay" (43) in an attempt to wrest power from nature. Shelley's novel begins with a "glorious expedition," a quest to discover and conquer unknown lands, and ends with that same expedition, the culmination of Victor Frankenstein's own journey to master the mysteries of reproduction. Both projects, Walton's and Frankenstein's, are colonial in intent, the former seeking to colonize new territory, the latter intent on colonizing another form of nature. As Kate Ellis has noted, the Monster's revenge story can be read as a protest narrative, a critique of "bourgeois domesticity that Mary Shelley had learned, principally from her mother's writings" (126). However, it may also be read as an allegory, a projection of issues regarding control over reproduction.

Unlike Morrison, however, Shelley writes within the constraints of an earlier age which does not allow her the buffer of historical perspective. Her voice is necessarily once removed from a reality, drawing upon the "double voice" (Lanser 618) or the polyphony of voices that cover or obscure less socially acceptable levels of meaning. Nonetheless, like Morrison's narrative, hers is also, to borrow from the work of Ellen Moers, a "horror story of maternity" ("Female Gothic" 83). As Moers documents, Mary Shelley's was a life in which death and birth were traumatically linked. Her own mother, Mary Wollstonecraft, died giving her life; Mary Godwin was only sixteen and unwed when she found herself pregnant by an already married Shelley, with whom she ran off. Several infant deaths and miscarriages later—punctuated by the suicide of Shelley's pregnant wife and the illegitimate pregnancy of her own stepsister, Claire, by an indifferent Byron—and the story of *Frankenstein* was born.

Consequently, what we find in both novels is a conflation of extremes in the images of nurturing mother and murderous monster. The former has almost an iconic status in both black and white cultures, serving as the cement that, theoretically, holds the family together. Sethe is described as having "milk enough for all" (100) with a capacity for love that was "deep and wide" (162) enough to encompass all her children. Yet, she is also capable of murdering her offspring, a violent political act in response to a system that leaves her little choice and no other role. Paul D sees it this way:

This here Sethe talked about love like any other woman; talked about baby clothes like any other woman, but what she meant could cleave the bone. This here Sethe talked about safety with a handsaw. . . . It scared him. (164)

It scares Paul D enough that he feels he must remind Sethe that she has "two feet . . . not four" (165). Sethe's pain and rage are often represented in animalistic terms, an aspect of her "monstrousness" which simultaneously calls attention to and then prevails over the negative stereotypes of chattel slavery. She crawls on her belly like a snake while laboring to give birth to Denver; she is ready to devour "like a snake. All jaws and hungry" any white boy who makes the mistake of coming near her (31). Sethe undermines the animal characteristics assigned to her by schoolteacher at Sweet Home by remaking those qualities and reinvesting them with an overpowering monstrousness. In Ohio, as he comes to retrieve his "chattel," Sethe can finally and definitively stop "him in his tracks"

(164), her murdered child in her arms, the symbol of the ultimate taboo and violation which sets her, and her remaining children, safely outside the social order. According to schoolteacher, not only is "the whole lot . . . lost now" (150) but the woman herself is useless to him given the primacy of childbearing to the perpetuation of slavery. Sethe's monstrous act has the effect of emasculating both nephews and the patriarchal system they represent.

The nephew, the one who had nursed her while his brother held her down, didn't know he was shaking. His uncle had warned him against that kind of confusion, but the warning didn't seem to be taking. What she go and do that for? On account of a beating? . . . But no beating ever made him . . . I mean no way he could have . . . What she go and do that for? (150)

Significantly, the nephew's syntax breaks down into "confusion," the language of the symbolic disintegrating and drained of its power to interpret and control. Nephew can neither interpret nor understand Sethe's monstrous act, as it belongs well outside the social order and, consequently, he can no longer control her or her children. Instead, he and the remaining white men back their way out of the woodshed, unable to meet the eyes of those who stay behind. Moreover, they are unable to look at "those of the nigger woman who looked like she didn't have any. Since the whites in them had disappeared and since they were as black as her skin, she looked blind" (150). Metaphorically at least, Sethe's act does blind her. The gaze, as the conduit to self-recognition, is dependent on the Other's gaze, the ideology of representation revolving around the perception of the subject (Mulvey 441). Within the symbolic, Sethe's identity as slave was produced within an economic framework and authorized at the scopic level. Now she cannot be looked at, that is, objectified as chattel, and her unseeing gaze no longer reflects the subjectivity of slavery formerly conferred upon her.

However, "monstrous" acts are not Sethe's alone. Her own mother resisted slavery by controlling, in a limited way, her reproductive capacity. She "threw away" all her infants except Sethe. "Without names, she threw them. You she gave the name of the black man" (62). Similarly, Baby Suggs serves as a matriarchal figure, nurturing her daughter-in-law back to life, sustaining neighbors, family, and friends, encouraging them to reclaim their lives from slavery. Yet she also had eight children by six fathers, one child that "she could not love and the rest she would not. 'God take what He would,' . . . . And He did, and He did, and He did" (23).

The conflation of nurturing mother and murderous monster is more opaque in Shelley's *Frankenstein*, a sleight-of-hand that redraws the conflicted boundaries of the socially constructed ideology of gender. As all too many critics have noted, the women in Shelley's text are "beautiful, gentle, selfless, boring nurturers and victims who never experience inner conflict or true desire" (Johnson 50). Similarly, Susan Wolstenholme has noted that the images of fathers in *Frankenstein* are explicit, suggested by strong male presence and also by the father-son relationships between Victor and his father, and Victor and the Monster (55), and also contrasted with the many stories told by men in the text while women seem unable to construct coherent narratives. Ostensibly, Elizabeth and her forerunner, Caroline, occupy the domestic hearth with a serenity that borders on the divine. Elizabeth's "saintly soul . . . shone like a shrine-dedicated lamp on our peaceful home. Her sympathy was ours; her smile, her soft voice, the sweet glance of her celestial eyes, were ever there to bless and animate us" (121). She also appears to have a love that is "deep and wide," ever available to her family, a passive victim to Victor's masculine ambitions and the Monster's insatiable vengeance. And yet, indirectly but inextricably, she is linked to the murder of little William; that is, she along with the many surrogate mothers in *Frankenstein* is implicated in monstrous acts that subvert the text's master (and masculine) narrative. It is Elizabeth who gives little William the miniature of his mother, the picture that allegedly incites the Monster to murder. After learning of the child's death, Elizabeth persists in "self accusations," insisting that "O God! I have murdered my darling child!" (55). That same miniature is placed by the Monster with the sleeping Justine, described as little William's "most affectionate mother" (63), who upon the morning of her execution believes herself to be guilty of infanticide. "I almost began to think that I was the monster," Justine confesses (65).

Perhaps the mystery here is, as in Edgar Allan Poe's "The Purloined Letter," "a little too plain" (*Collected Works* 136). The journey of Caroline's miniature can be linked to poststructural readings of Poe's short story, readings which trace the displacement of the signifier—the purloined letter—and its influence, in the words of Jacques Lacan, on "the subjects in their acts, in their destiny, in their refusals, in their blind spots, their end and fate" ("Seminar"). For our purposes, how does the displacement of Caroline's miniature determine the text's subjects in their acts, their refusals, and their fate? As it turns out, while the female subjects may appear passive and nurturing, the signifier, in this case the miniature, determines by its necessary and continued absence and deferral, the traces of their influence.

Caroline's absence, (she is already dead by the time William is murdered) offers a powerful subtext to *Frankenstein*, represented by her miniature which serves both as the image of the saintly mother, providing a brief moment of civilizing calm to the Monster, and as the presumed catalyst for the murder. From this perspective, Alphonse Frankenstein's lament takes on a new meaning when he says, "Thank God she [Caroline] did not live to witness the cruel, miserable death of her youngest darling!" (55). In a manner of speaking not only does she witness the murder, but she is also implicated, figuratively at least, in the act. The Monster, moved by her image and then angered by the beauty and gentleness that is denied him, wreaks his vengeance on the sleeping Justine by placing the miniature with her. "The crime had its source in her," he exclaims: "be hers the punishment! Thanks to the lessons of Felix and the sanguinary laws of man, I had learned now to work mischief" (103).

At one level, sanguinary laws may refer to the bloody acts of mankind that the Monster has already assimilated through his observations of civilization. However, the phrase also brings with it connotations of bloodlines, succession, and the kind of "mischief" that disrupts the patrilineal order. Just as Sethe murders her child to undermine the system of slavery and its commodification of reproduction, so too does the murder of William act as a staying hand on Frankenstein's overweening ambitions to control reproduction. Perhaps, then, it is no coincidence that the Monster kills William after the child boasts of his powerful "papa," thereby effectively cutting short a patriarch's dynastic hopes. It is precisely this papa, Alphonse Frankenstein, who after the murder of his son speaks of the law which will govern Justine's trial. "If she is . . . innocent, rely on the justice of our laws" (61), he claims. Justine, ironically and appropriately named, is indeed a "most affectionate mother" and innocent of the crime. However, she is punished because the evidence—the miniature of the mother—points to her guilt. Just as in Lacan's reading of Poe's story, wherein the letter is caught up in an endless circulation of meanings, so too does the circulating miniature unsettle and complicate Shelley's text, moving beyond any assurance of authorized control.

By following the displacement of the signifier, we find a subversive alliance among the women in *Frankenstein*, from Caroline to Elizabeth to Justine, women who, outside the law, undermine patriarchal control over birth, life, and death. It is interesting to note that Caroline first discovers and then chooses to adopt Elizabeth as her daughter. Alphonse comes home one day to find the young girl playing together with his son and then, after the fact as it were, gives his "permission" for the *legal,* formal adoption to proceed. On her deathbed, Caroline asks Elizabeth to serve as surrogate mother to the remaining family and all but decrees that Elizabeth and Victor wed. This semi-incestuous relationship, commented upon by numerous critics, is taboo within the symbolic order yet encouraged and sanctioned by Caroline.

In many senses, Caroline is stronger in absentia, in death, than in life. From this vantage point, it is necessary to reexamine Frankenstein's now infamous dream, the nightmare which occurs after he has just given life to his creation and, filled with dread, seeks a few moments of sleep:

I thought I saw Elizabeth, in the bloom of health, walking in the streets of Ingolstadt. Delighted and surprised, I embraced her; but as I imprinted the first kiss on her lips, they became livid with the hue of death; her features appeared to change, and I thought that I held the corpse of my dead mother in my arms; a shroud enveloped her form, and I saw the graveworms crawling in the folds of the flannel. I started from my sleep with horror; a cold dew covered my forehead, my teeth chattered, and every limb became convulsed: when, by the dim and yellow light of the moon, as it forced its way through the window shutters, I beheld the wretch—the miserable monster whom I had created. (45-46)

The conflation of images here is striking—Elizabeth, dead mother, the feminine symbol of the moon, and, finally, monster. In essence, this scene demonstrates that the social construct of "woman" can be both nurturing and monstrous, exerting a power both creative and destructive in its intent. The novel is less an indictment of "fathers as potential monster-makers" (Knoepflmacher 105) and more an exploration of the repressed, transgressive influence of the feminine.

These transgressive eruptions must be suppressed and controlled, a struggle that is best symbolized by Victor's "abortion" of his female creation, a monster so terrifying in its potential that "she might become ten thousand times more malignant than her mate, and delight for its own sake, in murder and wretchedness" (117). To neutralize this potential, Victor dismembers his female creation and, before dispatching her, waits until the moon—feminine symbol of regeneration—is obscured by clouds. Afterwards, he feels "refreshed" and filled with "agreeable sensations," secure in his observation that "clouds hid the moon and everything was obscure" (121).

The battle to control and contain the language in which the subjectivity of the female is constructed is an ongoing battle in both *Beloved* and *Frankenstein*. As Gayatri Chakravorty Spivak has shown, what is at stake for feminist individualism in the age of imperialism is "the making of human beings, the constitution and 'interpellation' of the subject not only as individual but as 'individualist.' This stake is represented on two registers: childbearing and soul making" (799). The relationship between sexual reproduction and social subject production, to paraphrase Spivak, is central to both Morrison's and Shelley's texts and reworked through culturally traditional feminine tropes of sewing and stitching, a form of "self-fashioning." Victor's need to dismember his female creation, in order to negate her potential, works in direct counterpoint to his feelings of "power" when assembling "a being like myself" (42). Yet his creature, the Monster, never feels whole, his alienation from society, his feelings of abandonment manifested in the hodge-podge, stitched, and tacked collection of limbs and features comprising his subjectivity. It is precisely his fractured appearance, his masquerade of coherence which literally demonstrates subjectivity as a construct, that evokes shock, revulsion, and earns him rejection from society.

Similarly, Sethe dismembers/disremembers her infant daughter, leaving Beloved with a scar where her head meets her neck, a mark which, appropriately, allows Sethe to begin recollecting and rebuilding her own fragmented subjectivity in terms of familial and cultural continuity. By reconnecting with the traces of disremembered history through Beloved, she begins to deal with the profound fragmentation of black female identity. Trying desperately to explain to Paul D the rationale behind her murder of Beloved, Sethe circles the subject by discussing instead a piece of calico:

Stripes it had with little flowers in between. 'Bout a yard—not enough for more 'n a head tie. But I been wanting to make a shift for my girl with it. Had the prettiest colors. I don't even know what you call that color: a rose but with yellow in it. For the longest time I been meaning to make it for her and do you know like a fool I left it behind? No more than a yard, and I kept putting it off because I was tired or didn't have the time. So when I got here, even before they let me get out of bed, I stitched her a little something from a piece of cloth Baby Suggs had. Well, all I'm saying is that's a selfish pleasure I never had before. I couldn't let all that go back to where it was, and I couldn't let her nor any of em live under schoolteacher. That was out. (163)

With her newly won freedom, Sethe endeavors to stitch together an identity for both herself and her children. Significantly, she forgets to bring with her remnants of slavery, the calico from Sweet Home's Mrs. Garner, and instead sews a shift for her daughter using fabric from Baby Suggs. This story serves as an explanation of her actions to Paul D, a narrative of self-fashioning that is less a selfish pleasure than a radical and necessary process of subject formation.

As a victim of slavery, marginalized as a woman and dispossessed as a consequence of race, Sethe's progress is marked by attempts to cobble together fragile fragments of identity. At Sweet Home, she craves a wedding dress and a ceremony as a means of defining herself and her relationship with Halle, something that would, symbolically at least, confer a familial identity, an unalterable connection. Under slavery this goal proves as elusive as Sethe's wedding dress, a patchwork of stolen fabric, pilfered pillow cases, dresser scarves, and mosquito netting, all of which could never be hers, but moreover only reflect her own status as chattel, a commodity in the same category as other household objects. Consequently, the sewing that Sethe does is always surreptitious, "on the sly" (10), as she must steal fabric fragments in the same way her potential subjectivity was stolen from her. Only when she gains the gift of remembering through Beloved does she openly and quite recklessly spend her life savings to cloak herself and her daughters in the language of ribbons and dress goods with "blue stripes and sassy prints" (240). In place of the discourse of "absence and negation" (Showalter 175) associated with "blackness," Sethe's and her daughters' attempt at fabrication leaves them looking like "carnival women with nothing to do" (240) and, more precisely, nothing to be. Without relationships and community, stealing scraps of fabric, sewing on the sly, or buying dress goods are simply transactions, once again reflecting the commodification of subjectivity. This process of envisioning the self emphasizes the influence of culture and language as the pattern from which subjectivity is stitched. It also underscores the inherent struggle in cutting against the grain in order to explore alternative possibilities of self-definition, which, as we see in *Beloved*, are not possible without relationships and community. Those possibilities are encapsulated in the words of Sixo describing his relationship with Thirty-Mile Woman, words which Paul D invokes at the close of the novel: "She gather me, man. The pieces I am, she gather them and give them back to me in all the right order" (272-73).

Getting the order right can be linked indirectly to the axioms of colonialism, in keeping specifically with Spivak's contention that "childbearing and soul-making" are among the hallmarks of imperialism. In that context, it is possible to argue that both *Beloved* and *Frankenstein* represent issues of racism and exploitation respectively, issues that connect with the power relations that create the colonial or postcolonial subject. Both texts focus on the commodification and/or colonization of reproduction, the effects of which are rewritten in terms of monstrousness—most specifically, figurations of rape. The conquering, domination, usurpation, and rape of Nature, traditionally figured as female, has long been seen as a sign of imperialism, a way of containing, subduing and, ultimately, exploiting Nature's fecundity. As a corollary to imperialism, the impact of institutionalized rape under slavery is a facet of colonialism that sharply marks the experiences and the identities of its victims. "When the enslaved persons' bodies were violated, their reproductive potential was commodified" (Barnett 419) along with their classification and categorization as chattel and property. As Pamela E. Barnett has clearly shown, sexual violation provides the framework of remembering for the black community in *Beloved*. Indeed, the memories of assault in Morrison's text present a litany of horrors: the boys who rob Sethe of her milk; Paul D's experience at the hands of white guards in Alfred, Georgia; Ella locked up and repeatedly raped by a father and son; Stamp Paid's wife, Vashti, forced into sex by her enslaver. Baby Suggs is compelled to have sex with her master and an overseer in an attempt to keep her child. Sethe's mother suffers at the hands of the crew during the Middle Passage; Sweet Home men dream of rape; Sethe fears for Beloved, anxious that white men will "jump on" (68) a homeless black girl. Sethe's feeling compelled to offer sex in exchange for the engraving on her baby's gravestone is a further exemplification of the commodification of human relations; sexual favors are as good as money when purchasing a name, that is, an identity for a baby.

Experiences of rape are certainly a traumatic trigger for communal memory, as Barnett concludes, and so paradoxically integral to subject formation in *Beloved*. Sexual exploitation for the purposes of subjugation and reproduction undermines the process of self-definition and yet forces the kind of crisis that does not allow forgetting of any kind. Paul D's greatest humiliation was being shackled with a bit in his mouth and "walking past the roosters" who seem to smile at him, making him feel that he is "something . . . less than a chicken sitting in the sun on a tub" (71-72). Repeatedly brutalized, Sethe's mother refuses the byproducts of rape but confers a fragile identity on Sethe by naming her after the black man, the one she put her "arms around" (62). Even Beloved is defined, not as a ghost, but as a black girl rumored to have been imprisoned and sexually enslaved by a local white man (119, 235). Horrifically, rape becomes a kind of definition, a brutal link between exploitation, power relations, and "the condition of traumatic return" (Barnett 425).

Exploitation by way of power relations also gives rise to Victor Frankenstein's monstrous creation, the discourse surrounding his enterprise decidedly phallic in tone. Walton notes Victor's capacity for "penetration into the causes of things" (28), while Victor himself remarks on "always having been imbued with a fervent longing to penetrate the secrets of nature," and longing to become like those "men who had penetrated deeper" (39). Victor also learns from "masters" of science who "penetrate into the recesses of nature and how she works in her hiding-places" (47) and he subsequently "pursued nature to her hiding places" (53). It is also significant that he exhorts Walton's men to "be more than men," while reminding them of their "glorious expedition" (150-51). The semiotic relation of the social to the discursive here reveals not only different concepts of social order but also the violence inherent in representation; that is, the power that lies behind the act of "authoring," not just in the sense of controlling a text but also in terms of self-fashioning. The monstrous acts of Sethe, the similarly monstrous influences of the female figures in *Frankenstein,* and the very creation of the Monster itself, serve to disclose the power structures that make commodification of human relations possible. Indeed, in the words of Victor Frankenstein, it is a filthy *business*, and one which brings the gothic, with its alleged allegorical and symbolic premise, irrevocably down to earth.

3

STORIES THAT WON'T TELL:
THE WITCHING HOUR, *FRANKENSTEIN*,
AND "THE TURN OF THE SCREW"

The power that lies behind the act of "authoring," not just in the case of controlling a text but also in terms of self-fashioning, is integral to an understanding of the American gothic. The monstrous acts of Sethe and the monstrous influences of the female figures in *Frankenstein* point to a subversion of ontological certainty that destabilizes the concept of subjectivity itself. Anne Rice's novel *The Witching Hour* is similarly a "monstrous creation" but one that goes a step further by testing the boundaries of gothic conventions and challenging our readings of them.

A sprawling, breathlessly flamboyant novel that some critics maintain is better relegated to the airport lounge than the lecture hall, Anne Rice's *The Witching Hour* serves best as a contemporary revisioning of the traditional gothic novel. The story of the Mayfair Witches, a saga spanning at least three centuries and tracking the tribulations of a powerful line of women, plays havoc not only with gothic conventions but also with the ways in which audiences have been taught to read and "interpret" them.

Interpretive challenges in Rice's novel, as in Toni Morrison's *Beloved*, once again trace the complex intersections of power, gender, and subjectivity. Just as Morrison's novel appropriates and subverts certain traditional discursive processes in its reworking of *The Scarlet Letter* and *Frankenstein, The Witching Hour* is also the scene of an "over-coding" (Eco 569) that sets up and dismantles frames for revisioning. In terms of discursive and literary relations, Rice's novel is seriously allusive, both a "monstrous creation" and a "story [that] won't tell" (James, "Turn of the Screw" 118), an amalgam that borrows from Mary Shelley's *Frankenstein*, Henry James's "The Turn of the Screw," Charles Brockden Brown's *Wieland*, and Edgar Allan Poe's "Ligeia" and reworks the mix to reveal how the subversion of ontological certainty destabilizes the concept of subjectivity, the foundation upon which social meaning and, in turn, the "self" is produced. Rice's text alludes to the forceful women of Poe, as well as to the embattled family of Brockden Brown's *Wieland* whose fate rests with the interpretation of a manuscript and who must also contend with a voice that seemingly comes from beyond the grave. Further, it takes up the issue of "the monster woman implicit in the angel woman" by invoking both James's governess at Bly and the gothic convention as a mediating concept open to revival and refashioning. More explicitly, *The Witching Hour* presents powerful (monstrous?) women whose material wealth, intelligence, and influence is unusual in the gothic genre, and who possess an authority that resides in the ability to interpret a text, that is, to control meaning, subjectivity, and resist the commodification of reproduction.

Rice begins an interrogation of the gothic by raising questions that reveal epistemological conflicts underlying attempts to constitute and validate meaning. The text, with its proliferating uncertainties, refuses to yield a univocal solution to the mysteries of the Mayfair family. Are the generations of Mayfair women actually "witches" or simply strong and intelligent women whose power threatens patriarchal norms? Is the family familiar, Lasher, a pagan spirit, a demon from hell, a projection of the family's "dark side," a scientific experiment, like Frankenstein's Monster gone awry, or a magical delusion like that visited upon the Wielands? Does Michael Curry, with his seemingly paranormal powers, experience apparitions and visions or simply hallucinations?

An amalgam of narratives told and retold from many points of view, Rice's text produces a tangle of interpretative problems and temptations that threaten to lead the reader down the predictable gothic path. The path, however, is more circuitous than straight, offering ambiguities that challenge canonic or normative methods of interpretation. The Mayfair "story" is presented to the reader and the novel's protagonists, Rowan Mayfair and Michael Curry, in the form of a text, a "file" researched and written by members of a semi-monastic order of scholars, the Talamasca. The "file" as such is open to interpretation, a biased and often personal reconstruction of the lives of thirteen witches, filled with gaps, voids, and slippages. In the words of Lasher, the file of the Mayfairs "is in a code. . . . Can you not see through the code?" (875) he asks. Reading, writing, and attempting to interpret the code remains the dilemma not only for Rice's embattled Mayfair family but also for the reader, who must wrestle with a frustrating multiplicity of interpretations—concerning both the text and the cultural practices that have produced the gothic genre itself.

To begin, where does a novel like *The Witching Hour* belong in the gothic panorama? In her study of Anne Rice, Bette Roberts argues that Rice borrows from the "male Gothic" example of Matthew Lewis, whose novel *The Monk* trades heavily in physical horror rather than the interiorized psychodrama closer to the Radcliffean model. Roberts cites the "distinction between the . . . psychological terror in the female Gothic novels and that of physical horror in those written by men" (16). Edward J. Ingebretsen, in his discussion of Rice's Vampire Chronicles, however, situates Rice's work in both traditions (94), adding that her novels also borrow tropes original to romance, the historical novel, and the sentimental tale/confession. Indeed, *The Witching Hour* contains multiple and sensationalized scenes of physical horror, including murder, rape, forced confinement, and kidnapping, but horrors nonetheless that are relayed against a backdrop of psychological terror evoked by ontological uncertainty. In this context, Brockden Brown's *Wieland* serves as an analogue for Rice's text, in terms not simply of plot devices but also in its preoccupation with interpretation, as Donald A. Ringe suggests: "The characters are mystified by the phenomena they perceive and, in some cases, interpret them as supernatural. . . . In *Wieland*, the problem of perceiving reality is of the utmost importance in the book" (48).

As with *The Witching Hour*, the source of the mystification stems from an allegedly supernatural occurrence haunting the family. When the elder Wieland dies under strange circumstances, the result of spontaneous combustion, the uncertainty begins. He leaves behind his own report, which is ambiguous, raising more questions than answers as to what transpired in his temple of worship prior to his demise. This ambiguity prompts the children to look for a supernatural element in his death, leaving them wide open to Carwin's hoax and ready to believe that the voices they hear are of supernatural origin. Clara, the narrator of the novel, spends much of her time deliberating over interpretations of anomalous occurrences and emerges as a strong woman who eschews superstition and tales of ghosts and apparitions. Not unlike Rice's creation, Rowan Mayfair, Clara struggles with the ambiguous manuscript left by her father and must do battle with madness caused by apparently inexplicable phenomena, the descent into which is fraught with threats of rape, the murder of her brother's wife and children, and separation from her lover. Conversely, Theodore succumbs to the madness, invests his faith in a voice whose origin is unknown, and follows its commands to murder his family. Because Brown's text emphasizes the question of supernatural intervention, the Wielands spend their time lost in a labyrinth of interpretation, left to construe the nature of the voice for themselves. As Ringe suggests, "Brown permits no easy solution to the problems he raises, and unlike the Gothic novelists from whom he derived so much, he retains an aura of ambiguity and uncertainty right to the end" (49). Carwin does emerge as the double-tongued deceiver, yet that does not do much to clarify the true impetus behind Wieland's murder of his family. In the British gothic strain, mysteries are usually resolved, brought about by a return to the rule of reason (Ringe 49), the ability to distinguish fact from fancy. However, Brown does not offer this easy way out, volunteering only an interpretative morass with which characters and readers must grapple.

The haunting of the Mayfair family by Lasher, another indeterminate voice from beyond, presents similar hermeneutic challenges that defy closure. For example, are Rowan Mayfair's admittedly extraordinary abilities as a doctor—to both heal or kill telekinetically—attributable to science or generations of evil? Is the pattern of incest peculiar to the Mayfairs simply a question of horror or a particularized psychological terror that, by destabilizing social norms, arouses readerly anxiety? Violence in *The Witching Hour*, as in *Wieland*, is never served straight up but becomes instead "an occasion for interpretation, a site for hermeneutic excavation" (Kowalewski 16) that opens spaces for less socially acceptable levels of meaning. That much of the violence is perpetrated by women in Rice's text is not in itself unusual in the gothic realm if we remember Sheridan Le Fanu's Carmilla or Dracula's Lucy Westenra or, for that matter, Poe's Madeline, who returns from the undead to finish the job. What is unusual, however, is that ambiguity serves as the moral fulcrum for Rice's "heroines." There are no attempts at rehabilitating Rowan Mayfair or her progenitors, as their fall from grace is a fall into empty metaphysical space where comforting polarities of good and evil come in shades of grey rather than black and white. The only certainty that emerges in Rice's text is the image of a family of powerful women whose descent is matrilineal and all of whom, male or female, must retain the name of the first Mayfair, the midwife who was burned at the stake for witchcraft in the seventeenth century.

Their power, symbolized by the Mayfair legacy, however, does not come easily or without price. It is a power that is bounded, conceived, and created by social norms and specific forms of discourse current at particular historical moments. In Foucaultian terms, the Mayfairs' power is filtered through the deployment of codes or disciplines such as the legal, educational, religious, medical, or political. Both Susannah and Deborah Mayfair are powerful "healers," but both are prey to the religious fanaticism that characterizes an age where powerful women risked the stake. They fall prey, as Petyr van Abel documents in 1689, to the superstitions promulgated by the Catholic church, codified more specifically in the writings of Father Louvier in his book on witchcraft and demonology. Reports van Abel:

This book has held this town spellbound, and . . . it was the old Comtesse who produced it, the very accuser of her daughter-in-law, who has said straight out on the church steps that were it not for this worthy book she would not have known a witch was living in her very midst. (261)

Susannah and Deborah are represented not only through van Abel's account, in his text belonging to the Mayfair file, but also through a network of historically determined relations. The church literally and figuratively constructs Susannah's and Deborah's subjectivity through Louvier's text with "skillfully done pictures of devils dancing by moonlight, and old hags feasting upon babies or flying about on brooms" (261). Similarly, when Deborah is unable to save her dying husband, the Comte of Montcleve, he declares her a witch on his deathbed. With that one declaration, she is no longer his wife, a comtesse, or a healer. Conversely, villagers who continue to represent Deborah as a healer are discounted, given that their access to a sanctioned discourse or code is comparatively limited. Consequently, it is through religious and legal codes that the nascent power of the two earliest Mayfairs is defined and thereby contained.

Three hundred years later, Rowan Mayfair inherits the abilities of her foremothers. She is described as "extremely healthy, brilliant, strong, and successful" (629), having transcended sexual stereotyping in her role as neurosurgeon. The Mayfair file includes commentaries from fellow physicians and nurses, all of whom "admired her for her exceptional accomplishments, no one thought of her as 'weird' or 'strange' or in any way connected with the supernatural" (609). Although the most powerful of all the Mayfair women, Rowan's abilities have been channeled through the medical and social codes of the latter half of the twentieth century, granting her a power authorized by prevalent social and political practices and symbolized by the honorific "doctor." That she is a genetic composite of her ancestors, as Rice's text makes abundantly clear, is immaterial; rather, how she is "read," and "interpreted," and subsequently, "documented" in the Mayfair file, determines the construction of her subjectivity.

With few exceptions, Rice's Mayfair women are portrayed as strong and determined, sometimes winning and at other times losing their battles across the centuries. They are the antithesis of traditionally gendered femininity, exhibiting characteristics and behaviors that veer toward the "monstrous." Charlotte Mayfair of the eighteenth century runs a plantation in Haiti with an iron will and much-envied success. She also holds her father captive, drugs and seduces him, and sets loose a torrent of spirits that hasten him to an early grave. In the twentieth century, Carlotta, in her own inimitable way of battling the influence of Lasher, drugs her niece Deirdre senseless; Rowan murders her philandering adoptive father and later, her aunt Carlotta. However, these examples of "monstrousness" are normalized in Rice's text, that is, naturalized in much the same way that conventional gothic texts "naturalize" traits emblematic of the feminine. More remarkable, the strength and sometimes "monstrous" abilities of the Mayfairs are accommodated by those around them. Michael Curry still loves Rowan Mayfair, although she isn't "like anyone else I've ever known. You're so strong."

"Yes, I am," she said thickly. "Because I could kill you right now if I wanted to. All your manly strength wouldn't do you any good." . . . He turned and looked at her, and for one moment in the shadows her face looked unspeakably cold and cunning, with her eyelids at half mast, and her eyes gleaming. She looked malicious . . . and he found himself shrinking from her, instinctively, every hair standing on end. (700)

"Manly strength" could very well be taken ironically here, as men in *The Witching Hour* fare poorly, not unlike *Frankenstein*'s women. Represented as morally upright, memorably handsome, and requisitely virile at the outset, their masculinity is gradually neutralized on a variety of levels. Petyr van Abel is forcibly drugged and confined by his daughter and lover; Mary Beth's husband, a brilliant architect, becomes a hopeless alcoholic; Michael Curry is debilitated by a heart condition. All the "nice" husbands are felled either by a wasting disease, yellow fever, alcoholism, or murder. Aaron Lightner, the scholar from the Talamasca, is eventually murdered in *Lasher*, while Julian Mayfair, the only male witch the family has ever known, is powerful but decidedly bisexual, rather than heterosexual, in his orientation. More important, the men whom Mayfair women marry not only take the name of Mayfair but also serve as surrogate fathers for offspring not biologically theirs. Instead, they act as smokescreens for the incest that genetically concentrates Mayfair power among certain of the family's women. This "inbreeding," which makes Rowan the "genetic beneficiary" of generations of Mayfair women, introduces the possibility of construction of the female subject through the dismantling of the patrilineal order. While the female body remains the site of continuity in *The Witching Hour*, it also emerges as the source of disruption and disintegration, subverting patriarchal lines of descent while asserting a female textuality. In other words, the matrilineal line offers the promise of textual inscription and, by trying to take control and make sense of the Mayfair story, Rowan endeavors to form a collective and female Mayfair subjectivity. The conflation of female figures, Rowan's ancestors,—Deborah, Charlotte, Mary Beth, Rowan or Deborah, Stella, Deirdre—operates as a communal polemic, a dialogization or conflict of voices revealing power structures as well as resistance to those structures.

A corollary to this resistance can be found in another aspect of Rice's revisioning of the gothic, that which Carol J. Clover defines as sensation or 'body' genre. Typically, the gendered woman in the gothic text is implicated in a repressed form of sexuality, forever the victim or "bad girl," as Poe's Madeline or Ligeia suggest, and forever punished for her latent libidinal impulses. Whether Madeline is read as the sister bent on incestuous relations who must be contained in a screwed-down coffin lid and secured behind an iron door or as an avenging succubus, the result is the same. She is defined/contained by her or the narrator's erotic impulses, which are deemed dangerously disruptive. The psychological state of the narrator in "Ligeia" is similarly all but irrelevant. Whether Ligeia truly does reanimate the body of Rowena or whether the narrator, prompted by his waking visions of her, hallucinates the episode, once again the results are the same—a dead woman who symbolizes or promotes dangerous libidinal drives that must be suppressed. In *The Witching Hour* Rice acknowledges this convention by borrowing from and unleashing Madeline's and Ligeia's nascent but potentially powerful eroticism. Mayfair women are sexually omnivorous, sampling lovers with a passionate deliberation that is simultaneously both male and female gendered. In Michael Curry's words, Rowan "look[ed] at him the way a man looked at a woman. Just as hungry and just as aggressive and yet yielding so magically in his arms" (690).

Rice's women are devoid of the sentimentality so long a hallmark of the gothic genre, and there are no examples of Radcliffean hand-wringing or sexual equivocation in *The Witching Hour*. Rowan "couldn't stop wanting him [Michael] physically" (668) and earlier in the novel her "couplings" involve a series of men with "roughened voices" and "heavy chests and powerful arms" (103). Those men are attractive not only for their physical attributes but also because, as firemen or policemen, "they save lives." "I like heroes," Rowan adds (103). With a deliberate nod to gothic convention, wherein the van Helsings of fiction are expected to rush in to save the day, Rice undermines the expected protocol by offering neither her male nor female subjects such recourse. Rather, ironically, Rowan saves Michael from drowning twice, the first incident involving her own sheer physical stamina and heroic prowess. Yet from the outset, the text engages in a subtle tug-of-war, inveigling the reader into a set of expectations about who will do the rescuing. Michael, appropriately named after the archangel who battled Satan

(928), is convinced that his mission in life involves saving Rowan from her fate by "driving the devil into hell" (918). He is presented as the quintessential hero, physically strong, handsome, and as "brave and good as anyone" (831) Rowan has ever known. However, he is robbed of his divine mission by Rowan herself, shunted to the sidelines while she does battle with Lasher on her own terms. In an inversion of the usual patriarchal relationship, she becomes his guardian, deciding that

she had to protect him now, because he couldn't protect her, that was plain. And she realized for the first time—that when things really did start to happen, she'd probably be completely alone in it. But hadn't that always been inevitable? (831)

Such inevitability is perhaps not only intended for Rowan but also for the Hester Prynnes, Madelines, and Ligeias, the result of the gothic genre's paradoxical impulse for containing women's potential power, positioning them as weak, victimized, and in dire need of rescue.

Traditionally, the need for rescue in the gothic genre was prompted by the threat of rape, loss of virtue, and sexual contamination. *The Witching Hour* addresses this convention with a graphic intensity that leaves plenty of opportunity for a diversity of response. Covering dangerous ground, Rice's text positions the representation of rape into the context of power and control, offering two frameworks within which to consider power relations. First, for all *The Witching Hour*'s comparative explicitness, sexual assault occurs "off screen," the rapes of Katherine by her brother Julian and Deirdre by her uncle Cortland (who is also her grandfather) relegated to the margins of the text. More difficult, however, is the Mayfair women's predilection for rape-like fantasies, their sexual appetites fed by Lasher's ability to interpret and act upon their desires. Projecting their fantasies and urges onto the family familiar, Mayfair women at once control the sexual action while becoming ensnared by it. "My world is pleasing you," says Lasher (899). "Shall I take a shape for you? Shall I make illusions?" he asks (899). Once again, in a reversal of gender roles, Lasher becomes the sexual canvas upon which Mayfair women draw their desires, the quintessential male concubine with whom any sexual activity, even fantasies of rape, is ultimately controllable and therefore safe. Outside the realm of reproduction, sexual congress with Lasher can result in no offspring while the "real" incestuous rapes of Katherine and Deirdre are deemed necessary to the perpetuation of the family line.

The dichotomy that is established underscores the text's relationship to social constructs of womanhood in terms of reproductive function.

What is Lasher if not a sexual fantasy turned monstrous creation, female sexuality used and exploited to ensnare and ensure the ultimate in reproduction? Having "bred" (931) Mayfair women through the manipulation of generations, Lasher's final objective is to be born through Rowan, to assume flesh and become a monstrous creation. As a late-twentieth-century reprise of Shelley's *Frankenstein, The Witching Hour* functions as yet another "horror story of maternity" (Moers 83) but with its own particular twist. This time the scientist and creator is a woman, a "doctor with the vision of a poet" (874), the "mother of disaster" (889). Rowan "dreams of Frankenstein-like discoveries" (186) and experiences the revulsion and attraction born of scientific ambition. Her "lust for power over the little fetal cells with their amazing plasticity" (183) is analogous to Victor Frankenstein's desire to "penetrate into the recesses of nature" (47).

As with Victor, Rowan is torn between the scientific and the domestic spheres, traditionally gendered as male and female respectively. As critics such as Stephen Berendt have noted, "home is fatal to male ambition" (53), and in Shelley's novel, represents a failure of traditional masculine ideology. Victor takes himself away from the domestic arena, requiring isolation from human contact in order to go about his "filthy business." On his deathbed, he exhorts Walton's hapless crew that to return home with anything less than victory would mean "the stigma of disgrace" (51). Rowan is similarly isolated, far away from her true family in New Orleans, living in coldly modern San Francisco, a city where she concentrates her powers and ambitions on the "horrors of Lemle's laboratory" (937) and gaining the scientific knowledge that Lasher needs to assume his own monstrous ambition.

It is no coincidence that, in another reversal of conventional roles, Michael Curry is quite literally a homebuilder, a contractor who lovingly restores old family homes, first in San Francisco and then later in his own birthplace of New Orleans. He undertakes the restoration of the ancestral Mayfair house in a symbolic attempt to banish its real or imagined ghosts and to provide a nurturing environment where Rowan can refocus her abilities on "redemption," on transforming the "Mayfair legacy . . . into healing" (772-73). Michael seeks a middle ground, a way of bringing science in from the cold, away from harvested fetuses in secret laboratories and into the realm of nature, which is typically gendered female. Yet ironically, he provides both the house and the baby that Lasher requires to assume human form.

In essence, Michael is a composite of *Frankenstein*'s Henry Clerval and Elizabeth, friend, fiancé, and confidant to Rowan, someone, as we shall later see, who brings "context" to her life. Like Elizabeth with

Victor, Michael serves as Rowan's only chance at salvation, offering the balance that might save her from her own ambitions. Significantly, on her wedding night to Victor Frankenstein, Elizabeth dies at the hand of the Monster, who ensures that his creator will be denied forever the nurturing domestic affection that has eluded him. Similarly, Lasher first makes his presence known to Rowan on her wedding night, and his appearance effectively marks the end of domestic affections between her and her new husband. As Bette Roberts points out, Rice's text, and we could include Shelley's as well, is predicated on "a kind of Hawthornian conflict of head and heart" (101) and, as with her Shelleyan counterpart, Rowan's scientific nature seems at first to prevail.

She is fascinated by the creature she creates with Lasher, speculating on the nature of his being as spirit and then later as human hybrid: "I need a microscope. I need to take blood samples. I need to see what the tissues really are now!" (936). While Frankenstein creates his monster with an eclectic collection of body parts, a masculinized technological project, Rowan's monster is created through her own womb, a womb which is violently and, quite literally, appropriated. This literal appropriation represents the symbolic culmination of the control and manipulation of women's reproductive functions, an echo both of *Frankenstein*'s rapacious project and *Beloved*'s treatment of the economics of reproduction. Unlike her Frankensteinian counterpart, however, Rowan does not turn away from the monster she helped create, a decision stemming not from any maternal "instincts" but from another source altogether. The social construct of maternity is effectively dismantled here, desentimentalized by Rowan's hard-eyed decision to accompany newly born Lasher as she walks through "the door she'd glimpsed a million years ago in her girlhood when she'd first opened the magical volumes of scientific lore" (937).

Once again, the text invites expectations that are summarily undermined. Rowan is simultaneously scientist and creator, an author in the truest sense. She takes ownership of her creation in a bid to control the story, that is, the text of the Mayfairs as set out by the Talamasca, a reflection of the communal polemic created by the cumulative efforts of her ancestors. At this point Lasher is connection to the family, "all the shiny-faced cousins . . . incapable of telling the whole story because they don't know it. They only know little glittering parts" (695). Lasher is an aggregate, a composite, and as Rowan's ancestor Charlotte notes:

all that he is proceeds from us. . . . That on its own it cannot think, do you not see? It cannot gather its thoughts together; it was the call of Suzanne which gathered it; it was the call of Deborah which concentrated it further. (341)

Or, in the words of Lasher to Rowan, he learned "all things from you. Self-consciousness, desire, ambition. You are dangerous teachers" (872). In a similar vein, Frankenstein's monster learns from dangerous teachers, in his case a collectivity that is capable of beholding, and therefore authoring, in a Rousseauian sense, "only a detestable monster" (Shelley 130).

The issue of authoring here is also closely linked to the Derridean idea of the law of the proper. Lasher's period of wandering is punctuated by his birth, or return, to the womb. "Word was finally made flesh, and I would be born" (930), he states imperiously. The thrust of this philosophical project depends on the notion of fall and redemption; that is, humanity is alienated from Truth (or God/Origin/Meaning) and enters into a period of wandering, a world of indeterminate representations and signs. The purpose of this wandering has to do with a longing to return to a proper place or origin wherein a proper, or literal meaning, can be resumed. In other words, there exists a paradoxical desire to reduce suspension, deferral, and delay of indeterminate meanings to one unique, literal meaning symbolized by a proper name, a presence. Significantly, Lasher reveals that he has "no need of a name" in his wandering, "no understanding even of a name. But in truth just no name" (861). *The Witching Hour* concerns itself with this drive to a final destination from the first Mayfair, Suzanne, to Rowan three hundred years later, a proper place where all misprisions and interpretations are thought to be resolved.

It is at this juncture that Rice's text engages an interrelational reading, one involving James's "The Turn of the Screw" and its concretization of the acts of reading, writing, and interpretation. James's narrative also concerns itself with the consequences of the law of the proper and attempts at constituting and validating meaning. As with *The Witching Hour*, "The Turn of the Screw" is a "story [that] won't tell," an exploration of interpretative challenges and temptations. As T. J. Lustig notes, "the idea is to establish *the* reading and if necessary to defeat other readings" (112). In other words, the reader's mission is to decide whether the governess is delusional, evil, or spot on about her own interpretation of events at Bly. A similar structure is established in Rice's text as the reader is invited to "reconstruct this sad tale" (621) and to "see through the code" (875), in essence, to determine a final reading or interpretation of the Mayfair family history.

On a rudimentary level, Rice has borrowed certain aspects of James's novella, allusions that are meant to invite an interdiscursivity, an interaction and questioning of gothic polarities. Both texts fall within the gothic genre, both working under a realist impetus that also contradicts and disrupts realist readings. While James's text announces itself as a ghost story in the frame, Rice's novel presents itself simply as a family history open to interpretation. Both texts have to do with a "written" tale involving the alleged sexual corruption of children by specters or ghosts that may or may not exist. The reading of the governess's story occurs on Christmas Eve in an "old House" (James 115); the denouement of Rice's text centers on Christmas Eve, which serves as a climax of the novel, and much of the action also revolves around an old house.

More striking, however, is that both texts are consciously "written" and conspicuous in their accumulation of proliferating uncertainties. "The Turn of the Screw" is a project literally concerned with the production of a narrative. "The story's written. It's in a locked drawer" (116), explains Douglas. He subsequently reads the governess's tale to the circle gathered in the old house and then transmits it, before his own death, to the narrator of the introductory chapter who finally makes an exact transcript of the manuscript. The governess struggles to produce a narrative, *her narrative*, and all we know of her life at Bly is her version of events in defiance of her employer's dictates. Significantly, her employer orders her to "never, never neither appeal nor complain nor write about anything" (122). Defiantly, the governess spends her time in his employ endeavoring to author a story wherein she is the hero, the protector of innocents corrupted by evil. She describes the specter of Peter Quint "as I see the letter I form on this page" (137). She comes upon Miss Jessel "availing herself . . . to the considerable effort of a letter to her sweetheart" (195). At one point, she and Mrs. Grose are ready to relay their suspicions to their employer, with the governess asking:

"Do you mean you'll write—?" Remembering she couldn't, I caught myself up. "How do you communicate?"

"I tell the bailiff. He writes."

"And should you like him to write our story?"

My question had a sarcastic force that I had not fully intended, and it made her after a moment inconsequently break down. The tears were again in her eyes. "Ah Miss, you write!" (199)

The bailiff and the employer underscore the conventional role of the governess in the gothic genre as a figure marginalized and often threatened by the same middle-class ideology that she is expected to reproduce in her charges. James's governess takes on an authorial function only after she arrives at Bly and receives the schoolmaster's letter concerning Miles. She deliberately, almost wilfully, confines the letter's "meaning," opting for her own interpretation, an interpretation that serves as the catalyst for her own "story."

The Witching Hour operates on an analogous level, the Mayfair women endeavoring to discover and interpret their family's "history" in order to assume authorial control of its writing. The text comprises portions of their story, continually reiterated, either by a different character or in a different setting; newspaper clippings, detectives' and doctors' reports, along with the Talamasca's scholars' contribution, comprise the "file" which remains unknown to the Mayfair family until Rowan's return to New Orleans. Rowan's ancestor, Deborah, on the night before her death, acknowledges the importance of writing what she knows and passing it along to her daughter (299). Conversely, generations later her descendent Stella confessed to not knowing the "meaning" of the manuscript left to her, a document subsequently destroyed by her mother, Mary Beth. Once they read the Talamasca file, however, Rowan and Michael see themselves as the "new chapter yet unwritten" and as having been "characters in this narrative for some time" (625). Rowan vows: "We're writing the file from now on" (710) and "it comforted her to think of the file" (737). To write the file is to create and control meaning rather than having the narrative take the form of, in the words of Aaron Lightner, "a horror story" (889).

Significantly, the story of the Mayfairs begins with misprision, with the seventeenth-century Suzanne's misunderstanding of a passage in Father Louvier's text on demonology. It is her misreading of this influential text that, ironically, allows her to summon the spirit of Lasher, whom she subsequently and significantly misnames. (He is named after Ashlar, a legendary folk saint.) This misprision marks the beginning of centuries of wandering from the sources, of attempts at establishing meaning. The Mayfair family's collective subjectivity is predicated on the concept of an absent core and a central enigma that, paradoxically, requires interpretation. Yet as Lasher justifies to Rowan:

There are many possible explanations. You shape the explanation by the question you ask. I can talk to you of my own volition, but what I tell you will have been shaped by what I have been taught through the questions of others over the centuries. It is a construct. If you want a new construct, ask. (860)

The construct refers to the codes or conventions that underlie texts, the sign systems that generate meaning. Lasher is no more the repository of determinate meaning than Michael's mysteriously empowered hands that can "read" the contexts of objects in an attempt to establish meaning. These attempts at interpretation underscore the condition of signification in general by emphasizing the likelihood of misinterpretation or misreading as being integral to all discourse.

Michael struggles to solve the Mayfair mystery, looking for a "literal interpretation" (914). Aaron Lightner confesses to "no certain interpretation of anything" but encourages Michael to "have an interpretation" (730). In moving to New Orleans from San Francisco, Rowan feels that she has "slipped into another interpretation" (712). During his final struggle with what could either be hallucinations or ghosts of Mayfairs past, Michael refuses the explanation that is offered him. "This is not the explanation. . . . This is not the final meaning" (947), he desperately maintains, amidst the onslaught of "hellish images" that he may or may not be creating himself. He only comes to terms with a reality that is an interpreted materiality mediated by both language and historical situation through his "contemplative relationship with the blank page" (956). It is only through his contribution to the Mayfair story that he can accept the indeterminate nature of his interpretation of the story of the Mayfair witches, a writing that "probably wouldn't stand up against the philosophers of the Talamasca. Maybe won't even go into the file. But it's my belief, for what it's worth" (964).

"The Turn of the Screw" sets up and undermines a similar realist referential doctrine of knowability. The letters referred to in the text are simultaneously absent from the text, either stolen, burned, concealed, or never completed and sent. Miles offers an explanation for his dismissal from school, one that focuses on language but refers to nothing at all, other than that "he said things" (135). From this confession, the governess decides that the message "can have but one meaning" (129) and proceeds to create ghosts as if they were texts. "It all lies in a half a dozen words" (180), she explains to Mrs. Grose about her interpretive strategy. As a referential reader, the governess "read[s] restlessly into the facts" (152), "extracts a meaning" from her charges' countenances (227), and "reads into our situation a clearness it couldn't have had at the time" (230). The result is that a socially marginalized figure becomes a hero in her own story, partially controlling, interpreting, and creating the language in which her subjectivity is constructed.

Both *The Witching Hour* and "The Turn of the Screw" self-reflexively critique not only the role of discourse in the creation of subjectivity but also the codes and cultural practices that have produced the gothic genre itself. As with Rice's text, James's novella establishes and dismantles conventional narrative frameworks to reveal the complexities of social relations generated by certain modes of representation. When the governess first meets her employer she presents as "a fluttered anxious girl out of a Hampshire vicarage" confronting "such a figure as had never risen, save in a dream or an old novel" (119). The text is invoking familiar gothic codes, Radcliffe and Brontë specifically, when the governess asks herself: "Was there a 'secret' at Bly—a mystery of Udolpho or an insane, an unmentionable relative kept in unsuspected confinement?" (137). The governess refers to Miles as a "little fairy prince" (179) and she is under the "spell" (169) of Fielding's *Amelia* (169) when she encounters Quint for the third time. Similarly, Rice's text makes overt references to *Frankenstein*, Dickens, and "cinematic" monsters (33, 64), keeping alive a constant and realist expectation that promises closure, that is, the moment when the story should become fully intelligible. Instead, the reader is offered no such relief but simply further evidence of the indeterminacy of language and the loss of a traditional basis for referentiality.

The resultant irony is a governess who writes herself a role, a hero without a cause (or reference for that matter), and a Mayfair witch who, in her quest for a definition of selfhood, escapes from the text with the monster she helped author. Together, Rice's *The Witching Hour* and James's "Turn of the Screw" resonate with the epistemological conflicts underlying attempts to constitute subjectivity and, in turn, validate meaning. In an amalgam that borrows from Shelley, Brockden Brown, and Poe, as well as James, Rice's text invigorates the symbolism and allegories of the gothic tradition by stripping away the distortions that inform our own readings of the genre. In the end, these are stories that simply "don't tell," revealing perhaps only one truth—that of the shifting social and cultural contexts responsible for our changing assumptions about and responses to the gothic.

4

THE AMERICA OF MY IMAGINATION:
BELLEFLEUR AND *ABSALOM, ABSALOM!*

I have chosen Joyce Carol Oates's text to punctuate the first section of my discussion of the contemporary gothic novel because it pushes at the boundaries of the genre in a way that is both parodic and postmodern. Once again we have a mother/daughter duality and a text that appropriates and subverts certain of the gothic genre's discursive practices. However, while Toni Morrison's and Anne Rice's novels are exercises in intertextual revisioning, which draw attention to the gothic genre as a historical and political construct, *Bellefleur* ventures further by adopting a stylized, metafictive intertextuality. *Bellefleur*'s overt stylization gives rise to textual interrelations that are necessarily parodic or ironic inversions (Hutcheon, *Theory of Parody*) gesturing to the ideological distance between a text and its precursor. While Morrison's *Beloved* and Rice's *The Witching Hour* fall along the gothic continuum as extensions or continuations of the genre, *Bellefleur* operates on a metafictional plane, using a discursive strategy of "subverting *from within*, to speak the language of the dominant order and at the same time suggest another meaning and another evaluation" (Hutcheon, "Introduction" 16).

More concretely, the distinctions among Morrison's, Rice's, and Oates's gothic texts can be explained another way. Morrison uses the transgressive aspects of the gothic genre, its repudiation of the "natural" and the rational, to create a history of the "Other," a story that otherwise could not be and, indeed, had not previously been told. The gothic genre allows her a space in which to give voice to that which has been silenced. Alternatively, Rice's expansive treatment of the genre, with her intent to humanize her preternatural subjects' conflicts in their search for self-knowledge, "opens up the possibilities of a genre increasingly narrowed by stereotypical conventions over the years" (Roberts 20). In other words, Rice makes relevant to contemporary readers the classic obsessions governing the gothic by reworking the clichés of vampires and witches as a means of cultural self-analysis. However, while Morrison and Rice work within the genre, Oates operates both within and outside, emphasizing contingency and multiplicity in her evocation of the America of her imagination. The result is a gloves-off critique, "a kind of necessary final act of destroying the past, required of all who belong to the tradition of the New" (Fiedler 16).

The America of Oates's imagination is not for the faint of heart. Rendered gut-wrenchingly violent and spiritually impoverished, Oates's terrain is riven with the profound "dualities at the heart of the American dream" (Creighton 39), "it's daylight and nightmare aspects" (Sjoberg 116). That Oates has chosen the gothic genre to throw into sharp relief the antithetical construct informing her "critique of America" ("Afterword" 562) is worth consideration, prompting an evaluation of the contexts responsible for our assumptions about and responses to a genre that, in Oates's hands at least, seems destined for weightier things than merely popular consumption.

However, one thing that is not new is her alliance of the gothic with the parodic. In *Love and Death in the American Novel,* Leslie Fiedler argues that the gothic mode is "essentially a form of parody . . . which simultaneously connects and rejects" (33). In turn, he cites the work of William Faulkner as the essence of all parody—conscious, unconscious and parody of parody (as in Sir Walter Scott consciously parodied by Mark Twain who is then inadvertently parodied by Ernest Hemingway). Implicated in this paradigm is Oates's *Bellefleur,* whose echoes are decidedly Faulknerian, culminating as a reiteration of *Absalom, Absalom!* with its grand plan gone awry, its rhetorical complexity, and its idiosyncratic treatment of time. Oates's revisioning of *Absalom, Absalom!* through *Bellefleur* lays bare what Fredric Jameson calls ideologemes or "the ultimate raw material" of cultural production (87), that is, the essence, spirit, or world-views that comprise texts. According to Julia Kristeva, there is a close relationship between the ideologeme and intertextuality: "We call the ideologeme the communal function that attaches a concrete structure (like the novel) to other structures (like the discourse of science) in an intertextual space" (313). In effect, then, *Bellefleur* is an imitative recasting of Faulkner's novel, an ironic inversion that engages the metanarrative that tells the "story" of America, its mythology, omissions, and distortions.

Oates's story is an almost overwhelming surplus of parodic gothic elements, found in the saga of the strange, multigenerational *Bellefleur* family with its power-hungry matriarch, Leah, and her psychic, hermaphrodite daughter, Germaine. A postmodern pastiche of walking ghosts, tenacious vampires, and logic-defying time warps, the text is an often confounding retelling of family tales that resembles more of a crazy patchwork quilt than any linear narrative. There is a gnome straight out of Washington Irving, a boy who regularly metamorphoses into a mongrel dog, a drum made of the skin of one of the Bellefleur patriarchs, a mad hermit, rivers that change direction, and mountains that shrink. In terms of the gothic tradition, what exactly is Oates doing and why?

John Gardner believes *Bellefleur* is Oates's "heroic attempt to transmute the almost inherently goofy tradition of the gothic (ghosts, shape-shifters, vampires and all that) into serious art" (99). However, he also levels the criticism that the author's heavy-handed use of "artifice undermines emotional power, makes the book cartoonish" (101). What Gardner is missing, perhaps, is the situational irony at work in the novel, wherein an artistic illusion is created only to be destroyed through the revelation of its own process of arbitrary construction. In other words, a "cartoonish" text defamiliarizes gothic clichés or stereotypes through profound exaggeration and hyperbole, the consequence of which pushes the reader, in the words of Adrienne Rich, to enter "an old text from a new critical direction" ("When We Dead" 90). I would argue that the old text in this case is Faulkner's *Absalom, Absalom!*

Faulkner's and Oates's forays into the gothic have much in common. As critics such as Leslie Fiedler and Irving Malin have noted, American gothic emerges from roots in the English post-Enlightenment, roots that when transplanted in the New World gave rise to a hybridization, and consequently, a new iconography. The truck and trade of English gothicism includes several basic elements, ranging from the spooky or medieval castle and ancient abbey to the somber ruin symbolizing the haunting past. As Malin has suggested, in the New World, the castle can be replaced with Sutpen's moldering mansion or Bellefleur's crumbling manor. Both Faulkner's and Oates's edifices begin as monuments to arrogance and pride before disintegrating first to ashes and then rubble, symbolizing in true gothic style the rise and fall of the houses, in this case, of Sutpen and Bellefleur respectively. Sutpen's Hundred deteriorates to "rotting portico and scaling walls . . . some desolation more profound than ruined" before its final conflagration (300). As Elizabeth Kerr notes, *Absalom, Absalom!* is "the only novel by Faulkner in which the entire history of the 'haunted castle' is given" (32). Bellefleur is also built around the single, controlling image of a "castle." However, Oates's ironic inversion of this theme manages to convey values directly opposed to those ostensibly presented, all the while giving readers a heavy dose of that which they have come to expect from the gothic. Faulkner's redaction involves Clytie's burning of Sutpen's mansion as a direct repudiation of the patriarch's "grand plan," a resounding finale that Oates borrows from and subsequently intensifies. *Bellefleur* concludes with a double-climax, a double-massacre with a full narrative accounting of the destruction of the Bellefleurs in 1825 and the destruction of the present-day Bellefleurs in Gideon's dive-bomb attack on Bellefleur Manor. The treatment of the gothic castle trope is exaggerated in the extreme. The patriarch himself, piloting his own plane loaded with explosives, destroys the "contorted and unnatural sight rising out of the green land" (552), the family house, hardly the "pretty flower" of the text's title, along with a battalion of Bellefleur "attorneys and brokers and financial advisers and accountants and managers of a dozen businesses and factories and mills" (547). The ultimate phallic symbol is turned in on itself, not once but twice, as the plane, the house, and all dynastic hopes are deflated. The conflagration is consumed by Lake Noir completing the picture, an allusion to Poe's "brackish tarn" into which the House of Usher eventually collapses. Clearly, Oates's text is a resounding echo of just about every gothic tale ever written, a self-reflexive amplification of the genre's tropes, in short, a way of recontextualizing the familiar.

The description of Bellefleur Manor could well be interpreted as a metaphoric accounting of the American gothic genre itself:

Bellefleur Manor was known locally as Bellefleur Castle, though the family disliked that name—for castles called to mind the Old World, the past, that rotting graveyard Europe . . . and when Raphael's grandfather Jean-Pierre Bellefleur was banished from France and repudiated by his own father, the Duc de Bellefleur, the past simply ceased to exist. "We are all Americans now," Raphael said. "We have no choice but to be Americans now." (4)

The manor is subsequently depicted as surrounded by wilderness overlooking Lake Noir and Mount Chattaroy, the tallest peak in the Chautauquas. Tellingly, it is "English Gothic in design, with some Moorish influence" (4), an amalgam of European and Orientalist motifs made real through imported labor and material. Although its battlemented towers and walls proclaim it a castle, the finished product is "a raw rugged sprawling beauty of a kind never seen before in that part of the world" (4). A hybrid, like the American gothic genre itself, Bellefleur Manor is emblematic of the myriad cultural conditions that inspired its development, and, just in case the reader has not made the metaphoric connection, it is described in the novel's penultimate page "like a castle composed in a feverish sleep, when the imagination leapt over itself, mad to outdo itself, growing ever more frantic and greedy" (552). The gothic castle within the English tradition represented the frantic greed of aristocratic power, the power of the past within the New World (Malin), and the power of the patriarchy in its creation of the domestic sphere (Moers), and it is this cultural heritage of class and gender that Oates manifestly dismantles. Faulkner's textual insurrection leaves behind Jim Bond, the ironic embodiment of all the taboos undermining social order, from miscegenation and illegitimacy to idiocy. In an irreverent but curiously more optimistic echo of the Sutpen debacle, Oates leaves the reader with a hermaphrodite version of Jim Bond and another version of Clytie, the passively aggressive and rebellious Sutpen family member who is also resolutely an outsider. Surviving the rubble of Bellefleur Manor's destruction is the child Germaine along with her intractable great-aunt Mathilde, who has lived on the other side of Lake Noir making crafts and quilts, determinedly refusing involvement in Bellefleur machinations. While Faulkner leaves the Jim Bonds "to conquer the western hemisphere" (302), Oates offers a small community of women as alternative voices to tell the story of America, "a tale still being told—in many voices—and nowhere near its conclusion" ("Afterword" 562).

Oates's and Faulkner's treatment of the gothic castle trope extends itself as well to the wilderness/quest theme that has characterized gothic fiction since Horace Walpole and Anne Radcliffe. The transition to American gothic involves the transformation of Old World forest into uncleared wilderness, the prairie, or mountain range. Power is wrested from the earth, from nature, which is usually gendered female. Nature's exploitation becomes a form of gothic horror in America, best symbolized by Sutpen and his "wild men" (27) who "overrun suddenly the hundred square miles of tranquil and astonished earth and drag house and formal gardens violently out of the soundless Nothing and clap them down like cards upon a table" (4). Rosa Coldfield emphasizes that Sutpen "tore violently a plantation" (9) in a foreshadowing of his "insult," that is, his coldly calculating intent to exploit her female reproductive capacities for his own dynastic purposes.

Oates turns up the volume on this New World gothic horror, given that Bellefleur is an unrelenting catalogue of exploitation and injustice against humanity and nature. The novel is full of massacres, from Franklin's "Narrative" to the historic exploits of John Brown, the 1825 Bellefleur massacre, the revenge massacre that followed, the massacre that left Jean-Pierre II in prison and the one that heralded his release. Workers "were slaves—they were parasites—they weren't human" (323), according to the avaricious Bellefleurs. Gideon and his brother win a little girl in a card game like so much human cargo and then proceed to rape her. Indians and Negroes are sold as slaves and "flogged to pieces . . . literally to pieces, to shreds, for wilfulness and sloth" (535).

Jean-Pierre, the first American Bellefleur, wrests three million acres from the wilderness and plans his own grand design "to control the northeastern border of what had newly become known as the United States of America (which meant control of waterways as well, and commerce with Montreal and Quebec)" along with a strategy "for breaking his wilderness kingdom away from the rest of the state, and even from the new nation, in order to establish a sovereignty of his own" (116). This megalomania is part of the historical record of the United States and yet, ironically, it is not out of place in the gothic genre. The feverish imagination that reconstituted the gothic in America was fueled in part by the very real horrors attendant on the nation's birth. To quote Jean-Pierre, writing to England about America:

There is only one principle here as elsewhere, but here it is naked & one cannot be deceived: the lust for acquisitions: furs and timber: timber & furs: game: to snatch from this domain all it might yield greedy as men who have gone for days without eating suddenly ushered into a banquet hall & left to their own devices. One stuffs oneself, it is a frenzy, the lust to lay hands on everything, to beat out others, for others are enemies. (534)

The exploitation of nature, "the lust to lay hands on everything," is closely allied with the gothic genre's tradition of the quest. It must be said, however, that the classic search for identity, parentage, or rightful heritage (Kerr 23) is reconfigured in American gothic to address flight—flight from oppression to freedom and a new Eden where nature waits to be conquered, exploited, and commodified. Flight in Charles Brockden Brown's *Edgar Huntly* is the backbone of the text, a pathology that finds echoes in *Bellefleur* with Jedediah's flight into the wilderness. Huntly's harrowing search for Clithero in the Pennsylvania back country projects fears of natural evil, symbolized by the Indian threat, as opposed to the traditional British gothic concept of social evil. While the natural threat is couched in symbolic terms, as an extension of the primitive and savage, it serves a practical and materialist purpose, that is, as an obstacle to progress and productivity that must be subdued or at least harnessed to some orderly design. Edgar Allan Poe's *The Narrative of Arthur Gordon Pym* follows along the same trajectory with Pym's flight into the heart of darkness of the region of Tsalal, with its "brilliant black" (88) natives who conjure in him a combined desire for and fear of blackness. "My whole soul was pervaded with a longing to fall; a desire, a yearning, a passion utterly uncontrollable" (198), says Pym in a paroxysm of dread. Not unlike the threat of the erotic, "nature" as represented by the Indian or the African must be integrated into the flow, circulation, and expansion of value. What better way than through the appropriation of land and enslavement, a strategy of sublimating the excessive and putting it to better, that is, economically productive use? The lust to lay hands on everything is also sanctioned by the New World's rejection of the old European order. Land and property in America are not inherited through family but rather appropriated, seized, worked, and sold for profit, and all the more reason that the patina of gentrification becomes a valuable commodity, a method of disguising the "lust" behind rapacious avarice. Sutpen's design in *Absalom, Absalom!* is fuelled by motives of revenge against the quasi-aristocratic world of the antebellum South represented by a black liveried servant's haughty demeanor and a closed door. He is an upstart, a crude *poseur* who parodies the concept of plantation gentleman lording over his slaves. The irony here is doubly acute given that the South itself is already a parody of European feudalism, with its attendant compulsions of *noblesse oblige* and patrician values.

Bellefleur throws into even sharper relief the parodic aspects of both America's history and its cultural manifestation in the gothic genre. "It had always interested me that in the nineteenth and early twentieth centuries in America wealthy men were eager to establish themselves as 'nobility' of a sort by reconstructing immense castles, and in many cases importing great sections of European castles for this purpose," Oates writes in the "Afterword" of *Bellefleur* (561). As we have already explored, the castle and its patriarchal connotations are the organizing principle around which Faulkner's and Oates's texts revolve. For the Bellefleurs, the family's line begins in America with Jean-Pierre's banishment from his homeland for his "'radical ideas' about individual rights" (116), a young man "repudiated by his own father, the Duc de Bellefleur" (3-4). However, unlike the Old World gothic predecessors, there is no restoration or recognition scene in either *Absalom, Absalom!* or Bellefleur, no room for a prodigal son or rightful heir, although Faulkner's text raises precisely this convention with regard to Bon. Instead, Sutpen and Jean-Pierre choose to stake their own claim, almost to the point of declaring sovereignty over their own hard-won "wilderness kingdom(s)." Ironically, their heirs are forced to repeat the pattern, either as unacknowledged offspring or as refugees from their heritages in an unconscious attempt to break the violent circle that is their legacy: Charles Bon, eldest son, and Jim Bond, only remaining male heir to Sutpen's grand design, are swept off the page. Bellefleur's Raphael disappears into Mink Pond; Yolande runs away to become a film actress; Garth marries Little Goldie and moves to "somewhere where no one knew the name Bellefleur" (446); Vernon leaves to write his poetry; Christabel marries her beloved and flees to Mexico while Bromwell escapes to pursue a scientific career. Even Jedediah Bellefleur, the mountain hermit hoping to escape his family and the world of America to find God, is denied any form of redemption. Ironically, while looking for God, he is reduced to the basest of bodily functions, to "What a mockery, that endless stream of food and excrement, given a human name! . . . He had become sheer sensation. . . . There was not a word left, not a syllable, not a sound! So God showed His face to His servant Jedediah, and forever afterward kept His distance" (439-441). Not unlike the presumed purgatorial existence of Henry Sutpen, Jedediah's wandering also involves flight from a woman who is forbidden to him. Here Oates ironizes the biblical quest theme, transforming it into a tragicomedy as a parody of man's quest for fulfillment, doubly so in that Jedediah is the rightful heir to a family, house, and fortune that no longer exists. "You have no family," says the messenger bringing him the news. "No family. Your brothers are dead, your father is dead, your nephews and your niece are dead: you have no family," he reiterates (554). Unlike the rightful heir in the traditional European gothic, who after successfully completing his test inherits his birthright, Jedediah must begin again with Germaine "waiting for him" (558). begin again as the lone individual carving out an existence in the wilderness.

A corollary to the traditional gothic quest and flight themes is the persecuted maiden in flight trope (Fiedler), descended from Horace Walpole's Isabella and Samuel Richardson's Clarissa. Fiedler has suggested that the gothic maiden is pursued both by the villain and the threat of violation as well as her own darker impulses. Ellen Moers has proposed that the villain actually allows for her liberation from her narrowly prescribed role, providing an appropriate context "where heroines could enjoy all the adventures and alarms that masculine heroes had long experienced, far from home" (126). In the American version of gothic tradition, the darker impulses seem to prevail, however, once again complicating fears and desires and pushing them into an arena where they may be safely repressed. Hawthorne's Hester Prynne, not a maiden but rather an adulteress, is constrained to deny her passion by the very man it threatens the most; his Beatrice Rappaccini and Zenobia both must die because their threat is that of the flesh; and Poe's Ligeia/Rowena combination expresses symbolically the erotic danger inherent in both the dark lady and the maiden, two sides of the same coin. In Faulkner's and Oates's texts the maiden in flight trope, its dark and light side, is defused through parody, a rereading and rewriting of a literary convention. It is interesting to note that Faulkner has his "heroine," Rosa Coldfield, fleeing from Sutpen and his outrageous proposal. However, Rosa is a maiden decidedly unpursued by the villain; she becomes "not mistress, not beloved, but more than even love; . . . all polymath love's androgynous advocate" (146), returning to her dead parents' house to live alone. Following in the American gothic tradition, she is desexualized, androgynous, described as a "crucified child" (4) entombed in her own version of history which she feels compelled to relate to Quentin, a history which he believes she would like published some day. It is precisely her degendered status as spinster and as self-cast outsider in Jefferson that allows her a voice of difference within a patriarchal text. "She wants it told" (5) becomes the subtext to the narrative, allowing for an interanimation of languages that is played off against any monologic intent. The usual gothic formula involving the maiden pursued has been up-ended; Rosa is not ravished, consumptive, or married off at the end of this tale—that is, she is not silenced in the way Ellen or Judith had been silenced through their assimilation to certain cultural codes such as mother and bride. More important, she does not allow her "desexualized" status to rob her of her agency.

While numerous critics have evaluated at length Rosa's "truthfulness," the veracity of her story when compared and contrasted with Mr. Compson's, Quentin's, and Shreve's versions, the discrepancies and contradictions nevertheless appear to mount. However, it is precisely the framework, no matter how flimsy, that Rosa offers within the first chapter of the text which provides for the dialogic confrontations that give rise to ideological points of view, directions, and values. Although Rosa's story is not necessarily what Quentin wants to hear, together an assemblage of discourses gives birth to a historical and social concreteness that is simultaneously relative and open-ended. Ironically, Rosa masters her villain by silencing him, disallowing him the words that could articulate for the reader the infamous "insult."

I will tell you what he did and let you be the judge. (Or try to tell you, because there are some things for which three words are three too many, and three thousand words that many words too less, and this is one of them. It can be told; I could take that many sentences, repeat the bold blank naked and outrageous words just as he spoke them, and bequeath you only that same aghast and outraged unbelief I knew when I comprehended what he meant; or take three thousand sentences and leave you only that Why? Why? And Why? that I have asked and listened to for almost fifty years.) But I will let you be the judge and let you tell me if I was not right. (134-35)

The blank, naked, and outrageous words are never repeated: the "maiden's" way of chasing down the villain, as it were, redressing the balance of power. Whether she is running from her own darker impulses, as Fiedler would have it, or enjoying what Moers might call a quasi-feminist liberation, is subordinate to the creation here of a subversive feminine voice that undercuts, and indeed, silences a dominant discourse and in doing so, undermines patriarchal, dynastic imperatives. In effect, Rosa as maiden is a parody, a not-wife, "old flesh long embattled in virginity" (4), simultaneously an evocation and displacement of a literary convention that allows for disruption of the text, the kind where difference, outside the traditional binary oppositions of gender, finds voice.

In the constellation of gothic devices, the persecuted maiden trope is further dismantled and neutralized in *Bellefleur*. While the trope is given center stage in Faulkner's text, the *raison d'être* for Rosa Coldfield's "impotent and static rage" (3), and the catalyst for the telling of the Sutpen story, Oates uses the device as a subplot, a demotion that ends in what can only be called burlesque or caricature. Leah and Germaine, the mother and daughter dynastic duo whom we will examine more closely later, take narrative precedence over the rather maudlin story of their poor relation Garnet and her below-stairs affair with the master-of-the-house, Gideon. The plot is stereotypically gothic, the heroine suitably fragile and wan yet passively aggressive. Garnet swoons, whispers, and half-heartedly flees her lover in the best gothic fashion:

So Garnet fled, in a paroxysm of shame, hardly knowing what she did, which turn in the corridor to take, which stairway to descend. She fled, too stupefied even to weep, and somehow found herself in an unheated back hallway, and then at a door, throwing herself against a door, as the dogs began to yip in a startled chorus. Gathering her cloak about her she ran across the lawn. Moonlight illuminated the long hill that dipped to the lake—illuminated the hill and not the surrounding woods—so that she had only one way to run. Now barefoot, her hair streaming, the skirt of her pretty silken gown beginning to rip, she ran, her eyes open and fixed. Somehow the cloak was torn off her shoulders—torn off and flung away. Still she ran, oblivious of her surroundings, knowing only that she must run, to flee the horror behind her, and to eradicate herself in the dark murmurous lake before her. Senseless words careened about her head: O Gideon I love you, I cannot live without you, I have always loved you and I will always love you—Please forgive me—(293)

Oates's parody of the fleeing maiden is evocative enough to grace the cover of the quintessential gothic book jacket, managing to pack in the requisite twisting, haunted passageways of the Gothic castle, vaporous moonlight, and a heroine simultaneously vulnerable and eroticized. However, the script does deviate in an example of intertextual irony, a way of marking difference, that is, critiquing in this case both trope and genre. First, Garnet's dramatic flight from Gideon is unnecessary in that he is long past pursuing her. As well, she is hardly a maiden having borne her lover a child which he, with help from his wife Leah, refuses to acknowledge. As luck would have it, the baby Cassandra is carried away by the Noir Vulture, leaving Garnet free to marry her real prince, the British Lord Dunraven, who first sees her "a ghostly figure running down the long, long hill—running barefoot, despite the cold—her hair flying behind her—her arms outstretched" (293) before saving her from drowning herself. It does not take long before Garnet is suddenly sensible, shifting her affections to Lord Dunraven just as seamlessly as Oates's script shifts from *Clarissa* to *Northanger Abbey*. This shift depends upon a double-voiced discourse wherein, to borrow from M. M. Bakhtin, "speech becomes a battlefield for opposing intentions" (185), a dialogism that is subversive by virtue of being parodic. In other words, when *Bellefleur*'s narrator insists that Garnet, the parentless servant girl, impoverished and "since the shame of her affair with Gideon Bellefleur and the birth of her illegitimate child, a figure of contemptuous pity" (470), "behaved honorably" toward Lord Dunraven, the reader is presented with a textual space that is dialogical, that is, where several "voices" can be perceived:

Of course there was a great deal of excited talk. And yet, oddly, very little of it was mean-spirited. For it seemed quite clear to the Bellefleurs, even to Leah, that Garnet had resisted Lord Dunraven's proposals; she had attempted to break off communication with him more than once; it was certainly not the case that she had seduced him, and cajoled him into marriage. She had, they felt, behaved honorably. Though Garnet was not a Bellefleur she had exhibited a Bellefleur's integrity—it was a pity, really, that they couldn't claim her for one of their own. (470)

The text here, with its heavy ironic overtones, invites multiplicity and ambivalence, and not just pertaining to Garnet's situation. Who is the seducer and the seduced in gothic convention? The pursuer and the pursued? The powerful and the powerless? The hero and the villain? At the center and in the margins? Are Hester and Garnet despoiled victims or powerful women whose potential is deemed dangerous? How does Rosa use her maiden status to redress the balance of power? Such questions undermine the status of the fleeing maiden trope, destabilizing gothic convention and thereby assisting in a reevaluation of certain social and ideological perspectives governing the metaphors for female experience.

As ironic inversion leads to reevaluation, so does the gothic theme of inheritance and dynastic hubris, in the hands of Faulkner and Oates, lead to a reconsideration of the metanarrative that tells the "story" of America. Malin has observed that disintegration, symbolized by narcissism and the breakdown of family, is reflected in new American gothic. *Absalom, Absalom!* and *Bellefleur* take up that thread both to unravel the American metanarrative with its claims to dynastic ambitions and to weave an alternative narrative that allows for dissenting and marginalized voices. In effect, we have texts that involve irresolvable contradictions wherein the process of difference is at work. Stated more concretely, we begin with stories that overtly concern patriarchs, dynasties, and grand designs and covertly end with women and alternative plots.

In both Faulkner's and Oates's texts, the American metanarrative is purposefully allied with biblical authority. As numerous critics have already elaborated (Fiedler, Malin, Kerr), the very title *Absalom, Absalom!* alludes to the third and illegitimate son of David, killed while leading rebellion against his father (2 Sam. 13-19). However, unlike David, Sutpen never does mourn for either of his sons, whom he considered only as conduits for his dynastic ambitions. Another biblical parallel concerns brother-sister incest, involving Absalom, his sister Tamar, and Amnon, another son of David. Absalom kills Amnon for violating Tamar. Analogously, Henry, desiring Judith himself and stand-in for his father, kills Bon to prevent miscegenation. Consequently, the patrilineal order, integral to the colonization, that is, the subjugation of the New World, is dismantled here by the taboos defined as outside the social (patriarchal) order. Minrose C. Gwin has suggested that the most subversive aspect of *Absalom, Absalom!* involves the father-daughter model as a trope for linking sexual difference to narrative process, wherein "the father's authoritative narrative is disrupted by the 'daughters' of his own creation" ("(Re)Reading" 240). This subtext flies in the face of those readings which see fatherhood and sonship in Faulkner as "deeply involved in the writer's venture and relate back to his maddest desire: the desire to seize the authority of an original author—the authority, that is, of an origin, a founder, a father" (244). Instead, Gwin argues that, through the creation of Rosa, Faulkner is able to become father and daughter of his own text. She is the feminine text of difference within patriarchal culture, maintains Gwin, while simultaneously her actions reinforce patriarchy's fixity and rigidity: "Her voice conveys her difference from the father, but it also reveals that she is still his daughter" (252).

Oates's text hinges on a fulcrum similar to Faulkner's, but this time mother and daughter (Leah and Germaine), rather than father and sons, parody the American metanarrative of "ambition for empire and wealth" ("Afterword" 561) and its cultural manifestation in what Gwin refers to as the "desire to seize the authority of an original author." Like *Absalom, Absalom!*, *Bellefleur* offers a biblical allusion to dynastic ambitions in the story of Leah and Rachel, who bore Jacob twelve sons who became the patriarchs of the twelve tribes of Israel (Gen. 25-35). Oates's Leah, married to her cousin Gideon, dutifully produces twins for the Bellefleur line, which "was not to dwindle away as so many New World aristocratic lines had" (36). Having but partially fulfilled this imperative, Leah is transformed into an empire-building autocrat after the birth of her last child, Germaine, from whom she seemingly draws mystical power and strength. Rather than weakening her position and role as a woman, Leah's last pregnancy gives her transformative powers symbolized by the monstrous ambition to reclaim the nearly three million acres of original Bellefleur lands and the primacy of the family. Her power, which is grounded in a devouring sexuality, inspires fear and compliance even from Gideon: "She was his height now or a little taller, a young giantess, beautiful and monstrous at the same time, and he did love her. And he was terrified of her" (55). Leah grows stronger as her pregnancy progresses, infusing her with a violent will to power that seems to emanate from "the child in her womb, who quivered with life—and in that instant she saw, behind her eyelids, the orangish-green flames of hell that licked joyously at everything within their reach" (66). She is both feminine and masculine, occupying both metaphorical designations for a subject's relation to dominant culture. Through a hyperbolic depiction of omnivorous female sexuality and fecundity linked to an equally overweening masculine ambition, Oates's text undermines the categories of gender by literally and figuratively exposing them as social and physical constructs. Indeed, Germaine is born both male and female:

The baby shrieked. Kicking, fighting. For breath. For life. Two somewhat abbreviated legs, and part of an abdomen, and rubbery-red slippery male genitalia, possibly oversized—it was difficult, with all the commotion, for Della to estimate—growing out of the abdomen of what appeared to be a perfectly well-formed, though somewhat large baby girl. (105)

Della solves the problem "with one, two, three skillful chops of the knife" (105). Della announces that the baby is now what God had intended:

"Now it's a she and not a he. I've had enough of he, I don't want anything more to do with he, here's what I think—" and with a sudden majestic swipe of her arm she knocked the bloody mutilated parts, what remained of the little legs, and the little penis and testicles and scrotum, onto the floor—"what I think of he."

Categories of both "he" and "she" give way in *Bellefleur* to the potential of androgyny. Germaine anticipates the elusive Mrs. Rache, in her costume of men's trousers, leather flight helmet, and courageous swagger, who is indirectly implicated in Gideon's aerial destruction of Bellefleur Manor. There is also the independent Brown Lucy, the vampiric Veronica, and the autonomous Aunt Mathilde, who maintains financial independence from the Bellefleurs across the lake from the family estate. In the words of young Bromwell, "the details of sex were of no significance, for wasn't life on this planet clearly a matter of . . . indefinable energy flowing violently through all things?" (287).

Just as Rosa Coldfield, identified as one of Faulkner's hermaphrodite figures, is desexed by virtue of her role as spinster and non-wife, that is, non-woman, Germaine and Leah transgress the boundaries of sexual categories through a parody of behaviors that are marked as masculine and feminine. Their mother/daughter relationship is an ironic inversion of the father/son alliance, satirizing certain patriarchal codes of behavior. Theirs was "the passion of absolute sympathy: absolute identity: as if the same blood coursed through both their bodies, carrying with it the very same thoughts" (385); their unity is symptomatic of the traditionally powerful role of consanguinity in the perpetuation of a hereditary line and, more important, the property that comes with it. Through her daughter's extrasensory powers, Leah intends to reclaim Bellefleur's "considerable empire!" (142), exploiting the baby's powers in order to move forward with her dynastic plans. Her objectives are turned aside, however, not only because most of the Bellefleur family is obliterated by its own patriarch, Gideon, but also because its younger generation refuses to play the roles assigned to it. Garth and Goldie, who wanted to live somewhere where no one knew the name Bellefleur move to Nebraska; Garnet leaves for England with Lord Dunraven; Christabel marries Demuth Hodge rather than Leah's choice, Edgar, despite his fortune and adjoining lands. "They are betraying us one by one, they must be stopped!" Leah insists (537). Finally, Germaine, the sole direct survivor of the Bellefleur line, begins "losing her 'powers'" (512), thereby thwarting her mother's ambitions. In the end the two people left to perpetuate the family line are the religious hermit Jedediah, who has managed to avoid most of his family's bloody history, and the androgynous child Germaine. Just as Sutpen's "whole ledger" (302) is cleared, leaving only Jim Bond, so too is the Bellefleur ledger wiped clean of the old generation and its destructive, hierarchical social order.

It is interesting that the witnesses to both the Sutpen and Bellefleur gothic histories are two women, Rosa Coldfield and Germaine Bellefleur. Both are described as androgynous and paradoxically child-like and adult. Rosa appears to Quentin like the "figure of a little girl, in the prim skirts and pantalettes, the smooth prim decorous braids, of the dead time . . . a child who had never been young" (14-15). Conversely, each of the five books in Oates's text symbolizes one year in the life of Germaine, each one ending with one of her birthdays. By five years of age, Germaine has witnessed the aging of her father, who is transformed from a virile young man to "Old Skin and Bones" (503), while, in the interim, her sister Christabel has reached full adulthood and her twin brother Bromwell remains continually a child. The complex narrative patterns of both *Absalom, Absalom!* and *Bellefleur* reinforce an alternative concept of time that "twists and coils and is, now, obliterated, and then again powerfully present" ("Author's Note" preface). Just as gender codes are transgressed, so too are the laws of temporality. "Time is a child playing a game of draughts; the kingship is in the hands of a child" begins the epigraph from Heraclitus in the foreword to Oates's novel. Alternate voices and alternate histories are allowed by what Bakhtin calls chronotopes or "time-space" (425), a strategy of translating the word into spatial categories and temporal relationships. In more concrete terms, *Bellefleur*'s chronotopic orientation can be seen as dissenting and anti-authority. In Bakhtin's analysis of Rabelais's work, and similarly fantastical tales of folk narrative, the idiosyncrasies of "fantastic realism" (168) work to purge the spatial and temporal world of the remnants of a transcendent worldview by chipping away at symbolic and hierarchical interpretations. The methodology for the purge, according to Bakhtin, involves the destruction of all ordinary ties, of all the "habitual matrices" (169), substituted with the creation of unexpected matrices and unusual narrative connections:

It is necessary to destroy and rebuild the entire false picture of the world, to sunder the false hierarchical links between objects and ideas, to abolish the divisive ideational strata. It is necessary to liberate all these objects and permit them to enter into the free unions that are organic to them, no matter how monstrous these unions might seem. (169)

What we have then in Oates's text is a repudiation of chronology: "the Bellefleurs, reminiscing, quite shamelessly jumbled 'chronological' order—indeed, they had a lofty contempt for it" (342). Dates revealed at the novel's outset make no rational sense as the text proceeds through layers of narrative that appear as continuations or repetitions of similar stories told from alternating points of view. Indeed, there is "a dizzying profusion of plots" (378), a "music composed of many voices" (268). Just as the history of the Sutpens is told through stories, the Bellefleurs themselves "were just stories, tales, anecdotes set in the mountains." The Bellefleur children would listen to stories "told and retold and embellished and pondered over . . . stories they'd heard months or even years and decades previously, laced with hilarity, or malice, or envy or simple frank astonishment at the pathways others' lives took" (69). However, the children would ask: "But did it really happen? Really?—what do you mean, really?" (19).

The idea of reality as simply a narrative construct, contingent on who is in charge of the telling, throws into sharp relief the "false hierarchical links" through which the "real" is read. *Bellefleur* includes "real" texts quoted from Benjamin Franklin's "A Narrative of the Late Massacres in Lancaster County of a Number of Indians, Friends of this Province, by Persons Unknown, with Some Observations on the Same" (388). Historical figures also make appearances, including Abraham Lincoln and John Brown. Fantastical stories are thrown into the mix, with Gideon's coming upon Rip Van Winkle only to kidnap one of Washington Irving's gnomes to bring home as a servant for Leah. A husband turns into a bear. A "Noir Vulture" "of steaming vapors, with a glaring red eye and daggerlike beak" (335) does away with a baby. Leah and Gideon's daughter Christabel ceases to exist in "reality" but returns only on the silver screen. In essence, Oates's text operates as historiographic metafiction (Hutcheon, *Poetics*), revealing a self-conscious concern with its status as fiction, a status heightened, ironically, by the integration of historical texts.

Aunt Mathilde's quilts represent the culmination of the narrative's preoccupation with time. Independent of the Bellefleurs on her side of the lake, Mathilde crafts "ingenious quilts that looked crazy to the eye" (328). Her work represents an alternative concept of time, one at odds with the "divisional ideational strata" (Bakhtin 323) that marks the world of the Bellefleurs. She teaches Germaine to "read" the asymmetrical squares by encouraging her to enjoy the different textures and colors that make up the "Celestial Timepiece," coaching her in an alternate way of understanding and perceiving the world (328-29). Not unlike Baby Suggs' quilt in *Beloved,* the patchwork construction of the "Celestial Timepiece" is a type of antinarrative, a repudiation of the linear, controlling narratives that govern and define the world. Just as Rosa Coldfield's seemingly hysterical and often incoherent accusations add a contrapuntal rhythm to Faulkner's narrative, so too does Mathilde's craft. Making a "kind of dizzying sense" (114), the quilt constructs its own story—a story that otherwise could not be told.

In essence, that story is a critique of America, a parodic recasting of *Absalom, Absalom!* which reveals the mythology, omissions, and distortions that inform our own readings of that particular culture. By creating what is in a sense an experiment, one that explores a self-consciousness which transcends mere solipsism, Oates gives a fictional language to the behaviors and beliefs that define economic and social relations in America. In that regard, her project is subversive, paradoxically engaging and contesting a literary legacy that is anything but "out of space . . . out of time." Oates's novel also serves as an appropriate platform from which to move to the next section of this discussion of the contemporary gothic novel—that is, from the realm of subversion to the dynamics of seduction.

II. SEDUCTION

We work in the dark.
—James, *The Middle Years*

In the hands of Toni Morrison, Joyce Carol Oates, and Anne Rice, a component of subversion emerges as an alliance of the erotic and seductive, a combination that has the power simultaneously to engage and disrupt a literary legacy. Yet, if we were to follow the trajectories mapped out by such critics as Richard Chase and Leslie Fiedler, there would be little of the erotic to be discovered in the American gothic novel. Allegedly, America is "desexed" (Fiedler 307), with thanatos taking over from eros and horror filling the vacuum. The terror, ostensibly, is a way of "mythicizing the brutality" (Fiedler 503) endemic to American experience long on rapacious capitalism and in stark contrast to claims of an utopian agenda. It would follow logically, then, that the erotic, as nonproductive, excessive, and anarchic, would stay repressed in an environment where economic outcome is privileged, the guarantor of survival and success in a raw New World.

Repression, however, leaves its traces. I would suggest that the specter of seduction has always haunted the American gothic novel, albeit indirectly, an influence that is disruptive to the process of commodity production and the circulation of value. From *The Scarlet Letter* to the tales of Edgar Allan Poe and to "The Turn of the Screw," the concept of seduction is implicated in what Jean Baudrillard would refer to as the semiological code of capitalism. According to Baudrillard, precapitalist societies were governed by a logic of symbolic exchange that valued waste and expenditure. Conversely, capitalist societies reduce those symbolic practices to the quantitative nexus of use- and exchange-value. From a Baudrillardian perspective, then, the gothic genre is transgressive in that privileges expenditure, sacrifice, and destruction as fundamental principles that happen to be antithetical to a materialist process of production. More concretely, seduction challenges the principles of production and consumption, reducing that which is gendered masculine, that is, the expansionist, materialist impulses predicated on commodification.

The chapters in this section trace the subversive tendencies that the process of seduction entails. The novels of Morrison, Oates, and Rice continue their subversive journey by disclosing the patterns of repression of the erotic in canonical works. The first chapter focuses on two canonical texts, *The Scarlet Letter* and "The Turn of the Screw," to establish this precedent by revealing an eroticism that is at once latent and manifest, simultaneously subversive and complicit. A discussion of Rice's *Interview with the Vampire* and Henry James's "The Jolly Corner" follows by taking up the patterns of dominance and submission, subject and object positions established in the novels of Hawthorne and James. In both Rice's and James's texts, specular seduction is the guarantor of subjectivity symptomatic of a long line of vampiric seductions (consumptions) that are inscribed in American culture. In the final chapter of this section, the work of Poe, Oates, and Morrison reveals how seduction is closely allied to a violence that is predicated on the operations of subjectivity as defined by commodity signs, encouraging deviation from social constraints and the responsibilities of ethics and conscience along with other forms of social affiliation.

5

DESEXED AMERICA:
THE DYNAMICS OF SEDUCTION IN *THE SCARLET LETTER*
AND "THE TURN OF THE SCREW"

According to Jean Baudrillard, seduction is the mastery of the world of symbolic exchanges, a transgression of the productivist code. Nathaniel Hawthorne and Henry James establish the outlines of this paradigm in a tentative acknowledgment of the erotic as nonproductive and therefore dangerous, a framework which finds consummation in contemporary gothic texts that allow the erotic its full, dissident, and also, complicit force. In Hawthorne, as we shall later see with Anne Rice's *Interview with a Vampire,* seduction operates on the level of the scopic structured by a symbolic order in which "the silent image of woman is still tied to her place as bearer, not maker, of meaning" (Mulvey 433). Along the same continuum, seduction in "The Turn of the Screw" operates on the level of subject/object positions, dominance and submission, echoes of which reverberate in *Beloved* and *Bellefleur.* What arises from the subtexts of Hawthorne and James carries over into Morrison's, Rice's, and Oates's revisioning of the gothic novel; what was once necessarily latent becomes manifest, an eroticism that is simultaneously subversive and complicit.

At the historical core of *The Scarlet Letter* rests a preoccupation with witches, that is, a fascination with male fantasies of women seduced by the devil (Schwab 171). As Gabriele Schwab convincingly argues, Hawthorne's narrative reveals the witch stereotype as a cultural pattern of interpretation "used against deviant women in general," while revealing fear of "seductive women . . . and of strong, independent women" (171-72). What Schwab sidesteps in her argument is isolating the nature and source of that particular fear. Within that context, my reading focuses on two aspects of Hawthorne's narrative; first, that he foregrounds the action of *The Scarlet Letter* in "The Custom-House" introduction, a setting that is suggestive of commercial activity, and second, that the text revolves around a very real seduction cloaked in the paraphernalia of the supernatural, one that takes place offstage but nevertheless involves the seduction of a clergyman by a married woman, an act which ultimately results in the birth of a child. In short, then, what we have is the juxtaposition of two Baudrillardian oppositions: production and seduction. Significantly, Hester Prynne, when facing her moment on the scaffold, is exhorted by the grim beadle to "show your scarlet letter in the market-place" (2206). Hester Prynne is in the "red" on two fronts; she is a scarlet woman who also owes a "debt" to society.

In this context, it is not incongruous that Hawthorne's text is prefaced by the "Custom-House" essay, which presents a setting that is distinctly commercial in nature, "worn by any multitudinous resort of business" (2179), where the shipmaster deals "in merchandise that will readily be turned to gold," and where the smart young clerk begins to acquire the taste of commercial traffic "as a wolf-cub does of blood" (2180). Our narrator is a "Surveyor of the Revenue" (2191) who, in his more thoughtful moments, equates "Uncle Sam's gold" with the "Devil's wages" (2199). The emphasis in the introductory essay is on commodification, that which is earned, produced, ordered, and taxed, a system that gives over little value and even less time to creative pursuits that are deemed unproductive. However, the narrator censures the officials who schemed to have him dismissed while exonerating himself as an artist. He finds in his work a "wretched numbness" (2196) which enervates him, drains him both of energy and time to devote to the literary life, something which he makes clear is poorly, if at all, rewarded. The paradigm in the "Custom-House" introduction is based upon establishing and then inverting the seduction theme. The young clerk in the Custom House is seduced away from his work by poetry (2192) while, in turn, the narrator finds himself enchanted by "Uncle Sam's gold" (2199), in danger of seduction and depletion as if from a demon that might claim his vital life fluid:

An effect—which I believe to be observable, more or less, in every individual who has occupied the position—is, that, while he leans on the mighty arm of the Republic, his own proper strength departs from him. He loses, in an extent proportioned to the weakness or force of his original nature, the capability of self-support. If he possess an unusual share of native energy, or the enervating magic of place do not operate too long upon him, his forfeited powers may be redeemable. (2198)

The narrator's relationship to his position foregrounds the seduction motif which is to come later. It is his stultifying work that drains him, and yet, ironically, he is seduced away from it by the scarlet letter, the red embroidered A, unearthed from a cabinet filed, significantly, among materials recording "statistics of the former commerce of Salem . . .

memorials of her princely merchants" (2192). The letter functions as "magic object," fixing the gaze of the narrator and negating his powers of reason in favor of his "sensibilities":

My eyes fastened themselves upon the old scarlet letter, and would not be turned aside. . . . I happened to place it on my breast. It seemed to me,—the reader may smile, but must not doubt my word,—it seemed to me, then, that I experienced a sensation not altogether physical, yet almost so, as of burning heat; and as if the letter were not of red cloth, but red-hot iron. I shuddered, and involuntarily let it fall upon the floor. (2197)

In effect, the letter has already seduced the narrator, tempting him away from his role as surveyor. It might be worthwhile to consider (after years of critics arguing for the plural and disseminal character of the letter A) that the literal meaning of the symbol is that of adulteress, a symbol which steadfastly attracts the gaze not only of the narrator but also of the entire Puritan community. Represented again in Pearl, in her lavishly embroidered garments as well as in the child herself, the letter connotes passion and rebellion. Pearl sees herself mirrored in the gold reflection of the letter on her mother's breast: "But that first object of which Pearl seemed to become aware was—shall we say it—the scarlet letter on Hester's bosom! . . . the infant's eyes had been caught by the glimmering of the gold embroidery about the letter" (2228). Consequently, Pearl, too, is seduced away from the Puritan path, refusing to let her mother remove the letter, a child of "preternatural activity" (2227) whose characteristics ally her with witches and the devil rather than with the hard-working and God-fearing populace of Salem.

Pearl is only integrated into the process of commodity production once the seductive spell of the letter A is lifted and she is claimed by her father, the Reverend Dimmesdale. A component of seduction, the secret, according to Baudrillard, creates a tension by that which is not revealed in the complicity of knowing silence. Hester, Dimmesdale, and Chillingsworth are part of a complicity which Baudrillard defines as "the opposite of communication, and yet it can be shared" (*Seduction* 79). Accordingly, the secret draws its strength from an "allusive and ritual power of exchange" (156); that is, seduction becomes a type of duel which never reveals the secrets that motivate it. However, once the enigma is resolved, the process of seduction is dismantled. Consequently, once the element of seduction has been eliminated with the revelation of Dimmesdale's secret, Pearl as subject is contingent on commodity signs. The elfin-child, the demon offspring, becomes through marriage "the richest heiress of her day. . . . Not improbably, this circumstance wrought a very material change in the public estimation" (2313). Within that material context of public estimation, Pearl's status and identity are subsequently commodified, described in terms of "articles of comfort and luxury" and "trifles, too, little ornaments, beautiful tokens" (2314).

Seduction in the Baudrillardian sense is conditional on the fabulousness or play of appearance, the idea of artifice, that which is "aleatory, meaningless, or ritualistic and meticulous, [a] circulation of signs on the surface" (*Seduction* 54). Hester's extravagant embroidery of the symbol A, "which drew all eyes" (2206), seduces the Puritan community by allowing for a circulation of signification, encouraging a projection of their fears and desires. Through the attraction of the symbol rather than words, Hester gains power over the magistrates and the regulations of the colony:

On the breast of her gown, in fine red cloth, surrounded with an elaborate embroidery and fantastic flourishes of gold thread, appeared the letter A. It was so artistically done, and with so much fertility and gorgeous luxuriance of fancy, that it had all the effect of a last and fitting decoration to the apparel which she wore; and which was of a splendor in accordance with the taste of the age, but greatly beyond what was allowed by the sumptuary regulations of the colony. (2205-6)

The symbol of seduction is so alluring that the magistrates allow Hester to embroider their ceremonial garments. Her embroidery is characterized as beautiful, sumptuous, and extravagant, in other words, art that, in the context of symbolic exchange, values excess and expenditure; her work is not "useful" but rather distracting and dangerous. Because the strategy of seduction is only ever a strategy of appearance and antagonistic to the principles of productivity, the power of the Puritan magistrates is moved to an arena of play and challenge, a diversion from the real, the "revenge of appearances over interpretation" (Baudrillard, *Seduction* 54). The original scene of seduction, to which the reader is not privy, is represented by the artifice of the letter A which, when first placed on Hester's breast, earns her the censure of the Puritan gaze. She does not reverse its codified meaning as critics such as David Leverenz, Gabrielle Schwab, and George Orians have argued, something which accounts for her refusal to speak out or protest, but instead, she allows the letter to play with the meaning that the Puritan community has conferred upon it. The letter operates as both the source and threat of seduction, indirectly winning (seducing) approval from the magistrates through its beauty and allure. Moreover, the letter represents the threat of seduction which is pervasive throughout the community. Hester seduces one of its religious leaders; Chillingworth, in the metaphoric guise of the devil, tries to seduce Dimmesdale's soul; Mistress Ann Hibbins attempts to lure Hester to sign a pact with the devil. By the narrative's conclusion, both the men with whom Hester has had contact are physically and symbolically drained. As though the prey of a succubus, Dimmesdale fades away to a "deathlike hue" (2308), and Chillingworth "positively withered up, shrivelled away" (2312).

Understandably, the Puritan magistrates perceive the dissident forces of seduction as hazardous to the productivity of their community, prompting the public drama of punishment visited upon Hester, a drama whose moral is ironically diminished as the adulteress begins earning commissions for embroidering magisterial garments. In other words, what begins with the punitive exposure to the community's gaze is reversed when the gaze is turned outward and the letter A exerts its seductive allure. Even after Hester is no longer required to wear the symbol, she continues to do so precisely because it is "looked upon with awe" (2314), drawing to her women who are wounded, wasted, wronged, or erring in sinful passion. Continuing to live outside Salem, she preaches that one day "a new truth would be revealed, in order to establish the whole relation between man and woman on a surer ground of mutual happiness" (2314). Although she allegedly disavows the role of prophetess, given that such a mission should be confided to a woman without sin, her subsequent actions belie her words, as she does not flee but operates as a counterpoint to the quantitative nexus of use- and exchange-value in the Puritan community.

The seductive appeal of Hester Prynne was apparently not lost on Henry James some decades later. He was to remember having seen a representation of Hawthorne's heroine in an exhibition at the National Academy, "a pale, handsome woman, in a quaint black dress and white coif" (*Selected Letters* 402). As the transgressive woman, Hester exercised "a mysterious charm" by which James reported being "vaguely frightened." Traces of the allure of the scarlet letter are found in "The Turn of the Screw" in the description of the governess's manuscript, which is written "in old, faded ink, and in the most beautiful hand" (117) and delivered in a package including "a thin old-fashioned gilt-edged album" with a "faded red cover" (122). The red and gold motif repeats the pattern of *The Scarlet Letter*, as does the frame chapter involving the discovery of a narrative and a secret. Most significant, however, are the covert scenes of seduction, which we witness in neither Hawthorne's nor James's texts. These Hawthornian traces once again reinforce the oppositions of production and seduction in "The Turn of the Screw" within the context of the social and economic role of the governess and, conversely, her role as a liminal figure "associated with disorder, misrule, inversion, and ultimately with the manifestations of social or literary crisis" (Lustig 151). She has been frequently read as a woman who is all too ready to fall from propriety to promiscuity, a creature both seduced and seductress, "a figure who epitomized the domestic ideal" and also "the figure who threatened to destroy it" (Poovey 127):

Saint or incubus? Hovering in the space between divergent, almost mythic archetypes, the governess is both picaresque antiheroine and melodramatic ingenue. . . . She is both the obedient servant and the adventuress, the reactionary and the revolutionary, puritan and prostitute, victim and violator, seduced and seducer. (Lustig 153)

In its own way, James's story is about the real material conditions of a woman who works for her living, although she occupies a different category from house servant, hovering in purgatory suspended between the upper and lower classes. Unlike fictional counterparts in the gothic pantheon, however, James's governess does not rise above her socially and economically dependent status through marriage or the discovery of lost wills or parentage. As Millicent Bell has pointed out, the suggestion that James's governess is delusionary or neurotically obsessed has a basis in the historic fact that many found their lives unbearable and suffered mental and physical anguish. In the 1840s more female inmates of institutions for the insane came from the ranks of governess than from any other occupation (Bell 3). Given their commodified status, they were vulnerable to exploitation, and indeed, to literal and figurative seduction. This dilemma is something to which James's narrator alludes as he listens to Douglas describe the governess's hesitation in accepting the position at Bly after her meeting with the master at a house in Harley Street:

"She was young, untried, nervous: it was a vision of serious duties and little company, of really great loneliness. She hesitated—took a couple of days to consult and consider. But the salary offered much exceeded her modest measure, and on a second interview she faced the music, she engaged." And Douglas, with this, made a pause that, for the benefit of the company, moved me to throw in—"The moral of which was of course the seduction exercised by the splendid young man. She succumbed to it." (121-22)

Critics have also succumbed to reading James's text as what must be a record series of seductions. F. W. H Myers blames Peter Quint and Miss Jessel for initiating and encouraging desires on the part of the children.

Robert W. Hill thinks it is a reasonable assumption that Miss Jessel, pregnant by Quint, died from an abortion, while Ned Lukacher speculates that "Miss Jessel became pregnant with Quint's child and was sent home, where she presumably died, as the result of either a miscarriage or an abortion." John Clair weighs in with the suggestion that Miles and Flora are the illegitimate children of the master and Miss Jessel, while Allen Tate assumes that the governess is trying to seduce Miles and Robert W. Hill believes it is Miles who is trying to seduce the governess (Lustig 158). The governess's text inspires such conjectures precisely because, to borrow obliquely from the narrator's words, the turn of the screw twists around the premise of seduction. The common denominator of all these speculations is the dominance and submission patterns that define seduction, and in turn, substantiate or vitiate power structures. What Fred G. See has observed about James's "brilliant heroines" in general can also be applied to the governess:

The problems faced by his brilliant heroines . . . is exactly a question of desire: they face, all of them, the gulf between desiring and being desired, a desperate experience which represents the difference between finding or losing, once and for all, desire's place in a world of forms, a vantage from which one may recognize and share the power of the self. (150)

It is precisely the chasm looming between the desiring and being desired that galvanizes James's text.

As for the nexus of power, it rests with the absent master whose "possession" of the actors at Bly is the catalyst of the seduction process. The concept of possession evokes both a supernatural and materialistic meaning; the former connotation involves the seizing of an individual's soul by a ghost and the latter has to do with the acquisition and retention of property. As James himself admitted, his tales embody both, "a strange mixture of matter and spirit" (*Henry James* 122), the symptoms of which demand "the inquisition of signs not as objects but as evidence of an excluded ideality which aims to reclaim them" (See 154). For our purposes, then, the alleged preternatural activity swirling around the inhabitants (past, present, and absent) of Bly emanates from a power struggle at whose core sits the absent master. He exercises his powers of possession, which are of course sanctioned both economically and culturally, over the material reality of Bly, oversees its operations through his servants, Quint, Miss Jessel, Mrs. Grose, and the governess, and exercises jurisdiction over his two wards. Most significantly, the symbol of his ultimate power of possession is his interdiction against writing, an authoritarian edict that, at the same time, inhibits the right to speak, to interpret, and to confer meaning. It is precisely this interdiction which sets in motion the epistemological whirlpool that is "The Turn of the Screw," driving the governess (and subsequent critics) into feverish attempts to assign an ultimate meaning to the events or nonevents at Bly.

The governess struggles against this interdiction, this symptom of possession, by conjuring the scenes of seduction which simultaneously attest to the master's power and yet undermine the processes which serve it. Hers is a revolt, and while she never successfully sends a letter outlining her suspicions to the master of Bly (Miles intercepts it), she does produce a narrative which, while never ultimately assigning an unequivocal meaning to events, nevertheless allows an arena for interpretation with the specter of seduction as its key. Similarly, she refuses to play the passive gothic heroine, unlike her predecessor, whom she perceives as having been seduced and abandoned. Instead, she "bounds" around Bly (142, 192, 235); she "seizes" characters and suppositions (214, 232, 236), "throws" and flings herself about (187, 203). With her words, she figuratively delivers a blow to Mrs. Grose's stomach (156), pushes people to the wall (162), and holds Miles under fire (179). Unwilling to fall into the role of seduced and despoiled governess, she summons the scenes of seduction which define the commodified status of governess in order to authorize her own rewriting not only of the traditional gothic scene but also of authentic material conditions.

The introduction to "The Turn of the Screw" and the governess's manuscript sets up the parameters which are to be undermined. Our governess is the "youngest of several daughters of a poor country parson," while the master of Bly "proved a gentleman, a bachelor in the prime of life, such a figure as had never risen, save in the dream of an old novel, before a fluttered anxious girl out of a Hampshire vicarage" (119). She is infatuated with him, but then in just the first of a series of transitions, she transfers her hopes, expectations, and dare we say, vengefulness onto her new charge, the master's nephew and heir. As Mrs. Grose elaborates:

"You will be carried away by the little gentleman!"

"Well, that, I think, is what I came for—to be carried away. I'm afraid, however," I remember feeling the impulse to add, "I'm rather easily carried away. I was carried away in London!"

I can still see Mrs. Grose's broad face as she took this in.

"In Harley Street?"

"In Harley Street."

"Well, Miss, you're not the first—and you won't be the last."

"Oh I've no pretensions," I could laugh, "to being the only one." (126)

The governess is conscious both of the materiality of her situation and the architecture which keeps her and her kind in their proper social place. Conversely, she is also aware of the danger and power inherent in being "carried away," an awareness which she displaces in her description of Bly as both a "castle of romance" and a "big ugly antique but convenient house, embodying a few features of a building still older, half-displaced and half utilised, in which I had the fancy of our being almost as lost as a handful of passengers in a great drifting ship. Well, I was strangely at the helm!" (127). Indeed, she is at the helm, more so than Miss Jessel ever was. From Mrs. Grose the governess infers, rightly or wrongly, that Miss Jessel became pregnant with Quint's child and was sent home, where she presumably died, as the result of either a miscarriage or an abortion. Her fall from innocence also implicates her in the alleged seduction of the children. Consequently, the governess holds her precursor in disdain and contempt, and as Ned Lukacher has suggested, her mind is full of gothic stereotypes when envisioning Miss Jessel (123). In the eyes of the governess, Miss Jessel is a "vile predecessor," "dishonoured and tragic," an "awful image," "dark as midnight," with a "haggard beauty" expressing an "unutterable woe" (196). I would like to suggest that the governess's aggression stems from projection and her refusal to reprise the role suggested by her vile predecessor.

As archetypal fallen woman, seduced by Quint, who, many critics have pointed out, is a convenient surrogate for the master of Bly, Miss Jessel is at once the seduced and the seductress, who in the eyes of the governess is continuing to exert an unwholesome interest upon the children from beyond the grave. This is the particular archetype that the governess refuses and rebels against, despite the insistent reminders that there is not much separating the two women. She accuses Flora of being able to see Miss Jessel "as well as you see me" (213). Mrs. Grose stares into the eyes of the governess "as if they might really have resembled" those of Miss Jessel, and the governess gazes back as if, within her gaze, "Miss Jessel again appeared" (157). Miss Jessel was also "almost as young and almost as pretty" as she is herself (129), and their resemblance is reinforced when the governess collapses on the stairs in the same place and posture as Miss Jessel on her second appearance. She also covers her face with her hands (187), exactly as Miss Jessel does on her second and third appearances (173, 196). Most significantly, the governess catches sight of the "spectre of the most horrible of women" seated at her own table, whom, at first glance, she mistakes for a housemaid purloining her pens, ink, and paper to compose "a letter to her sweetheart" (195). Miss Jessel's look appears to say that "her right to sit at my table was as good as mine to sit at hers" (196). This experience convinces the governess that, more than ever, she must remain at Bly to save the children from seductive supernatural influences and, unconsciously, that she must also remain to save herself.

As the master's "'own' man, impudent, assured, spoiled, depraved," Quint exercises the displaced influence of his employer. Mrs. Grose explains that Quint and the master "were both here—last year. Then the master went, and Quint was alone. . . . Alone with us. . . . In charge" (147). The valet wore his master's waistcoats, was a "hound" (159), according to Mrs. Grose, and was responsible for Miss Jessel's demise. However, as the governess suggests, the master is ultimately culpable, and more so, as the "everyman" that appears to her in the guise of Quint: "He remained but a few seconds—long enough to convince me he also saw and recognised; but it was as if I had always been looking at him for years and had known him always" (142). The master, Quint, and everyman are conflated to represent the perils for women like the governess, economically dependent and vulnerable to exploitation. Instead of succumbing, however, the governess turns her sights on the children and, more specifically, Miles in an attempt to contest the "machinations of a decadent patriarchy" (Lukacher 128). Hence, we see her metaphoric seduction of Miles, another of the master's surrogates: "Turned out for Sunday by his uncle's tailor, who had had a free hand and a notion of pretty waistcoats and of his grand little air, Miles's whole title to independence, the rights of his sex and situation, were so stamped upon him that if he had suddenly struck for freedom I should have had nothing to say" (189). He is the "little fairy prince" (179) from whom the governess seeks a "magnificent little surrender" (189) and their repartee often resembles that of a bored gentleman attempting to rid himself of the now unwelcome attentions of a former lover. He refers to wanting to move on (190-92) away from her company, exhorting her "to let me alone" (203) regarding "this queer business of ours" (200). In a reversal of roles, the governess all but stalks him in the candlelit darkness, visiting him in his bed, trailing him outside in the middle of the night in true gothic fashion. At one point, she describes the two of them as resembling "some young couples . . . on their wedding journey" (227).

The governess's fight for Miles's surrender is fueled by a curious amalgam of rebellion, revenge, and seduction, a response not unlike Hester Prynne's refusal to relinquish her letter and, more important, its meaning. Miles's surrender is more significant than his empty confession, which, after all, reveals exactly nothing other than a governess who revels in the "desolation of his surrender," a woman "infatuated" and "blind with victory" (234). The nature of her conquest lies in her penultimate words: "I have you" (236). This time, with the boy "dispossessed"

(236), she is in possession, both in the material and supernatural sense, truly at the helm, in a reversal of roles that traditionally would have the governess at the feet, or in the arms, of her employer.

However, unlike *The Scarlet Letter*, the Baudrillardian secret is never revealed in "The Turn of the Screw," wherein seduction continues to create a tension, a type of duel driven by the unknown that motivates it, a cypher that continues to lure readers into a field of conflict where patterns of dominance and submission, shaping material and ideological practices, are drawn.

6

VAMPIRE VOYEUR:
SPECULAR SEDUCTION IN
INTERVIEW WITH THE VAMPIRE AND "THE JOLLY CORNER"

As Rosemary Jackson explains, the gothic has long been preoccupied with "problems of vision" (45): "In Fantastic art, objects are not readily appropriated through the look: things slide away from the powerful eye/I which seeks to possess them, thus becoming distorted, disintegrated, partial and lapsing into invisibility" (45-46). In terms of the American gothic, this preoccupation is made manifest in Henry James's "The Jolly Corner," a text which foregrounds the function of the specular in Anne Rice's *Interview with the Vampire*. In both texts, the gaze or the look is both implicit and explicit in the process of seduction/consumption, the correlative of subjectivation and the death drive, and integral to the Lacanian concept of "seeing oneself seen" (Lacan, *Seminar I* 244).

The impulse toward specular seduction in both James and Rice is paralleled by the texts' narrative drive. Narration can provisionally constitute subjectivity, a way of "seeing" the subject's story so as to affirm the fiction of consciousness. The premise of *Interview* is based on an act of narration as seduction, the confessional mode of subject/object positions, involving the young journalist who is lured by the vampire Louis's compelling tale. Similarly, James's story begins and ends with Spencer Brydon confessing his fears and spectral experiences to Alice Staverton. In the words of Peter Brooks, "some narratives pretend pointedly to be oral storytelling rather than acts of writing in order to seduce the reader into a transferential relation" (236). Transferential relation, by which I mean the seduction/submission function, operates on the level of the scopic in James's and Rice's texts, that is, eroticization at the level of the gaze. The desire that drives the subjects of these texts is propelled by Lacanian misidentification, leaving the subject permanently fragmented and in perpetual slavery to desire.

"The Jolly Corner" sets up this dichotomy nicely. James's story grew from a suggestion that he follow up his tale "The Turn of the Screw" by writing an international ghost story. James had returned to

America in 1904 after twenty years in Europe. In his effort to reorient himself to his native country, he wandered through Washington Square, his old neighborhood in New York, in a reconnaissance which prompted a tale that would reverse the international themes that encompassed his earlier fiction. The premise of "The Jolly Corner" is related to James's novel *The Sense of the Past,* in which a young American finds himself at night in his ancestral home in England, his identity exchanged for that of a forebear whose portrait he had admired. Conversely, in "The Jolly Corner," Brydon returns to New York after thirty-three years abroad to confront an apparition, which he refers to as "his alter ego" (718), in his ancestral home. This horror is a fusion of what Brydon sees around him in America and appears as a version of Brydon's American self. In America, Brydon encounters the kind of unbridled mercantilism that might have consumed him had he not left for Europe. Those values "assaulted his vision wherever he looked" (713), but he admits it was precisely those "monstrosities" that had lured him back, his properties and their respective rents, those "flourishing New York leases" that had allowed him to live a leisurely life in Europe. Upon returning home, Brydon, ambivalently, becomes subsumed by the demands of commerce and building his apartment house, finding in himself "a capacity for business and a sense for construction . . . to 'go into' figures" (713). Indeed, the language of commodification controls James's text. Alice Staverton's neighborhood is reduced to "some vast ledger page" (713). Alice archly mentions that had he but stayed at home in America, Brydon would have "discovered his genius in time really to start some new variety of awful architectural hare and run it till it burrowed in a gold-mine" (714). In a similar vein, Brydon notes that his staying in New York would only have been a matter of money, "inevitably a reason of dollars. . . . There are no reasons here but of dollars. Let us therefore have none whatever—not the ghost of one" (716).

The conflation of the ghostly with commodification is made manifest through Brydon's alter ego, a horrific apparition that stands in for Brydon's American, mercantile self. That Brydon stalks his Doppelgänger is indicative of a desire of identificatory unification, a longing for a unified self and for an integrated consciousness through the fulfillment of desire. "He knew what he meant and what he wanted; it was as clear as the figure on a cheque presented in demand for cash. His alter ego 'walked'—that was the note of his image of him" (718). This quest finds its theoretical origins in Lacan's mirror phase, which forces a split between the "I" that is perceived and the "I" that is perceiving. In the mirror stage, the gaze is the conduit to self-recognition, the self, in effect, becoming the object of an Other's gaze. Permitting an illusory sense of unity, this "identity" is formed and authorized by the level of the scopic, with the gaze already the gaze of the Other. Or to borrow from Lacan, "in the scopic relation, the object on which depends the phantasy from which the subject is suspended in an essential vacillation is the gaze" (*Four Fundamental Concepts* 83). In other words, the relationship of the self to the world, of the ego produced within a social frame, is revealed through the perception of an Other. Interestingly, then, while hunting his ghost, his "duplication of consciousness" (720), Brydon was "kept in sight while remaining himself—as regards the essence of his position—sightless" (719). The play on "eyes" and seeing is reinforced; Brydon closes his eyes in "terror of vision" and in almost catching the apparition "he felt his eyes almost leave their sockets" (721). When ultimately catching the "opposed projections of him" (721), Brydon is undone by the gaze, the glare, the dangling, double eye-glass, the bared identity that is his alter ego. "He had been 'sold'" (724), he decides, before losing consciousness.

The apparition, with its deformed hand missing two fingers, convex pince-nez, and "poor ruined sight," is a "ravaged" (725) figure, whose ruin more than hints at corruption at the heart of his million dollars a year. This denouement represents a reversal of James's usual thematic predilections that concern innocent American protagonists full of dangerous illusions about the complex European order. Here it is the specter of America that is called into question. In this instance, the mirror-doubles represent the subject's attempt to master his own lack, the lack of a fixed or posited identity which might be cemented in its own specular image. However, the rejection of that image is an acknowledgment and repudiation of the conflation of desire and commodification. Brydon feels both attracted and repelled by his alter ego; he hunts him down in an elaborate gothic dance of stairways and darkened corridors, drawn by the "horrors" of commodification that his own personal specter implies.

I would suggest that an analogous desire propels Rice's vampires wherein specular seduction operates as the guarantor of subjectivity. Similar to Brydon's own history, Louis's myth of a unified self is initially dependent on the gaze of the Other, reflected in the eyes of Lestat or Armand. However, that illusory self is soon fed by cultural commodities; this particular alter ego is a totally commodified reflection. As Linda Badley has written, the vampire becomes, among other things, "the yuppie, addict, and conscience-stricken consumer" (109), reflecting a "predatory consumer culture" (111). Louis becomes as cold and distant as "strange modern paintings of lines and hard forms . . . as alien as those hard mechanical sculptures of this age which have no human form" (339); he becomes a disembodied voice on tape. Similarly, in *The*

Vampire Lestat, Lestat is reborn as a leather-clad rocker-demon on a Harley-Davidson motorcycle, a commodified objective correlative of the late-twentieth-century North America he inhabits. Rice's vampires, and even Brydon's specter, exemplify Baudrillard's concept of simulacrum, neither copy nor original, simultaneously less and more real, hyperbolic facsimiles of the "human" condition. Consequently, *Interview* reflects a fascination with seduction and simulation, with displacements and dissolutions of boundaries between the real and its simulacra, between the authentic and the counterfeit, and between the subject and the object of consumption.

Seduction and consumption, literal (blood) and figurative (commodity), are integral to vampires' survival as subjects, not unlike Brydon's survival in Europe was contingent on his "flourishing leases" in America. The vampire's "self" can only survive through the "dark trick," the consumption of blood that is predicated upon his or her talents for seduction. It is seduction that operates as the guarantor of subjectivity in *Interview,* and those elements of seduction give the text its "unrelenting erotic nature" (Liberman 117) encompassing all libidinal options. Lestat seduces Louis and a series of young men and women; the child-vampire, Claudia, must seduce her victims by pretending to be a helpless little girl. As the scene at the Théâtre des Vampires also reveals, vampiric eroticism can seduce an entire mortal audience. During a performance, a vampire dressed as death lures a mortal woman on stage and seduces both the woman and the audience into believing that the proceedings are simply an act. It would seem that in all these instances of the "dark trick," seduction exploits the desire for submission, the need to yield the fragmented self into the body of the Other in an attempt at an ideal unity.

Rice's text implicates the vampire, his victim or object of desire, and the reader in a closed circuit of scopic identification which underscores a relationship of specular seduction. As Jackson notes, that which is not seen or which threatens to be un-seeable has a subversive function in "relation to an epistemological and metaphysical system which makes 'I see' synonymous with 'I understand'" (45). As with "The Jolly Corner," *Interview* is bracketed by the recurrent image of seeing, in the opening words of the vampire Louis's "I see" to the catalytic "visions" (9) experienced by his brother, and to the penultimate question of the novel asked of the young journalist by Louis, more exhortation than query, "Do you see?" (344). The term *inter/view* further presents intriguing possibilities, "expressing mutual or reciprocal act or relation, or among, between" (*OED* 437), thereby uncovering the potentiality of an economic, libidinal, and specular exchange. *Inter,* taken as a verb rather than as a prefix, gestures as well toward another way of seeing, suggesting an interstitial vantage point from the grave or "other" side.

Lacanian emphases on the importance of the gaze accommodate the modes of seeing explored in Rice's text. Louis's quest, at its most basic, is the drive toward subjectivity through a symbolic order wherein identity can be at least provisionally reconstituted and represented. His desire mirrors the desire of the modern age which finds a marked absence at the heart of the secular world. Louis's sense of loss and alienation, as Armand reminds him, "is the very spirit of your age. Don't you see that? Everyone feels as you feel. Your fall from grace and faith has been the fall of a century" (288). The novel's resonance, according to Jean Marigny, stems precisely from its "interrogation douloureuse, ce qui est peut-être la marque d'une civilisation qui a perdu ses certitudes immuables" (591). Cast from the comparatively secure moorings of the Enlightenment "I," that eighteenth-century faith in the transcendence of the subject, Rice's novel exposes a divided subject situated within a divided text, poised on the dividing line between Romanticism and modernity. (It is not coincidental that Rice's vampires were "made" at the time of the French Revolution, representative perhaps, of the beginnings of the modern world.) As with James's text, Rice's novel draws upon the Romantic device of the Doppelgänger or double image; Louis's encounters with other vampires and specters on his journey represent manifestations of his divided self. *Interview* explores the power of the gaze in uncovering the overflow of possible but nonetheless shifting subject positions which Louis, as modern infinitely divided "self," takes up and which Lestat in postmodern self-reflexiveness ridicules. Louis's quest, his search for the vision that might provide the potential for the unified self, falls short into the limits of language, resulting in the perpetuation of divisions and self-reflexiveness. "A *spectre* with a beating heart" (168, emphasis added) whose "seeing" offers only an illusory promise of identificatory unification, Louis's gaze reflects a longing for a unified self and for an integrated consciousness through the fulfillment of desire.

Interestingly, then, one of the "greatest pleasures of a vampire, is that of watching people unbeknownst to them" (42). "I was always looking" (51), Louis tells the young journalist. He is vampire/voyeur who observes "with fascination" (78) as Lestat seduces and kills two women in their New Orleans townhouse. He watches human lives "through glass" (87), seeing himself being seen, his "identity" reflected in their eyes. As the plantation Pointe du Lac is burning, Louis encounters the overseer, Daniel, who "looked at me with eyes of glass. I was a monster to him" (53). Yet, Louis confesses that when alive "I gazed at nothing, not even a mirror . . . especially not a mirror . . . with a free eye" (46). (It is interesting to note that traditional vampire lore does not allow the vampire a reflection at all; he stands totally outside society [the symbolic] in a space where identity is meaningless.) Explained another way, Rice's vampires transgress the boundaries delineating the imaginary and the symbolic. At once part of a pre-oedipal state characterized by the anarchic, incestuous, sadistic, and pregendered, they also anticipate entry into the symbolic and its required repression by the signifying obligation.

This modality, oscillating, as we shall soon see, between the real, the imaginary, and the symbolic, plays itself out more specifically in the critical passage chronicling the murder of Lestat's *blind* and ailing father. The scene opens with an encounter between Louis and the plantation's overseer, Daniel. Confirmed as a monster in the overseer's eyes, Louis, true to his provisionally "monstrous" self, plunges a knife into the overseer's heart at the precise instant of seeing "Lestat's figure emerge in the mirror over the sideboard" (54). At the moment of identification with Lestat's image, Louis is ordered by Lestat to murder the blind patriarch. Reluctant and appalled, Louis nonetheless stands in as son, whispering the word "father" to the dying man, who is unable to identify him visually, before dispatching him. Assuming a false identity, which can be neither authorized nor challenged by a blind and failing patriarchal symbol, Louis as ersatz son denies the Name-of-the-Father and inclusion into the symbolic order. Consequently, the murder of the old man is both a repudiation of the Law and an ambivalent attempt at subjectivation.

The instances of the mirror-doubles in this passage also represent the subject's attempt to master his own lack, the lack of a fixed or posited identity which might be cemented in its own specular image. As Jackson documents, gothic fantasies of dualism and mirror images work as a "powerful metaphor for returning to an original unity, a 'paradise' lost by the 'fall' into division with the construction of a subject" (89). While the mirror stage positions the subject within a physical space, it does not offer the agency to participate in social or symbolic exchange with others. Louis's momentary identification with the overseer, in whose eyes he sees reflected a monster, indicates his own inner "reality" turned outward to be reflected through the gaze of the Other. His murder of the overseer prefigures his identification with Lestat, foreshadowing the ersatz son's murder of the father. Importantly, after the deed is done and Louis decides to "torch the house" (57), which is representative of family and patrilineal identity, he vows to "turn to the wealth I'd held under many names, safe for just such a moment."

Thereafter, Louis attempts identification not with the Name but with "many names." The hunt for origins, the "who made us" quest, echoes throughout the text, a search for "a hundred things under a hundred names" (340) that takes Louis and Claudia to Eastern Europe and Paris. Lestat, characterized by his excessive, seductive, and sadistic tendencies, significantly betrays no interest in either his human father or his vampire origins in *Interview*. He is the ultimate seducer, marked by the chaotic pre-mirror stage that Lacan has linked with *jouissance,* "a radically violent pleasure which shatters, dissipates, loses—the ego" (Barthes 91). This domain, centered upon an original, primary narcissism, obstructs possibilities of symbolic, that is, societal imperatives. Lestat stands firmly in the oedipal, that imaginary realm, a young man whose father had disowned him and "would not acknowledge any mention of our names" (*Lestat* 61). He is a young man linked stubbornly to his mother with whom he had "a powerful understanding" (Lestat 27), a relationship precluding speech and transgressing incest taboos. Lestat's quest is propelled by a longing for the imaginary, a return to undifferentiation and the primary (m)other. Consequently, Lestat's journey is marked by sadism, horror, or that which suggests or projects "the dissolution of the symbolic through violent reversal or rejection of the process of the subject's formation" (Jackson 91).

Conversely, for Louis, the images of seeing and mirrors mark a process of *méconnaissance* or misrecognition that relentlessly emphasizes the subject's lack. Louis creates a set of false identification strategies that lead exactly nowhere. The pilgrimage to Eastern Europe ends with an encounter with a primitive vampire, in whose eyes Louis hopes he may find the recognition necessary to make him "whole." "Close your eyes for an instant, and then open them slowly. And when you do, you will see it," Claudia counsels, as Louis turns his gaze on the creature silhouetted in the moonlight: "For one full instant he looked at me, and I saw the light shining in those eyes and then glinting on two sharp canine teeth; and then a low strangled cry seemed to rise from the depths of his throat which, for a second, I thought to be my own" (191). The aim of the subject's desire is to fuse with the Other, in this case the mindless corpse of the primitive vampire whose strangled cry Louis momentarily believes to be his own. Shortly thereafter, Louis also "identifies" with the grieving mortal, Morgan, with whom he does "a strange thing. I told him my name, which I confided in almost no one" (176). The scene in which Louis encounters the now dying Morgan is once again replete with specular imagery:

. . . it was Morgan, whose pale face showed now in the moon, the marks of the vampire on his throat, his blue eyes staring mute and expressionless before him. Suddenly they widened as I drew close to him. "Louis!" he whispered in astonishment, his lips moving as if he were trying to frame words but could not. "Louis . . ." he said again . . . he reached out for me. I turned and ran from him. . . . "Louis," he called out again, the light gleaming in his eyes. He seemed blind to the ruins, blind to the night, blind to everything but a face he recognized, that one word again issuing from his lips. I put my hands to my ears, backing away from him. (193)

Louis's anguish at hearing his name is an implication of the paternal metaphor in the symbolic debt whose acceptance would confer a Name and an authorized speaking position. In the order of symbolic functioning, the Other is embodied in the figure of the symbolic father who seeks to mediate in narcissistic and imaginary identifications and gratifications. It is interesting to note that Morgan/Other has difficulty formulating words, that is, speech, other than the one name which Louis is desperate to deny, his given Name. Explained otherwise, here exists the threat that "the mirror might be splintered by the word" (Ragland-Sullivan 279), that is, by the symbolic. Significantly, Louis tells his young interviewer, "we had no name" (208).

In yet another quest to shore up his fragmented sense of self, Louis's meeting with his Doppelgänger, the vampire Santiago, triggers another play of misrecognition that once again disrupts his fantasy of completion. The gaze and the mirror become once again an unreliable medium of interpretation:

He [Santiago] was enormous in height though gaunt as myself... black eyes staring at me in what seemed undisguised wonder. . . . And then suddenly I realized that not only was his black hair long and full and combed precisely like my own, and not only was he dressed in identical coat and cape to my own, but he stood imitating my stance and facial expression to perfection . . . as I barely moved my lips, he barely moved his lips, and I found the words dead and I couldn't make other words to confront this, to stop it. And all the while, there was that height and those sharp black eyes and that powerful attention which was, of course, perfect mockery, but nevertheless riveted to myself. He was the vampire; I seemed the mirror. (213)

Again, speech is precluded, words are necessarily "dead," and conscious perception has been disorganized by another's gaze in a play of self-idealization and misrecognition. Desire in relation to the other is found in the "observation of observation" (Lacan, *Seminar II* 312). Brydon's encounter with his Doppelgänger is positioned in much the same way:

Rigid and conscious, spectral yet human, a man of his own substance and stature waited there to measure himself with his power to dismay . . . So

Brydon, before him, took him in; with every fact of him now, in the higher light, hard and acute—his planted stillness, his vivid truth, his grizzled bent head and white masking hands, his queer actuality of evening-dress, of dangling double eye-glass, of gleaming silk lappet and white linen, of pearl button and gold watch-guard and polished show. No portrait by a great modern master could have presented him with more intensity. (724)

Which is more "real"—the mirror and the portrait or Louis and Brydon? Interpreted more directly, both Louis's and Brydon's subsequent panic is prompted by the disintegration of even a provisional subjectivity which has undermined the reality of the "moi," self as object and Other, leaving only a symptom, in the case of Louis, a "perfect mockery" of himself which reveals him as a "complete fool" (215), and in the case of Brydon, weak denials as he lies prostrate in Alice's arms. Similarly, an encounter with and seduction of an artist in Montmartre culminates in a portrait of Louis, "captured perfectly" but with "nothing of the horror in it" (260). The end result of a vampiric seduction, the likeness operates once again as a symptom, the product of misrecognition.

Louis cannot assimilate the fiction of his subjectivity as represented by the disorienting gaze, that is, the mocking Santiago and the portrait. Similarly, Brydon cannot assimilate the image presented by his alter ego, a reflection of the fiction that his own subjectivity presents. "It's not me," he intones repeatedly to Alice. The disorienting gaze of the Other coincides with Lacan's concept of the real, the domain of the inexpressible, or that which cannot be symbolized (Benvenuto 166). According to Lacan, that which has been foreclosed from the symbolic returns to the real (*Four Fundamental Concepts* 38), usually in terms of a threat. Or to borrow from Ellie Ragland-Sullivan, the "Other (A) is the place of the unconscious and thus is either a dark-faced and absent part of oneself which one must flee or a mysterious force which one renders divine and proceeds to worship" (297). Brydon tries to flee the dark-faced and absent part of himself. Louis flees the threat represented by Santiago, a seemingly inescapable confrontation or conflation of self with Other, but is compelled to love and follow Armand, to see in him "the reflection of myself" (309), allowing "my eyes [to] penetrate his eyes" (319), thereby seduced by and surrendering to a deceptive, identificatory fusion. On the banks of the Mississippi years later, the illusion is finally acknowledged and relinquished in the words of Armand to Louis: "I have the dreadful feeling that I don't exist at all. And you are as cold and distant from me as those strange modern paintings of lines and hard forms that I cannot love or comprehend. . . . I shudder when I'm near you. I look into your eyes and my reflection isn't there" (339). The illusion of subjectivity as conferred by the gaze is revealed more pointedly by the intrusion of the Real which cannot be translated to support the subject's "reality" or fiction. It rests beyond any hope of representation into which, for example, Armand had hoped to insert himself.

Analogously, Louis cannot articulate the actual experience of his preternatural transformation, a narrative that comes with its share of blanks and frightening elements which carry the potential of undermining his "reality": "I can't tell you exactly. . . . I can tell you about it, enclose it with words that will make the value of it to me evident to you. But I can't tell you exactly, anymore than I could tell you exactly what is the experience of sex if you have never had it" (14). Indeed, the Real is connected to the concepts of death and sexuality, a union which yields a surplus pleasure, a *jouissance* which is denied the speaking subject but available to the subject in the Imaginary and the Real. This pleasure is driven by a desire or yearning for original unity which can never be fulfilled. Seduction is its modus operandi: "I kill humans every night. I seduce them, draw them close to me, with an insatiable hunger, a constant never-ending search for something . . . something, I don't know what it is . . ." (*Interview* 125). Or to paraphrase Lacan, the yearning for this unity is the primary desire of the subject, but, at the same time, an irreducible deferral of gratification.

Outside the symbolic, *jouissance* transgresses the Law-of-the-Father, moving beyond the pleasure principle into the orbit of the forbidden. Beyond the Law, Rice's vampires exist in a realm that is characterized by the anarchic, incestuous, sadistic, oral, and pregendered. Without the phallus, the indicator of difference, Rice's vampires cannot take up a gendered position that is socially and culturally (symbolically) constructed. The phallus is literally and figuratively missing in Rice's text, beginning with the ancient king and original vampire, Osiris, who was dismembered by his brother Typhon and subsequently pieced together again by the faithful Isis: "As for the missing part of the body, the part that Isis never found, well, there is one part of us which is not enhanced by the Dark Gift isn't there? We can speak, see, taste, breathe, move as humans move, but we cannot procreate" (*Lestat* 289).

Consequently, the text offers the androgynous, polymorphous sexuality that transcends notions of hetero- and homosexuality as well as the incest taboo. It exemplifies a decadence that flies in the face of the traditional vampire myth as a cautionary tale against incest (Twitchell). Rice's vampires cannot be destroyed by a fatal and phallic stake-through-the-heart in a world where seduction is oral. "Let the flesh instruct the mind," Claudia, child vampire, counsels more than once

(123, 154). In the moment of *jouissance,* driven by the pre-oedipal impulse integral to vampire existence, the oral, rather than the phallic, is the controlling principle: "I sucked the blood from Lestat's wrist and felt his heart pound with my heart. It is again and again a celebration of that experience; because for vampires that is the ultimate experience. . . . The sucking mesmerized me" (28-29). As Marigny notes, the analogy between the vampiric act and the sexual one in Rice's test is made abundantly clear: "On y trouve en particulier un même mouvement rythmique qui va en s'amplifiant, symbolise ici par le battement des deux coeurs, puis qui se calme subitement, aboutissant à un état extaltique d'apésanteur qui s'apparente à l'orgasme" (554). An aura of sensuality, of a feverish eroticism, infuses the vampiric quest. Seduction is at its center, allowing for a temporary but blissful illusion of fusion with the Other.

The preeminence of orality over the phallic manifests itself in other ways in Rice's text. The concept of family as delineated by the Law and the symbolic is radically undermined and reconfigured by the two "fathers" who wrest the girl child, Claudia, from the arms of her already dead mother. Distilled in Louis's initial attraction to Claudia is a perverse reenactment of the original mother/child dyad, another manifestation of the desire for a pre-symbolic wholeness. The relationship between Louis and Claudia is subsequently described in incestuous terms as "Father and Daughter. Lover and Lover" (102). When Claudia asserts herself as her mamma's daughter, Lestat replies: "No, dear, not anymore. . . . You're our daughter, Louis's daughter and my daughter, do you see? Now, whom should you sleep with? Louis or me?" (95). Claudia's malleability, which allows her to be at once doll-like, child-like, seductress, mistress, paramour, and daughter, enacts a performance upon which Louis's and Lestat's lack is projected, performances which not only transcend taboos enacted by the Law but also allow for the mirage of stable identities. To draw upon Lacan, "in the life of a man, a woman is something he believes in. He believes there is one, or at times two or three" (*Feminine Sexuality* 186). Claudia is necessary to both Lestat and Louis in order to keep the fiction of an authentic subjectivity alive. Doll, daughter, or seductress, she exists to satisfy and fulfill Louis's and Lestat's versions of themselves, "à la fois l'innocence et la perversité . . . à l'image de la femme-enfant, frivole et coquette" (Marigny 231). Claudia cannot exist without them; she is the Lacanian concept of woman as symptom. "As much as I hated him [Lestat] with him we were . . . complete," she says. "No," responds Louis, "only you were complete. . . . Because there were two of us, one on either side of you from the beginning" (200-1). When she is finally abandoned for Armand, she turns to ashes; no longer necessary to "complete" Louis, her reason for being dissolves.

Claudia's attempt at authentic subjectivity hinges upon her seduction of Madeleine, a dollmaker who makes the same doll again and again in an attempt to remake the daughter she has lost. In turn, Claudia asks Madeleine to create for her a "lady doll" to fill the void of both her dead mother and the woman she might have become. As Badley points out, "Claudia desires Madeline [sic] much as Madeline desires her, not as a mother or a lover but as an image to complete the self" (131). Nonetheless, this desire translates into a vampiric seduction whose goal is subjective insertion in society and ideology. Claudia wishes to escape from the doll-like prison created for her by Lestat and Louis, a purgatory that represents the passive and truncated characterization of woman as little girl. She tries on for size the socially inscribed roles of mother/daughter/adult woman only to find these identities as fragmentary and untenable as the roles written for her by her vampire "parents." As she explains to Louis:

"A beautiful child," she said glancing up at me. "Is that what you still think I am? . . . Yes I resemble her baby dolls, I am her baby dolls." Something seemed to shift suddenly, something within the very walls of the room itself, and the mirrors trembled with her image as if the earth had sighed beneath the foundations. . . . And then I saw what her still childish figure was doing: in one hand she held the doll, the other to her lips; and the hand that held the doll was crushing it, crushing it and popping it so it bobbed and broke in a heap of glass. . . . She wrung the tiny dress to make a shower of glittering particles as I averted my eyes, only to see her in the tilted mirror over the fire, see her eyes scanning me from my feet to the top of my head. She moved through that mirror towards me and drew close on the bed. "Why do you look away, why don't you look at me?" (210)

Louis averts his gaze from the guarantor of his provisionally unified consciousness, away from the wholeness of the metaphoric mirror that is now shattered, the multitude of shards, no longer an intact doll, but reflecting the infinitely divided nature of the self. Yet Claudia, according to Louis, provides him with an illusory self and thereby "made it mean something" (239), conferring signification and identity as a paradoxically unifying force through her many roles. Both the fragility and power of the gaze may manifest itself, to borrow from Ragland-Sullivan, as fragments in hallucinations, dreams, or memories (95). In Louis's memory of Claudia, he had "the most disconcerting sensation . . . she would look up from that game of solitaire, and the sockets of her eyes would be empty" (337). She would be, finally, incapable of the consolatory illusion of authentication.

The impulse toward specular seduction in *Interview* is paralleled by the text's narrative drive. Narration can provisionally constitute subjectivity, seducing the Other into "seeing" the subject's story so as to underwrite the fiction of consciousness. This desire prompts Louis to say to the young journalist at the outset of their interview, "let me take things in order" (15), or in other words, let me construct a coherent identity for you to believe in and authorize for me. Alternatively, Louis asks: "Is this what you want? Is this what you wanted to hear?" Then he feels panic at the journalist's lack of response/authorization: "You don't answer me. I'm not giving you what you want, am I?" (67). The desire to narrate the "true" self is answered, appropriately enough, by the presence of the tape recorder, the material manifestation of the identity which Louis so craves. The machine registers every word that is eventually transformed into a novel, a best-seller which everyone reads but nobody believes to be anything but fiction.

This fictional identity is commodified on tape and eventually in best-seller format, the product of a long line of vampiric seductions (consumptions) that, I would suggest, are socially, economically, and historically inscribed in American culture. Beginning with James's "The Jolly Corner," specular seduction is an element in the gothic narrative that underscores the uncertainty and dislocation of the self which can only find temporary surcease in a conflation of desire and material consumption. As Bette Roberts has noted in another context, Louis's seduction by Lestat and then by Armand is reminiscent of another form of "enslavement" (95), recalling a tradition including *Narrative of the Captivity, Sufferings and Remarks of Mrs. Mary Rowlandson* and *My Life and Bondage* by Frederick Douglass. In these texts, the reality of captivity is as harrowing as Rice's gothicized and supernatural version, a historical template that perhaps serves to emphasize the relationship between the consumption of blood, metaphorically and figuratively, and the construction of the self. "But it's not me," insists James's Brydon, desperate to separate himself from that particular image. Nonetheless, despite Brydon's and the reader's unease, the power of the American gothic rests precisely in its ability to hold up a mirror to an experience of commodification from which we should have difficulty turning away. As the next chapter reveals, seduction is closely allied to a violence that is predicated on the operations of subjectivity as defined by commodity signs—conferred by the ownership of slaves and withheld as a consequence of race and gender.

7

WICKED LIASON(S):

BELLEFLEUR, BELOVED, POE, AND THE VAMPIRE / SUCCUBUS

As we have already seen, there are several connotations relevant to the concept of seduction; it challenges the principles of production and consumption and, yet, it is implicated in the network of commodification and consumption. Contextualizing the work of Edgar Allan Poe, the novels of Joyce Carol Oates and Toni Morrison explore further the implications of seduction by thematizing the "wicked liaisons" (Oates 201) that operate against the grain of traditional interpretations of the gothic. The place to begin here is with the theorists who locate the original seduction theory in Freud's attempts to explain certain behaviors in his female patients with regard to sexualized relationships (whether real or imaginary) involving dominant men within their immediate familial circles. The result of these sexual encounters, according to Freud, was hysteria. In order to uncover the aetiology of hysteria, Freud found himself dealing with issues of power and domination in society, and as Martha Noel Evans has suggested, his discomfiture with his findings is made clear in his writings, which make use of the word "seduction" to refer to what is, after all, a theory of trauma: "The shift in Freud's vocabulary from words denoting injury to one implying persuasion and even possible assent can be seen as part of a widespread social pattern which minimizes the sexual exploitation of women by men" (Evans 74).

In itself ambiguous, Freud's legacy has been variably absorbed and reconfigured by literary theorists who focus primarily upon the implications of seduction and the politics of interpretation. Madelon Sprengnether, for example, has noted the significance of Freud's linguistic influence over his by-now-famous patient, Dora, through his role of analyst as interpreter. The pattern of dominance and submission operates as the foundation of the seduction process. The form of seduction via interpretation (Sprengnether), that is, the right to speak, to interpret, and to confer meaning, is culturally encoded as a male prerogative marked by these patterns of dominance and submission. Because subjectivity is constituted through language, denial of the right to speak, interpret, and confer meaning influences the very real, material ways in which women and men are socially constituted. These material practices are the issues that Morrison and Oates explore through the use of a traditional gothic trope, the female vampire or succubus. Specifically, my focus will be Beloved and her vampiric relationship with Sethe and Paul D and Oates's twist on the vampire theme in *Bellefleur*'s "Room of Contamination" and "Bloodstone" chapters. These texts allude strongly to Poe, drawing on his female creations, those women who play at but refuse to stay dead. Poe's abstractions of fetishized gender imagery find their way, although in different form, into Morrison's and Oates's texts to reveal more clearly the economic and social violence through which women are constituted as subjects or, conversely, denied subjectivity.

Traditionally, this trope has found shape as a sexualized demon that drains the vital life fluid, either blood or semen, from her victims (Guiley 92). She has also made an appearance in African American literature, prominently in Charles Chesnutt's *The Conjure Woman* (1899) (Puckett 568) as a shape-shifting witch who "rides" her victims at night. In *Beloved* and *Bellefleur* she is more obviously the seductress, an overtly eroticized figure who is less specter and more temptress, a figure conjured along both realistic and fantastic lines. She seduces in order to drain her oppressors, to rob them of their subjectivity and to contest the patterns of dominance and submission that shape material and ideological practices such as slavery, racism, and sexism. Unlike her gothic foremothers, Morrison's and Oates's vampire/succubus is the specter of womanhood that, this time, refuses even to play at being dead. Poe's protagonists, for example, struggle in fairy-tale-like circumstances, out of space and out of time, with women who reject being contained. Poe's fiction is structured around evasion and allegorical displacement, a gothic play of terror and exaggeration that keeps the reader and the protagonist at least at arm's length from however many versions of the truth there might be. "The Fall of the House of Usher" is allegorical in nature, the interpellation of the "Mad Trist" story and Madeline's resurrection only hinting at the incestuous decadence of an antebellum South. What does emerge, however covertly, is that Madeline and her counterparts Ligeia, Berenice, and Morella suggest different interpretations of the erotic, interpretations which throw into sharp relief deep anxieties concerning women's libidinal appetites as potentially destabilizing forces in society. These forces were to be contained, negated, or neutralized to maintain at least surface control not only over narratives but also social constructs. A woman on her wedding bed or funeral bier suggests immobilization, Coventry Patmore's "Angel in the House" reconstituted.

There are clearly elements both of the vampiric and the erotic in Poe's female figures, traces of which can be found in Morrison's and Oates's texts. However, Poe etherealizes his female subjects, while conveniently etherealizing, obscuring, or better yet, draining his text of its potential meanings. I would suggest Morrison's and Oates's texts accomplish the opposite, reenergizing or revivifying the seductive vampire/succubus trope by linking it with the economic and social violence through which women are constituted as subjects or, conversely, denied subjectivity. In "House of Usher," Poe's abstractions or elisions begin with the narrator's reluctance to make meanings or connections from "fancies and superstitions" "the shadowy fancies" (*Collected* 267). Quite obviously, the house is drawn as a fairly explicit composite of the inner workings of a man's mind—windows like eyes, vines growing in profusion, similar to the arabesques of Roderick Usher's own hair, a tower (phallic) poised over the female image of a tarn, and so on. The narrator also denies the strange feelings he experiences during the first and only encounter with the living Madeline; similarly, Roderick has cut himself off from any sensory perceptions so that his thoughts are purely abstracted, exemplified in his portrait of an idea and his poem describing reason's topple from the throne. As well, the "Mad Trist" allegory is one step removed, a "weak specification" that only insinuates meaning which is deliberately held at bay, much like Madeline herself. However, the narrator cannot prevent Madeline from actually intruding and writing in the margins of the text that is both "Mad Trist" and "The House of Usher." Her cries encroach on the master text, and the narrative concludes with the house folding into itself, a symbol of incest as well as devouring, insistent femaleness as represented by the tarn. By literally running away, the narrator refuses to confer meaning upon or offer explanations for his story.

Similarly, "Ligeia" traces the parallel processes of the etherealization of the female subject and the draining of meaning from a text. A dead woman for Poe is a good woman in the same way an obscure text which elides certain social issues serves as an avoidance mechanism masked in gothic terms. Typically, Ligeia is first idealized by the narrator, her face and form like marble, lily white. She is Astarte, a goddess who finds her consummate form in death. Her poem "The Conqueror Worm" is both her attempt to stay alive, at least through authorship, and her own incursion into the master text. Ligeia imports meaning into a text that is ostensibly about death and decay by suggesting images of phallic oppression. Her return, conjured by the narrator's invocation of her name, gives her, literally, the last word, a signifier for the signified, in a text where both meaning and women are symbolically depleted. Ligeia is the agent, the vampire who manages her own "return," although at Rowena's expense.

Poe's short story "Morella" finds echo in the Sethe and Beloved duality of Morrison's text. Morella is the "worm that *would* not die" (69), a woman who feeds upon the narrator, who first grows pale (64) and finds that his "wife's manner oppressed me as a spell" (65). After an earthly struggle, it is Morella who conveniently begins to "pine away daily" (66) before succumbing simultaneously to what is both death and birth. She fights the narrator's wish for her demise: "Shall I not then say that I longed with an earnest and consuming desire for the moment of Morella's decease? I did" (66). As her vitality flows away, she gives birth to a daughter who seems to take her place. Just as Sethe is depleted by Beloved, who takes on physical size and power as her own is diminished, Morella's daughter grows "strangely in stature and intelligence. Strange, indeed, was her rapid increase in bodily size" (68). The daughter is the mother reanimated, the woman who refuses to stay dead, a conflation of female identities that struggles against literal and figurative containment.

As a predecessor to Morrison and Oates, Poe was influenced by issues of gender and race. Joan Dayan notes the important presence in Poe's life of "the black woman in the house" while Poe was growing up ("Amorous Bondage" 264). She maintains that the presence in African American stories of "the angry dead, sightings of teeth, the bones of charms, the power of conjuring" influenced Poe's interpretation of the gothic (265). Borrowing from these tropes, Poe denaturalized the "natural order of things" (249) by actively illustrating how women were converted into property or possessions. However, much as Poe's female subjects are robbed of their vitality—their subjectivity as it were—Morrison's Beloved sets up an interesting opposition wherein the female vampire/succubus figure actively resists this depletion by depleting the power of the patriarchal order. In other words, the story doesn't end with her coming back to life; in effect, her coming back to life propels the story forward. "We can describe the title character as a witch, a ghost a devil or a succubus" and "the point of view of the narrative encourages us to see her as the traditional vampire" (155), suggests Trudier Harris. As Pamela E. Barnett has argued, *Beloved* exploits the succubus figure to represent the effects of institutionalized rape during slavery (see chapter 1 above). Along the same continuum, Beloved's role of vampire/succubus calls into question the complex of social networks and real conditions that help to reproduce relations of race and gender. Her seductions of Sethe and Paul D work simultaneously to reveal and problematize the ideology allowing for the commodification of reproduction and slavery. By consuming Sethe's vitality and Paul D's semen, Beloved gains the material to construct a language and hence a subjectivity that takes the form of an alternative story that, otherwise, could be neither remembered nor passed on. Beloved's form takes on the "shape of a pregnant woman" (261), her body protruding like a "winning watermelon" (250); she carries within her the collective experiences of her race. Consequently, when she disappears like the vampire or succubus of a "bad dream" (274), "they couldn't remember or repeat a single thing she said, and began to believe that, other than what they themselves were thinking, she hadn't said anything at all." (274). Through her seduction of Sethe and Paul D, Beloved gathers others' "thinking," and their memories, when concentrated, form the fragile basis of self-definition through a collective consciousness outside the imposed social constructs of gender and race.

This process is exemplified by Beloved's desire, her appetite for seduction that introduces the longing for the unattainable original presence beyond the symbolic. She seduces Paul D, forcing him from Sethe's room to the cold house where she exhorts him to "touch me. On the inside part" (263). He succumbs, convinced he is doing so against his will: "something is happening to me, that girl is doing it . . . she is doing it to me. Fixing me. Sethe, she's fixed me and I can't break it" (127). The spell of seduction, the fact that Beloved is constantly aroused or "shining" (57), is vampiric in nature. In the daylight, Paul D "can't imagine it. . . . Nor the desire that drowned him there and forced him to struggle up, up into that girl like she was the clear air at the top of the sea. . . . It was more like a brainless urge to stay alive" (264). Similarly, Beloved literally sucks her mother dry, an impetus foreshadowed in the scene where Sethe's water breaks and Beloved "walks out of the water" (50) and then consumes numerous glasses of water. She is hungry for her mother, who is "licked, tasted, eaten by Beloved's eyes" (57), and she seduces her as Sethe is "sliding into sleep" and experiences a "touch no heavier than a feather but loaded, nevertheless, with desire" (58). Beloved's desire to kiss Sethe on the neck in the clearing is also clearly vampiric in nature, paralleling her insatiable appetite for her mother's stories. Significantly, she has a "thirst for hearing":

It became a way to feed her. Just as Denver discovered and relied on the delightful effect sweet things had on Beloved, Sethe learned the profound satisfaction Beloved got from storytelling. It amazed Sethe (as much as it pleased Beloved) because every mention of her past life hurt. Everything in it was painful or lost. She and Baby Suggs had agreed without saying so that it was unspeakable; to Denver's inquiries Sethe gave short replies or rambling incomplete reveries. Even with Paul D, who shared some of it and to whom she could talk with at least a measure of calm, the hurt was always there— But as she began telling about the earrings, she found herself wanting to, liking it. Perhaps it was Beloved's distance from the events itself, or her thirst for hearing it—in any case it was an unexpected pleasure. (58)

The conflation of pleasure and thirst underscores Beloved's seduction of Sethe, who goes into a decline as Beloved's strength grows. However, the pleasure and the thirst are both theirs; for Sethe, the thirst is the need to remember, and the pleasure emerges from communion with her daughter. For Beloved, her thirst is for hearing, and her pleasure derives from reclaiming her mother. But paradoxically, seduction also connotes both pleasure and pain, a yielding and diminishment of Sethe's fragmented self comprising the painful and the lost, the unspeakable. In the final scene of the novel, Sethe reenacts the image of the vampire's victim, a fading figure whose gradual enervation parallels her vampire's increasing force. That power is symbolized by Beloved's pregnant shape, the ripening womb of a collective identity that undermines the economics of reproduction experienced as slavery. She stands "thunderblack and glistening . . . her belly big and tight. Vines of hair twisted all over her head. Jesus. Her smile was dazzling" (261). Having fed from the stories and memories of her race, Beloved emerges as a goddess figure capable of bringing into being, forfeited through slavery and dispossession, a lost African self.

Conjuring images of both the supernatural and rebirth, the text's exorcism scene also doubles as a scene of birth. Just as Sethe commits infanticide as a desperate attempt to assert ownership over the products of her body and just as her own mother "threw away . . . without names" the babies she could not by rights claim, so too does Beloved demand retribution from a system which reduces human beings to objects, possessions, and property with only economic value. Significantly, the exorcism scene is a rewriting of an earlier episode in which Sethe attempts to save her children from a non-life of slavery. Now Sethe is the "little girl" and imagines that schoolteacher rather than abolitionist Edward Bodwin has returned for her "best thing" (262). While the former encounter resulted in a child's murder, the latter results in a birth. In effect, it is Beloved's "pregnancy" that signifies the "dead coming back to life" (35), a continuation of the vampiric theme that marks the text. The women gathered to exorcise the ghost of Beloved are also the midwives who attend to a birth that they may now claim as theirs. While the women assemble outside the house on Bluestone, Sethe ministers to

Beloved as though she were in labor. Beloved is "sweating profusely . . . sprawled on the bed in the keeping room, a salt rock in her hand" (261). The gathered women, in a rite of exorcism and delivery, are searching for

the right combination, the key, the code, the sound that broke the back of words. Building voice upon voice until they found it, and when they did it was a wave of sound wide enough to sound deep water and knock the pods off chestnut trees. It broke over Sethe and she trembled like the baptized in its wash. (261)

The cadence here is that of parturition, the image of water breaking integrated with the recurring water metaphor that dominates Morrison's text. Beloved has sucked Sethe dry in order to forge a collective consciousness and, earlier, Sethe sought liberation from the river of life that is the Ohio which she crosses to gain freedom; at the river her water breaks and she gives birth to Denver. She also drinks water from the river, the flow that symbolizes emancipation, a form of ritual cleansing that is reenacted when Baby Suggs bathes her. Water is a life force, baptismal in nature and, significantly, linked to the vampire trope in terms of its capacity to sustain or end life. Beloved takes Sethe to the brink of death, drinking her life as she once drank her milk. Ironically, the "undead" is required to give life, that is, to seduce, consume, and, ultimately, begin the reintegration necessary for the lost African self. Consequently, the women assembled outside 124 find the "right combination," a communal building of "voice upon voice" that delivers the words and the language, the instruments of power crucial to self-definition.

The specter of Beloved disappears with the birth of "remembering," a challenge to a world in which the value of humanity is nonexistent other than in purely economic terms. Remembering is crucial and yet understandably painful. Consequently, the black community deliberately tries to forget her "like a bad dream" (274) and "like an unpleasant dream during a troubling sleep" (275). However, like the vampire of myth, Beloved continues to disturb them in sleep, ensuring that footprints, the "photograph of a close friend or relative" (275), and the traces of the disremembered and unaccounted for are reclaimed and reintegrated into a newly emerging community. She continues the painful work through seduction, with the "rustle of a skirt" and "knuckles brushing a cheek in sleep," and with "certainly no clamor for a kiss" (275).

The trope of seduction, as a means of subverting patterns of dominance and submission that shape material practices such as slavery, racism, and sexism, is reworked once again in *Bellefleur* with a decided debt to Poe. Just as Beloved's seduction of Sethe and Paul D reveals the ideology allowing for the commodification of reproduction and slavery, so too does Oates's treatment of the vampire/succubus myth. Oates predicates her manipulation of the myth on the psychological and sociological connections between the sexual exploitation of black women and the etherealization of white women, an issue Poe would explore in the context of his female figures again and again. As Minrose C. Gwin has suggested with Poe in mind, "it is not the smallest irony of the slavocracy that its codes of conduct demanded moral superiority from white women and sexual availability from black" ("Green-eyed Monsters" 39). Similarly, Katherine Fishburn notes that southern society denied women of both races the opportunity for self-determination: "Whereas the lady was deprived of her sexuality, the black woman was identified with hers" (39). White women were expected to reflect "delicate constitutions, sexual purity and moral superiority to men," while black women were "subhuman creatures who, by nature, were strong and sexual" (39).

Ostensibly, it is this picture that *Bellefleur* re-creates in two of the multilayered narratives that comprise the novel. In "The Room of Contamination" we see the scion of the Bellefleur family seduced repeatedly by the specter of a black woman until he fades away and literally disappears. Conversely, we also have the story of "The Bloodstone" and great-aunt Veronica, a perennially girlish figure and unclaimed treasure whose "perpetual virginity" (360) is assured only by her family, who steadfastly refuse to see her vampiric nature. In effect, then, we have the sexualized figure of the black specter and the etherealized white lady, the "whore/virgin dichotomy" (Gwin) that Oates rewrites. Situated within that dichotomy is Oates's rendering of sexuality or "how sexuality contributes to, or often mocks, our attempts to order our lives" (Waller 17). As critics such as G. F. Waller have acknowledged, Oates's texts adumbrate "possibility and power" in sexual relations, or what Oates herself terms "the totally irrational, possessive, ego-destroying love, which can't be controlled and is, perhaps, a pathological condition of the soul" (18). Such is the power of seduction in *Bellefleur,* "an attraction of person to person so violent that it expresses itself as obsession and takes on the quality of fatality" (Kazin 43).

The link which yokes eroticism with violence in Oates's text allows for the undermining of the hierarchical, competitive, and acquisitive Bellefleur family agenda. As Marilyn C. Wesley has noted, "Oates's obsessive theme and plot is the American family and the misuse of power" (141). That process begins with the questioning of gender construction, as evidenced by the hermaphrodite Germaine, the androgynous Mrs. Rache, the aggressive Brown Lucy, and the avariciously ambitious Leah. As the precocious young Bromwell Bellefleur asks: "What was sex? What were the sexes? The details of sex were of no significance, for wasn't life on this planet clearly a matter of . . . indefinable energy flowing violently through all things?" (287). The concept of violent energy, in this case as it relates to the vampire trope, literally and figuratively effaces the power relations defining the Bellefleur world. The "Room of Contamination" chapter effectively sets up two competing values, one of consumption conducted at the level of commodity-form within the constructs of society, and the other of desire theorized as an anarchic arena outside social definition. In a network of associations, the text juxtaposes that which can be purchased or commodified and, in effect, defines the social order and that which resists such definition. This opposition is established at the outset of the chapter, simultaneously invoking imagery of the phallic in the form of the "immense muscular grace of the cedar of Lebanon" overlooking the Turquoise Room and, conversely, in the distance, the "mist-shrouded slopes of Mount Chattaroy" (191). Significantly, the blue-green gemstone after which the room is named symbolizes in Western tradition the planet Venus (Biedermann 357), gendered female and associated with eroticism and desire.

The apartment is outstanding in its luxuriousness, its costliness, and its value as an objective correlative for Bellefleur family status. It was constructed originally for the illustrious guests, the Baron and Baroness von Richthofen, and "it was rumored that more than $150,000" (191) went into its construction and furbishment, which included an elaborate Italian Renaissance mirror, expensive paintings, and turquoise and gold ornamentation. The other aspect of the room concerns its alleged contamination, symbolized by the manifestation of a "black woman—a Negress—but not a slave" (201), who proceeds to seduce Samuel, the only son of Raphael Bellefleur. Her presence is marked by an odor, an indefinable scent of erotic excess that contaminates the room, and ultimately robs it of its status. The contamination begins one night before the Civil War when the room plays host to three former slaves, members of John Brown's insurgent army. Although a northern family, the Bellefleurs shared the common viewpoint that "Negroes were the sons of Ham, and accursed," and that slavery supported the "hierarchy" established by God (196). However, the Bellefleurs are also quick to give short shrift to any form of ethics or religion in deference to economic efficacy. As Samuel remarked about Raphael, "you'd think he wanted a monopoly on lumbering in the mountains only to further God's work on earth" (193). To that end Raphael Bellefleur "opposed slavery because he opposed the Democrats; privately he knew the system to be an enviable one—it answered the only important moral requirement that might be reasonably asked of an economic strategy: it worked" (197). His belief in the power of economics translates into his opinion that, if freed and left to his own devices, the "black man . . . he'll soon have his own slaves" (197). Just as for Gideon Bellefleur, who violates Little Goldie, a child he acquires as the result of a poker game, and as for Jean-Pierre II, who ends a Bellefleur labor dispute by killing fifteen of the striking fruit pickers with a hog-butchering knife, for Raphael life is literally and figuratively cheap and can be assigned a dollar figure, not unlike any other commodity. As the narrator ingenuously remarks:

It was characteristic of Raphael's studied generosity that, in 1861, he would hire to take his place in the 14th Regiment of the Seventh Corps of the Union Army of the Potomac not one but two bounty soldiers, and that though he contracted to pay them a fairly small, fixed price, he in fact paid them far more, on the condition that they tell no one—no one at all—exactly how much he was paying. And since one of the soldiers died almost immediately, in Missouri, and the other was to die at Antietam, under McClellan, the extent of Raphael's largess was never known. (191-92)

Morally flexible and crudely mocking, the patriarch Raphael acquiesces cynically to his younger brother's request to shelter Brown's escaping "soldiers" in the splendid Turquoise Room. These "runaway slaves with skins of an unimagined blackness" (195) spend the night, but after their departure, subsequent guests, all of whom are of course white and men of wealth and power, report strange "presences" and odors (199). Once again, the text juxtaposes, as we shall see, the erotic, couched in gothic terms, with commodity culture. The room's first visitor after the departure of the runaway slaves is Senator Wesley Tidd, who comes to visit to discuss "the logistics of a partnership with Raphael Bellefleur in an iron-ore mining operation" (198). The narrator notes that, as a result of this partnership, the mines produced iron for military equipment and that "two hundred thousand tons were to be extracted annually . . . before the mines wore out" (198). Both human beings and nature clearly exist to be exploited. However, after a night in the Turquoise Room, the senator finds his own resources depleted: "he seemed drawn and tired, and apologized for 'not being himself.' His head ached, his eyes watered, his stomach was upset, he had suffered unpleasant dreams" (199). Similarly, some months later, Hayes Wittier, who would one day "speak in support of the Secretary of War Cameron" (199), reports having spent "a somewhat unusual night" haunted by a "number of presences . . . you might characterize them as *foreign*" (199).

Tidd and Wittier foreground Raphael's son Samuel's own contamination and eventual "dissolution" at the hands of the succubus in the

Turquoise Room. As the heir to Raphael Bellefleur's fortune, he represents the pinnacle of his father's "considerable financial success" (193), having graduated with honors from West Point and having been promoted to the rank of first lieutenant at the age of twenty-six. He is also engaged to the youngest daughter (who significantly remains nameless) of Hans Dietrich, "whose fortune and castellated mansion" (194) rivals that of Raphael. Dietrich's considerable holdings are itemized by the narrator: his ten thousand acres, his initial investments into hops and wheat, the fact that he was "outlandishly rich" (194). However, Dietrich loses his fortune and the engagement between his daughter and Samuel is broken off: "Samuel was halfway tempted—for he did think highly of the girl, despite knowing her only superficially—he did love her—to insist upon the wedding in the face of his father's and even the Dietriches' opposition: but in the end nothing came of it" (194-95). Love without the taint of ambition or acquisitiveness never enters into the equation and, once again, we are only to learn that the Dietrich property is auctioned off "for a fraction of its price" and eventually sold to another businessman who "had made his fortune in bricks" (195). At this point, the text reads like a ledger; everything has a fixed price and cost, including human relations, an example of moral turpitude which can only be "contaminated"—that is, mitigated—by the Turquoise Room. Samuel's immersion in its tainted atmosphere is symbolized by his relationship to the "Negress," who first appears to him in "that enormous intimidating mirror" (199). In European iconography, the significance of mirrors takes in two extremes. The mirror appears in the hands of deadly sirens of antiquity, or of Luxuria, the personification of lust and vanity, but it can also denote the virtues of self-knowledge, truth, and prudence (Biedermann 223). The Turquoise Room's Italian Renaissance mirror allows for both connotations. It is through its seductive powers that Samuel, and through him, Raphael, are forced to confront, at least unconsciously, the dissonance inherent in their worldviews. Or, in the words of Marilyn C. Wesley, "beyond the mirror of the Bellefleur ego . . . lies all that is disregarded by their political system: the black, the poor, the powerless, the female" (140). However, the Negress's power over Samuel does more than simply symbolize the plight of the disenfranchised. As a succubus, she seduces and consumes the Bellefleur heir; their "wicked liaison" (201) culminates in his ultimate "dissolution," thereby driving Raphael to destroy the mirror, representing the erotic, that which is outside social control and resists commodification.

The Negress's overpowering allure, symbolized by a sensual odor emanating from the Turquoise Room, acknowledges and then contests the stereotypical view of black women as "subhuman creatures who, by nature, were strong and sexual" and readily exploitable. She appears to Samuel as a black woman "but not a slave—evidently not a slave" (201), her earthy sensuality a force to be reckoned with. The tables are turned and this time it is the white male, scion of a powerful family, whose boundaries are threatened. Samuel is seduced and reduced to a puerile figure:

He stood immobile, waiting for her to speak—what if she called him by name, what if she claimed him!—his thumbnail now jammed between two of his lower teeth. . . . He remained immobile . . . his legs slightly bent at the knee as if their strength were draining from them; and the thumb pressed against his teeth. But you have no *right* to be here, he whispered. (201)

Unfortunately for the Bellefleurs, the Negress has a right to redress those patterns of dominance and submission created by the social order the family supports. As a succubus, she appropriates the sexist and racist image of the sexualized black female. Her power derives from her status as a supernatural figure, enabling her to destabilize the forces which define the material and ideological ways in which society is constructed.

The Negress's power is palpable. Samuel is lured back into the Turquoise Room again and again, entering another dimension where the erotic holds sway over the commodified world of the Bellefleurs: "They could smell the woman on him [Samuel]—they could sense his erotic gravity—a sensuousness so powerful, so heavy, that it held down his soul like an enormous rock, and would not allow it to float to the surface of ordinary discourse" (201). The Negress's influence pervades the house and "even in the breakfast room, that incontestable rich ripe overripe fairly reeking *odor* that emanated from Samuel, stirred by his every movement, wafted about in the most innocent of atmospheres" (202). Far from innocent, the world of the Bellefleurs becomes "contaminated," profaned by the excessive, nonproductive, and polymorphous slowly and inexorably encroaching on a world defined in purely economic terms. Not only does an odor suffuse the house but also time takes on a different dimension in the Turquoise Room. "Time was different there," remarks Samuel, who disappears into the chamber for "longer periods of time, for days at a stretch" (203). Samuel begins to fade away, in tandem with an alternative clock that refuses to adhere to the Bellefleur's sense of time. He believes he disappears into the room for two hours but according to "*their* calculations he had been gone for four days" (203). As I have already explored in chapter 4, Oates's text is a repudiation of chronology. The concept of reality as simply a narrative construct, contingent on who has the power to tell and interpret, is culturally encoded as a male or patriarchal prerogative. By forcing an alternative version of time, the Negress introduces the concept of radical possibility—order, hierarchy, the commodification of human relations, all of which can be undermined. Or in the words of Samuel: "Time is clocks, not a clock. Not your clock. You can't do anything more with time than try to contain it, like carrying water in a sieve" (203). Plurality suddenly becomes a possibility.

The possibility of alternative views and social constructs finds its apotheosis in Samuel's dissolution. His mother, Violet, is first convinced that " a filthy wicked slattern" is out to "destroy Raphael's heir" (202), and finally he disappears into the Turquoise Room and never reemerges: "The boy had simply disappeared. He no longer existed. There was no trace, no farewell note, there had been no significant final remark: Samuel Bellefleur had simply ceased to exist" (203). Through her seduction and consumption of Samuel, the succubus has undermined the patrilineal order in an ironic inversion of a system that promotes the commodification of female reproduction. The available black woman, readily exploitable for her reproductive and sexual capacities, rewrites the scenario by using seduction as a means to spirit away an heir valued only for his role in a dynastic continuum. Appropriately enough, after his son's disappearance, Raphael smashes the mirror with "spasmodic blows" using "his gold-knobbed cane," the phallic symbolism underscoring the patriarch's violent opposition to the erotic and alternate forces that "had taken his son!" (204). Raphael can only conceive that his son has been "taken," that is, stolen from him in much the same way as any of the valuable objects in the Turquoise Room could conceivably be taken. Unable to confront the truth of the chamber, faced with "nothing more than the mirror's plain oak backing, mere wood, two-dimensional, reflecting nothing, containing no beauty, but badly hacked by the spasmodic blows of his cane" (204), Raphael orders the room locked up.

The refusal to acknowledge alternate visions by resisting divergent concepts of order is important to the preservation of the status quo. The succubus that haunts the Turquoise Room in *Bellefleur* is matched by the vampire, great-aunt Veronica, who lives among the Bellefleur family. Just as the Negress appropriates the cultural construct of the sexualized black woman, Veronica's unacknowledged existence as a vampire plays with the stereotype of the delicate, sexually pure, and morally superior girl/woman. In her youth, she is seduced by the predatory Ragnar Norst, becomes a vampire, and subsequently leaves behind a curious trail of dead fiancés, a series of events no one in the family sees fit to question. The text's blanks and omissions only hint at Veronica's career as a succubus. The narrator and the Bellefleur family insist on keeping alive "the myth of her girlish fastidiousness" (361), her "*ordinariness*" (360). She embodies several stereotypes at once, the girl-child, the delicate woman, and the aging spinster on the shelf. She "of course . . . never exercised. It seemed to tire the poor woman even to walk *downstairs,* which she did with an air of listlessness." She gossips about relatives and neighbors with "an air of languid incredulity and could not tolerate anything but the finest linen against her skin. Her manners were mincing" (361). Several times she is described as a "frightened child" (364), "delighted as a child" (367), and "prankish as a child" (374). However, her physical condition belies the image of "girlish fastidiousness" and suggests images of a voluptuous, sensual woman. She is a "plump, full-hipped and full-breasted woman of moderate height" (360), with a "full, comfortable figure, and the suggestion of a second chin, and her obvious air of superb health" (361). Obviously, as a predatory vampire, Veronica does well satisfying her unusual appetites in a way in which society would never allow her to satisfy libidinal ones. The irony is that the Bellefleurs can readily ignore a succubus in their midst but would have trouble accepting a sexual woman. (Even Leah's passionate nature is transformed early on, her energies properly transferred to satisfying dynastic ambitions.) Accordingly, Norst's vampiric seduction of the young Veronica is couched in erotic terms; the concept of vampiric seduction as sexual congress is hardly new. With Norst, Veronica "seemed to lose all her powers of judgement. . . . His voice was liquid and sensuous . . . even *seductive*" (363). He would leave her feeling "quite drained" with talk about "kindred souls and mutual destiny and the need . . . to surrender" (364). Of course his visits to Veronica are nocturnal, appearing to her in her "most secret dreams" (369), his eyes glowing "with an unspeakable lust" (367).

However, Norst's seduction of Veronica, whether vampiric or carnal, triggers in the young woman the enervated, consumptive state so familiar in Poe. She is transformed from a vibrant and sensually curious woman into an etherealized state marked by "languid, sweet melancholy" (371), her "soul swooning downward, gently downward" (372). Typically, her etherealization makes her "more beautiful than ever" (372) "despite her pallor and the hollows around her eyes" (373). When she is hospitalized just in time, the doctors studiously ignore "high on her breast, a curious fresh scratch or bite" which of course "had nothing to do with her serious problems of anemia and pneumonia" (374). True to Poe's aesthetic that "the death . . .of a beautiful woman is, unquestionably, the most poetical topic in the world" ("Philosophy" 19), Veronica finds her recovery disappointing:

Her thin cheeks were growing rounded again and her dead-white skin was turning rosy but the mirror's image did not please her: she saw that it was uninteresting, banal, really quite vulgar. She was uninteresting now, and her lover, if he returned, if he happened to gaze upon her, would be sadly disappointed. (375)

A woman's full-blown sexuality is ambivalently perceived, at once threatening and alluring, necessitating control and containment, a condition which comes full circle and back to Poe. As Cynthia S. Jordan points out in her reading of "The Fall of the House of Usher," the narrator and Roderick are complicit in Madeline's premature burial: "We have put her living in the tomb." Her interment beneath the narrator's "sleeping apartment" suggests "a consciousness plagued by its repressed underpinnings" (Jordan 141). In Jordan's view, the narrator becomes the true "madman," consumed with "fear and hatred of . . . female sexuality incarnate in Madeline Usher" (141). Madeline's sexuality is also allegorized as vampirism; Lyle H. Kendall reads Madeline as "a vampire—a succubus—as the family physician well knows and as her physical appearance and effect upon the narrator sufficiently demonstrate" (450). Similarly, J. O. Bailey itemizes the vampiric décor of Poe's tale, including Roderick's wanness, his cadaverous complexion, the family illness, not to mention the more obvious details as Madeline's body in the vault and the final "somewhat erotic embrace" and "moan of pleasure" as commonplaces of vampire lore (445-58). Not unlike Madeline, Veronica is transformed once more, from the iconography of "fastidious girlishness" to a dangerous woman, from prey to predator. Her sexual appetites, allegorized as vampiric cannot, however, be interred and contained in some Bellefleur vault. She refuses to be objectified or etherealized, and the deaths of her numerous fiancés significantly and resoundingly indicate her repudiation of marriage, wherein she would be commodified, that is, converted into property or chattel.

An inversion of the Victorian tableau of woman in her wedding bed or funeral bier, Veronica and Beloved veer off the beaten path of traditional gothic narrative first broken by Ligeia, Morella, and Madeline. Poe's denaturalizing of the "natural order of things" (Dayan, "Amorous Bondage" 249) disrupts the patterns of dominance and submission, opening a space that reveals a struggle, a resistance to societal strictures that demand women to remain silent, powerless, and passive. The trope of sexualized demon that drains the vital life fluid from her victims is reconfigured both in Morrison and Oates and linked with the economic and social violence, once again the patterns of dominance and submission, through which women are constituted as subjects or, conversely, denied subjectivity. The implications of seduction are thrown wide open, thematized as "wicked liaisons" which do happen to "lead astray" and away from conventional interpretations of the gothic genre.

III. THE CULTURE OF CONSUMPTION

All your Demons are visible
All your Demons are material.
—Anne Rice, *The Vampire Lestat*

Examining the gothic genre through the prism of commodity culture reveals some of the key dynamics underlying our perceptions and definitions of horror. To trace the genesis and progression of the American gothic text is to trace the modes of discourse based on simulacra, the Baudrillardian idea of the counterfeit, an empty symbol repeatedly recreated and manipulated. What is the gothic, after all, but a collection of simulacra, specters, witches, and vampires conspiring to undermine the reader's ability to distinguish the real from the unreal?

The concept of simulacrum in the gothic operates as a facet of subversion, concerning itself with seduction on two levels, one that marks it as disruptive of the process of commodity production and circulation of value and the other that implicates it within the semiological code of capitalism. The result is a continuum that reveals a cultural process increasingly dominated by the consumption of signs themselves. In essence, that cultural process is an aspect of the horror conjured in the American gothic. The horror that is simulacrum finds its source in the loss of foundational meaning. Frankenstein's Monster, a patently artificial creature, is at least once or twice removed from his creator's original vision. The Wieland family invests its faith in a voice whose origin is unknown. The revenants that populate Poe's fiction are ghostly imitations of sisters, wives, and daughters who refuse to keep their place, both figuratively and metaphorically. On yet another level, the symbols of the gothic, Hester's scarlet letter, Sutpen's dynasty, and James's governess are referents to now empty antecedents, essentially resymbolizations (or simulations) of that which is more counterfeit than real, aging and European-based concepts of signification that hark back to another age that may have only existed in the overwrought imagination. From a more theoretical perspective, simulation is the ungrounding of Western discourse in a hyperreality of signs referring to other signs with no recourse to an absolute origin, "a nostalgia for a natural referent to which the image might not really be connected (Baudrillard, *Symbolic Exchange* 51). Consequently, the contemporary gothic is strewn with empty relics, the vampires who now laugh at the symbol of the crucifix (itself an empty relic in the belief system of the twentieth century), the ghost of a baby that crystallizes the horror of commodification of human capital, and the crumbling New World castles that are trapped in the economic logic of a culture of consumption.

The American gothic, as a reflection of economic and cultural antecedents, finds itself impounded in a world where production and consumption are necessarily followed by the simulations that simply gesture to a commodified universe. In this Baudrillardian arena, signs and modes of representation come to constitute reality; signs interact with other signs, referring to and gaining their significance in relation to other commodity signs. In the first chapter of this section, *Bellefleur* and Hawthorne's *The House of the Seven Gables* serve as stops along that continuum which ultimately veers into a realm increasingly dominated by semiological relations or, in other words, into a process involving the consumption of signs themselves. The juxtaposition of *Beloved* and Melville's "Benito Cereno" focuses the concepts of appropriation and value and the relationship of gratuitous expenditure to actual configurations of power, revealing a violence that serves as a rebuke to a system defined by commodification and consumption. The apotheosis of that system is disclosed in the final chapter of this section, in Rice's *The Vampire Lestat* where "cool" seduction, to borrow from the Baudrillardian lexicon, has formed a pact with simulation in a conflation of desire and consumption. Lost in a world governed by a commodified system of sign values, Lestat's story belongs to the order of the hyperreal and of simulation. Ironically, the gothic genre which begins its career as being "unreal" emerges in *Lestat* as a close approximation of reality, depicting our world as the simulacrum that pervades postmodernity itself.

8

THE LUST FOR ACQUISITIONS:
BELLEFLEUR, THE HOUSE OF THE SEVEN GABLES,
AND NEW-WORLD GOTHIC HORROR

The governing tropic structure which underlies Oates's *Bellefleur* is a gothic conflation embodying images of consumption and eroticism, imagery situated in the recurrent metaphor of "devouring jaws" and yet another expression of the "lust for acquisitions" that haunts the Bellefleur family and the gothic novel in America. To borrow from Baudrillard, we are what we consume, and American gothic can be read as a continuum of feeding desire within a culture of consumption. *Bellefleur* and Hawthorne's *The House of the Seven Gables* serve as stops along that corridor, ultimately veering into a realm increasingly dominated by semiological relations and into a cultural process involving the consumption of signs themselves.

To begin, the two texts share a haunted house, a family curse, and an intense involvement with claims of property. The Bellefleurs are entangled in a multigenerational quest that is driven by *"insatiable* interest" (117), a frenzied desire for empire and wealth. The Pyncheon property claims are similarly based on theft and falsehoods. Both narratives are filtered through heterodiegetic narrators (Genette) who are absent from the stories they present (as opposed to homodiegetic narrators who are present as characters in their own story). Point of view in both texts reveals useful conceptual information about the conventions through which meaning in narrative is produced, tracking the culture of consumption through the relationship of perception and discourse. Significantly, the Bellefleur saga is presented by an overbearing, pseudo-Victorian narrator whose intrusive tone threatens to leave the reader in a permanent midnight of parodic gothic embellishment. An example of historiographic metafiction, the stability of point of view in *Bellefleur* is undermined through an "overt, deliberately manipulative" narrator (Hutcheon, *Poetics* 160) whose semblance of control is simply that —counterfeit. In this context, point of view, comprising those aspects of narration that concern the textual presentation and representation of speech, perception, and event crucial to the production of literary meaning (Lanser 114), allows Oates's text to be read against itself through its tropological structure. The narrator simultaneously inflates and deflates tropes, through numerous parenthetical asides and ironic understatement, with the result that the text retains the illusion of reality while exploiting the potential for ideological response. More to the point, as John Goode argues, point of view is "what articulates the relationship of the text to ideology itself" (218). In effect, then, what does Oates's narrator, armed with editorial omniscience, accomplish? As Susan Lanser suggests, there are three issues focusing a narrator's ideology: the way it is expressed; how its "content" relates to the cultural text, and the position of authority held by the particular voice. Further, the expression of ideology may be explicit or more deeply embedded in the narrator's speech activity (216). Embedded ideology is revealed through value-laden lexis, register, and subordinated syntax, while explicit ideology is specific and categorical, present on the surface level of the text. *Bellefleur*'s narrator, who holds sway over the text's point of view, has it both ways, seemingly supporting ideological constructs while undermining them. I suggest that her voice is largely parodic, that is, a caricature of the traditional third-person narrator, conventionally omniscient with unimpeded access to every character's mind and with no responsibility to account for information or the story's ultimate outcome. The narrative "truth" emerges through devices of formal realism to the point of parody, wherein "the parasitic text [is] dependent for its meaning not on the real world but on the conventions of literature itself" (Lanser 164).

In terms of Oates's text, those conventions are rooted in Hawthorne's and, as we have seen earlier, Faulkner's renderings of gothic voice or point of view. In all three texts, the point of view revolves around a family that has inscribed itself in history through possession and consumption, through metaphorical jaws that relentlessly devour land, people, and finally, capital. *The House of the Seven Gables,* with its dead man's hereditary curse and a dynasty founded on pious theft, is a precursor to *Absalom, Absalom!* In the Pyncheon house, the symptoms of this possession can be found in the symbol of an Indian deed as well as in the dead Judge. Similarly, Sutpen's claim is as tenuous as that of the Pyncheons. In essence, all three novels can be read as treatises regarding property—owning, stealing, inheriting, and marrying it—but disquisitions nonetheless rendered by points of view that restore connections between ideology and technique.

In the case of Hawthorne and Oates, although with different results, their texts borrow from the nineteenth-century tradition, a moralist Victorian aesthetic that sought to ensure readers receive morally appropriate bromides. Point of view was to create both realistic illusion and ideological control. Conversely, point of view in *Absalom, Absalom!* ushers in a modernistic aesthetic, an indirect narrative method translating the increasingly perceived unstable external world into the arena of private consciousness. From Sartre's insistence that fiction portray experience rather than a formulated consciousness to New Criticism's emphasis on the autonomy of the text, the instability of point of view, as exemplified by Faulkner's text, creates not one fixed perspective but an overlapping of many voices. As we have seen in chapter 4, point of view is decentered in *Absalom, Absalom!,* allowing for an interanimation of languages that is played off against any monologic intent. The discrepancies in Mr. Compson's, Shreve's, Quentin's, and Rosa's stories provide the framework that gives rise to contrasting ideological points of view. *Bellefleur*'s point of view is a postmodern amalgamation of both narrative methods, simultaneously achieving a semblance of "authorial" control that paradoxically pluralizes and problematizes the private and public histories of America with the consequence that "the ideological and the aesthetic have turned out to be inseparable" (Hutcheon, *Poetics* 178). As Linda Hutcheon points out, postmodern fiction exploits "both distancing irony . . . and technical innovation, in order both to illustrate and to incarnate its teachings" (181).

However, rather than a didactic element, there is a provisional quality to Oates's text despite the narrator's blandishments. The "devouring jaws" metaphor in *Bellefleur* emerges as a semiological enigma that makes it difficult for either literal or figural meanings to prevail. The Bellefleur "saint" Jedediah dies with the words *"The jaws devour, the jaws are devoured"* on his lips (30). Leah is momentarily derailed from her rapacious ambitions by the same words, a litany or mantra that she cannot exorcise from her unconscious mind (403). Metaphorically, devouring jaws make an appearance in the Noir Vulture, who snatches and kills the baby Cassandra, in the figure of the Doan boy, who metamorphoses into a predatory hound, in Vernon's impassioned poetry delivered to exploited Bellefleur tenant farmers whom he refers to as "The Mud-Devourers" and likens to "shocking images—jaws devouring jaws, wormlike men crawling on their bellies . . . creatures who devoured filth and declared it manna" (323). Then there is the chapter entitled "The Jaws," which traces Jeremiah's attempt to breed silver foxes and make millions only to have the animals escape one night and devour one another in cannibalistic frenzy.

This trope of "devouring jaws" is foregrounded in *The House of the Seven Gables,* both figuratively and literally. The Pyncheon family lives under a curse not unlike the Bellefleurs, one which has visited "the clutch of violence upon his [Colonel Pyncheon's] throat" (17) and threatens to repeat itself every generation or so: "If one of the family did but gurgle in his throat, a bystander would be likely enough to whisper, between jest and earnest—'He has Maule's blood to drink'" (21). As with the Bellefleurs, much revolves around the possession of property and the waxing and waning family ambition of "ultimately forming a princedom for themselves" (*House* 19). As Robert K. Martin has shown, Hawthorne's novel was written in the midst of a national debate over the right to property, that is, private versus communal, and the right to own and sell slaves (131). In *The House of the Seven Gables* property is obtained by legal or illegal means, by land grant or purchase or through labor. Unlike the great castles of the traditional gothic past, in America property is simply bought and sold without any claim to hereditary or natural right. As with the Bellefleurs, the Pyncheons find themselves prey to the economic marketplace and under pressure to find the original land claim or, as with the Bellefleurs, to reclaim (purchase or steal) territory. The colonel's willingness to return the house to the Maules if he can repossess his lands in Maine indicates the role of a capitalist economy in which inheritance is greatly subordinate to colonial mercantilism. As Martin emphasizes:

That the almost mythic lands in Maine . . . can be claimed only through a missing Indian deed underlines the role of national theft and genocide. These "vast," "unexplored and unmeasured" lands are what remains of the colonial dream of America, the imposition of European property rights on native peoples; they are also a fantasy of the wealth of the "east" that awaits the merchants of Salem.

It is the cultural work of the text to resolve the dilemma of the stolen land, and it does so in a way that evades the issue of the Indian lands by staging a conflict between two white families in the absence of now dispersed and dispossessed Indians. (132)

It is fitting that the alleged curse manifests itself in images of devouring blood, a gorging that causes asphyxiation in the case of the colonel and several of his descendants, and an almost cannibalistic, vampiric frenzy on the part of the Bellefleurs. As Oates comments in the novel's "Afterword," "we have known people who want to suck our life's blood from us, like vampires; we feel haunted by the dead—if not precisely by the dead then by thoughts of them" (562). The dead that haunt these two gothic texts are incarnated in "the jaws devour, the jaws are devoured," embodying a cyclical sense of socio-economic horror, associations of the uncanny, of remembering and return. At the close of Hawthorne's text, Judge Pyncheon is dead, Clifford is free, Holgrave marries Phoebe, and they all leave the house and, presumably, the cycle. Similarly, "One by one the Bellefleur children free themselves of their family's curse" ("Afterword" 562). Raphael disappears into Mink Pond; Yolande runs away to become a film actress; Garth marries Little Goldie and moves to "somewhere no one knew the name Bellefleur" (446); Vernon leaves to write his poetry; Christabel marries her beloved and flees to Mexico while Bromwell escapes to pursue a scientific career. The references to race and the commodification of human relations in *The House of the Seven Gables* and *Bellefleur* underscore the insistent presence of history which new generations strive to forget.

Significantly, the houses that represent the "lust for acquisitions" that propel the Pyncheons and Bellefleurs are canceled out at the conclusion of both texts. (It all but requires high explosives to remove Bellefleur manor from the American countryside.) By marrying Phoebe, Holgrave, the last of the Maules, inherits the Puncheon estate and recovers the Maule claim. In other words, capital, not real estate nor the moldering castle of the gothic tradition, is exposed as the next step in the modus operandi of a commodified culture. Along the same continuum, the Bellefleur fortunes are first built upon the exploitation of land and workers but, as the children's fates soon reveal, they are themselves consumed into a Baudrillardian hyperreality that is dominated by an indeterminant play of simulations. The beginnings of this process are found in Hawthorne's reluctant acknowledgment of the role of commodification in American culture. The narrator's description and interpretation of genteel Hepzibah's first day of "setting up shop" reveals the delicate balance between ideology and point of view:

The inevitable moment was not much longer to be delayed. . . . The town appeared to be waking-up. A baker's cart had already rattled through the street, chasing away the last vestige of night's sanctity with the jingle-jangle of its dissonant bells. A milkman was distributing the contents of his cans from door to door; and the harsh peal of a fisherman's conch-shell was heard far off, around the corner. None of these tokens escaped Hepzibah's notice. (40)

The exploration of absence here, that which that text leaves unsaid, uncovers a system of values which makes the textual perspective appear "natural" rather than ideological (Todorov). As Tzvetan Todorov might explain it, it is the perspectival vision that allows a text to present potentially threatening material in such a way as to neutralize it. As Hepzibah gathers her courage to open her shop, the town comes alive through the activities of commerce whose literal dissonance, the "jingle-jangle" of bells and the "harsh peal" of a fisherman's conch shell, underscores the rather genteel sensibilities of the narrator, who, in turn, interprets Hepzibah's reluctance to join in the economic activities of Salem. "We are loitering faint-heartedly on the threshold of our story. In very truth, we have an invincible reluctance to disclose what Miss Hepzibah Pyncheon was about to do" (34), he confesses:

Our miserable old Hepzibah. It is a heavy annoyance to a writer, who endeavors to represent nature, its various attitudes and circumstances, in a reasonably correct outline and true coloring, that so much of the mean and ludicrous should be hopelessly mixed up with the purest pathos which life anywhere supplies to him. What tragic dignity, for example, can be wrought into a scene like this! How can we elevate our history of retribution for the sin of long ago? (40-41)

What precisely is the sin of long ago that the narrator delicately refers to? The original Pyncheon cheating the original Maule out of his rightful claim? Significantly, the first of Hepzibah's transactions is the sale of a gingerbread Jim Crow, an allusion to slavery as one of the origins of New England's prosperity. Ned's consumption of the gingerbread figure is an allegorical reiteration of consumption patterns that marks the economics of America. The body is first commodified and then consumed, as the references to Ned as a "cannibal" (50) reinforce. Typically, the narrator reveals that Hepzibah's "old gentility was contumaciously squeamish at the sight of the copper-coin" (50), but upon the reappearance of the little cannibal looking for another Jim Crow, she demands payment. However, as she drops "the first solid result of her commercial enterprise into the till," that first transaction gives her a "copper stain" (51), one that figuratively implicates her in the slave economy. The point of view here is both ideologically explicit and embedded (Lanser):

The little schoolboy, aided by the impish figure of the negro dancer, had wrought an irreparable ruin. The structure of ancient aristocracy had been demolished by him, even as if his childish gripe had torn down the seven-gabled mansion! Now let Hepzibah turn the old Pyncheon portraits with their faces to the wall, and take the map of her eastern-territory to kindle the kitchen-fire, and blow up the flame with the empty breadth of her ancestral traditions! What had she to do with ancestry? Nothing;—no more than with posterity! No lady, now, but simply Hepzibah Pyncheon, a forlorn old maid, and keeper of a cent-shop! (51)

This passage incorporates both diegetic and mimetic discourse, including narrated speech that allows for greater ideological possibilities. The point of view is a combination of the narrator's values, his belief that the gingerbread transaction has sullied Hepzibah's lineage, reinforced by her own thoughts and feelings filtered through the narrator's consciousness.

However, the embedded discourse points to another related, although more ideologically loaded meaning. If we were to read the same passage ironically, making the ideological link with slavery, then turning the Pyncheon portraits to face the wall and burning the map of the eastern territories makes sense in quite a different way. In other words, the shame of commerce arises from its link to the commodification of human relations, another measure of "the empty breadth" of ancestral traditions in the New World.

The ideological implications of the consumption of the gingerbread Jim Crow and the Pyncheon curse with its "clutch of violence upon [his] throat" (17) are mediated through a diegetic authority, the narrator, who carries the ontological status of historical truth. To some degree this status is also conferred upon *Bellefleur*'s narrator, but in a way that makes us much more aware of the existence of "discourse," that is, the historical conditions of meaning and the positions from which points of view are both produced and perceived. In a parodic reprise of the omniscient narrator, Oates's text calls attention to the links among authority, knowledge, and power. As Hutcheon points out, historiographic metafiction "is always careful to 'situate' itself in its discursive context and then uses that situating to problematize the very notion of knowledge—historical, social, ideological" (*Poetics* 185). In this context, the point of view established in *Bellefleur* presents and then undermines the text's ostensible direction, positing that which is presumably "natural" within a certain historical context just before forcing the reader to question the text's alleged authority. The Bellefleurs "naturally" believe that "Negroes were sons of Ham, and accursed; they didn't feel pain or exhaustion or despair like the white race, not even like Raphael's Irish laborers, and they certainly did not possess 'souls'—though it was clear they were more highly developed than horses and dogs" (196-97). This declaration is almost immediately paired with an allusion to the historical John Brown and his followers whose failed attempt to attack Harper's Ferry and put an end to slaveholding by establishing a "second government" (196) is deemed unthinkable and unimaginable by Raphael Bellefleur. Raphael refers to Brown as "a maniac and a murderer," a perfectly "natural" assumption given the historical context but one which is undermined by the overt parody of the point of view. "Parody's contradictory ideological implications (as 'authorized transgression,' it can be seen as both conservative and revolutionary)" invite a paradoxically "conservative installing and then radical contesting of conventions" (Hutcheon, *Poetics* 129).

Correspondingly, the conflation of consumption and eroticism, with the former winning out over the latter, is similarly naturalized. The depiction of the young bride Leah as a woman of voracious libidinal appetite is presented as natural in the context of the Bellefleurs' natural appetite for acquisition. As a storm rages on the night of Mahalaleel's arrival, she and Gideon veer from a violent argument to a "passionate heaving ecstatic labor":

Leah, sobbing, struck Gideon with her rather large fist . . . and Gideon . . . threw her back hard against the headboard of their antique bed (Venetian, eighteenth-century, a canopied intricately carved gondola outfitted with enormous goose-feather and swansdown pillows, one of the silliest of Raphael Bellefleur's acquisitions, Leah's favorite piece of furniture, so wondrously vulgar, so lavish, so absurd . . .)

And then it was over, and both were asleep, Gideon swam effortlessly, through what must have been a flood; but he was untouched by uprooted trees, debris, even corpses flung along by the current; his heart swelled with triumph. It seemed that he was hunting the Noir Vulture once again. That enormous white-winged creature with its hunched shoulders and mottled, naked, monkey-ish face. . . . (9)

The point of view adumbrates the various levels of meaning in the trope of "devouring jaws." The narrator paradoxically inflates and deflates the trope through numerous parenthetical asides, acknowledging, naturalizing, and then contesting the construct. Leah's "insatiable interest" is first allied with passion and then merged with the commodities that will soon define her passion. After the birth of Germaine, Leah's libidinal energies (she banishes Gideon from her bed) are sublimated into a passion for consumption. In this context, Gideon's postcoital dream of the predatory Noir Vulture and the apocalyptic flood, leaving the detritus of nature and corpses in its wake, is liberally suggestive, multiplying the potential for ideological response. On an explicit level, what could be more natural for an American family such as the Bellefleurs than a healthy appetite for dynastic ambition? Yet on another level, the embedded ideology challenges this "natural" assumption by invoking the image of the Noir Vulture, a carrion bird which by nature feeds upon flesh. The whole concept of what is natural is called into question in both Hawthorne's and Oates's texts, mediated by a gothic perspective that naturalizes, that is, commodifies, the grotesque or supernatural. The Maules are a family of wizards capable of cursing the Pyncheon family for generations. Yet, Holgrave normalizes those supernatural abilities through his work making daguerreotypes and, more importantly, he exorcises the haunting past by marrying Phoebe and inheriting the Pyncheon estate while recuperating the old Maule claim. Ultimately, he no longer has any need for wizardry or mesmerism once he has "mastery over Phoebe's yet free and virgin spirit" (212), for he has something even more powerful—money. Analogously, Germaine's preternatural abilities are put in the service of Leah's empire building, but when her powers disappear so too does Leah's empire collapse. Clearly, New World gothic horror comes in two formulations that are closely linked, the supernatural and the economic.

This recurrent pattern is once again reinforced by a point of view that paradoxically naturalizes and defamiliarizes the horror intrinsic in commodification. Most notably, the episode in which the silver foxes devour one another in cannibalistic frenzy is presented disingenuously, as though the reader would have a difficult time believing in such an occurrence. "Giddy with expectation, quite certain that they would become millionaires within two or three years," Jeremiah expresses the appropriate incredulity:

He had never seen anything like it. Why, the creatures were cannibals, they were monsters. They appeared to have devoured, or attempted to devour, their own off-spring—! Acres of carcasses. Bloody strips of flesh . . . a sight too hellish to be borne. Jaws devouring jaws . . . And then, the next day, to learn that Horace had taken what remained of the money (hardly more than $500, in Jeremiah's vague estimation) and fled to Cuba with his fifteen-year-old mulatto mistress. (510)

The shock is quickly undercut by the mention of money and a young mulatto mistress almost in the same breath. In the interim, the silver foxes' cannibalistic frenzy allegorically summarizes the Bellefleur saga in several sentences. Which is the more horrific? Like the young boy devouring the gingerbread Jim Crow, the Bellefleurs devour land, people, and capital with an intensity that far outstrips that of any ghost, vampire, or metamorphosing entity the gothic imagination could possibly deploy.

The transformation of the gothic into the economic implies a further step, one that introduces a realm increasingly dominated by semiological relations, a process involving the consumption of signs themselves. First the jaws devour and then, the jaws are devoured in another variation of the Baudrillardian universe in which signs and modes of representation come to constitute reality; signs interact with other signs, referring to and gaining their significance in relation to other commodity signs. The gingerbread Jim Crow and the copper penny transaction point to a com-modification that constitutes a totalizing social process, one of alienation and exploitation (reification), in which objects come to dominate sub-jects. The Bellefleur saga is punctuated by the disappearance of its younger members, many of whom flee from a mode of production only to exchange it for what Baudrillard would refer to as a code of production. They disappear into a hyperreality dominated by an indeterminant play of simulations, into an illlusion of identity that is fed by cultural commodities. The young Yolande seemingly leaves the Bellefleur clan only to resume her existence on celluloid. A number of the younger cousins had seen a film and speculated on the young actress's identity: "for *was* she Yolande, or did she merely *seem* to be Yolande?" (340). Still trapped in a culture of consumption, the younger Bellefleurs are devoured by a proliferation of models and simulations, as counterfeits within a circular system. Individual family members are frequently conflated with cars, the metaphoric twentieth-century engine of the American economy: "It was in a handsome two-seater Buick, canary-yellow, with rakish wire-spoked wheels, that Garth and Little Goldie eloped, and in a smart little fire-engine-red Fiat with a cream-colored convertible top and polished hubcaps . . . that Christabel and Demuth Hodge eloped one fine autumn morning" (340). Yolande is also allegedly spied on screen in a "supercharged Auburn, chalk-white, with gray upholstery and exposed exhaust pipes, of gleaming chromium" (340). Salvation for the young Bellefleurs comes ironically and not unexpectedly in the form of the automobile, simultaneously the sign of American upward mobility and escape. "One by one they disappear into America, to define themselves for themselves. The castle is destroyed, the Bellefleur children live" ("Afterword" 562). Paradoxically, they may escape from the Bellefleur lust for acquisitions only to find themselves defined by the next stage in the production and consumption continuum.

In one of the final chapters of the novel, the young genius Bromwell Bellefleur, after disappearing from home years before, publishes a monograph entitled, "A Hypothesis Concerning Anti-Matter" about a "mirror-image universe of anti-matter" (545). As yet another attempt at escape from the "remorseless claims of blood" (545), and from the remorseless claims of a commodity culture, Bromwell's monograph reflects the impossibility of release from a deterministic universe of simulations. He dreams of a "god of sleep who swallowed them up one by one by one" and, "oddly, that the water (but the water was only a metaphor!) had frozen, and those who clung to its surface, upside down, were trapped beneath the ice, their heads lost in the chill shadow, the soles of their feet pressed against the ice" (545-46). Perhaps Bromwell's dream is the end result of a long historical process of commodification and simulation, beginning with Jim Crow and ending with a consumer society devoured, inextricably trapped, and endlessly reflected in the economic logic of a culture of consumption.

9

APPROPRIATION AND VALUE
IN *BELOVED* AND "BENITO CERENO"

In the previous chapter, Hawthorne's *The House of the Seven Gables* summons the image of a gingerbread figure, the consumption of which by young Ned serves as an allegorical reiteration of consumption patterns that marks the economics of America. The body is first commodified and then consumed, as the references to Ned as "cannibal" reinforce. Both Melville's "Benito Cereno" and Beloved offer variations on that particular theme, depicting a world delineated by the arbitrary and dangerous constituents of ownership, an arena in which the dangers and violence of possession and consumption (literal and figurative) are played out both in gothic and realist terms. To the men and women who are defined as objects, possessions, and spiritless bodies with economic value, "slavery foregrounds the literal marketplace and makes selfhood meaningless" (McKinstry 260). That is to say, slavery is implicated in that which Baudrillard refers to as the political economy of the subject:

Far from the individual expressing his needs in the economic system, it is the economic system that induces the individual function and the parallel functionality of objects and needs. The individual is an ideological structure, a historical form correlative with the commodity form (exchange value) and the object form (use value). The individual is nothing but the subject thought in economic terms, rethought, simplified and abstracted by the economy. The entire history of consciousness and ethics (all the categories of occidental psychometaphysics) is only the history of the political economy of the subject. (*For a Critique* 133)

In essence, human subjectivity is commodified and reproduced in the form of labor and power, a process that, according to Baudrillard, may only be averted by refusing participation in the circuit of production, acquisition, and exchange. That noncompliance figures both in Melville's and Morrison's reading of America's experience of slavery, an interpretation that acknowledges the role of violent excess inherent in capitalism, that is, the relation of gratuitous expenditure to actual configurations of power. More specifically, it is the recognition of the radicality of death, its otherness, and its manifestation in the supernatural that can be seen in *Beloved* as opposing the rationality and linearity of the economic system. Analogously, Don Alexandro's murder and implied cannibalization in "Benito Cereno," imbued with ritualistic and sacrificial overtones, lowers the bar between life and death, enacting a violence that destroys a world of autonomized relations. In Baudrillardian terms, the power over death provides an archetype of the power of society over the individual "because it is in the manipulation, in the administration of death that power is founded in the last instance" (*Symbolic Exchange* 201). Once the bar between death and life is lifted, "this tollgate and this control between the two banks" (Genosko 1) is eliminated.

In this context, both "Benito Cereno" and *Beloved* lift that bar, turning the system of economic relations between slaves and whites inside out. This transformation is heightened by the gothic indeterminacy of Melville's story on two levels, the epistemological and the ideological. The Spanish slave ship, the *San Dominick,* is encountered by a northern American captain, Amasa Delano, whose misreading of the situation on board the ship slowly unfolds. In the morning mists, the ship first appears to him as a monastery perched on the Pyrenees, inhabited by cowled monks and, subsequently, as an ancient, deserted chateau, with formal gardens of trailing seaweed and wormy balustrades. He also perceives the ship to be hearse-like with a wen on its side and a ship's bell that has a graveyard toll. In effect, Delano begins his misreading of the story guided by the empty iconography of the gothic, the images of monasteries, castles, and coffins. Those hollow signifiers serve only as simulacra, underscoring the loss of foundational meaning with no recourse to an absolute origin. What did all these "phantoms amount to," including the "central hobgoblin of all," the Spanish Captain Don Benito (2515-16)? Delano asks himself. He learns that what haunts the *San Dominick* has nothing to do with monasteries or crumbling ruins and everything to do with the double horror of slavery and insurrection, an uprising that has turned the world upside down. The ship's oval stern-piece figuring two masked bodies, one of whom is holding his adversary down with a foot to the neck, suggests the roles are reversed, and that the slave Babo is the master of all. Returning to the sternpiece motif at the story's denouement, Melville has Delano with his foot on the neck of the unmasked Babo, implying the collusion of the northern United States in the institution of slavery. At every turn, the symbols of the gothic are linked not to some imaginary past, out of place and out of time, but to referents of a present-day horror. The image of the ship as monastery points to the role in the history of the Americas of Dominicans, who proposed that slaves be imported from Africa in order to save the Indians from slavery and extinction. The image of a decaying chateau implicates the corruption of colonial empires while hinting at the corruption which lies in the hold of the *San Dominick* itself, just as its resemblance to a coffin points darkly to the demise of Don Alexandro.

Indeed, in misreading the story of the *San Dominick,* ironically, Delano assists our rereading of the gothic. He naively refers to his initial perceptions of the ship as fanciful "enchantments" when, in the next moment, his eye falls upon the vessels' corroded main-chains, "rusty in link, shackle and bolt" (2520) Obviously, the step from enchantment, being held spell-bound, to being held in chains, is only a matter of degree. As Joseph Adamson has noted, Delano finds himself captured in a state of fascination, enchantment or captivation, particularly when Babo is present: "If Babo exploits to his destructive and vindictive ends a fascinatory, exhibitionistic power that aims at magically overwhelming his victim, Captain Delano unwittingly does his very best to help him along" (232). As Adamson points out, the deception practiced on Delano by Babo depends largely on optical effects, a specular seduction of sorts that delivers the captain into Babo's hands. Consequently, the gothic's links to the imaginary world of castles and friars are all the more tenuous, its links to more immediate horrors made stronger through Delano's gradual discovery of the transposed power relations aboard the ship. Those power relations are defined by the murder of Don Alexandro, inspiring a rereading of the message "follow your leader," both by Don Benito's crew and, subsequently, by Delano. His corpse "prepared," Don Alexandro's skeleton is substituted for the ship's proper figurehead, the image of Christopher Colon, the discoverer of the New World. The ritualized murder of Don Alexandro, to which we shall return shortly, is the mechanism that allows Babo to rebuff Delano's offer to purchase him for fifty doubloons. "Master wouldn't part with Babo for a thousand doubloons," says the erstwhile slave, in a direct rejection of the dictates of capital within a slave economy.

Morrison's narrative is based on a similar equation. Beloved's murder is a necessity, a rejection of the dictates of capital, its attendant values and practices, and a rebuke of a system of sign values whereby individuals are situated within a consumer society and must submit to its domination through the activity of consumption. As with Babo and the slave cargo of the *San Dominick,* both Paul D and Sethe's worth is measured as market value, that which they can produce and which in turn might be consumed. Paul D "has always known or believed he did, his value—as a hand, a laborer who could make a profit on a farm—but now he discovers his worth, which is to say he learns his price. The dollar value of his weight, his strength, his heart, his brain, his penis, and his future" (226). In turn,

Sethe's "price was greater than his; property that reproduced itself without cost" (228). Slaves are literally commodified subjects turned objects, "men and women were moved around like checkers":

Anybody Baby Suggs knew, let alone loved, who hadn't run off or been hanged, got rented out, loaned out, bought up, brought back, stored up, mortgaged, won, stolen or seized. So Baby's eight children had six fathers. What she called the nastiness of life was the shock she received upon learning that nobody stopped playing checkers just because the pieces included her children. (23)

Rented, loaned, bought, stored, mortgaged, won, stolen, seized—the language is ideologically marked, contextualizing and historicizing the workings of power relations within and outside slavocracy. In a painful irony, slaves can only have agency in the world of capital exchange, in which they are commodities to be produced and regulated, by selling themselves as objects. Halle buys his mother by working during his free time and Sethe buys Beloved's tombstone with her body, all of which operates as an inversion of how Halle's time is eventually reclaimed by his new masters and Sethe is exploited as an object of reproduction. Halle and Sethe's attempts to play the system, to take control of the surplus, that is, the profits, are counterproductive. Halle realizes that once he has bought his mother out of slavery, he will never be able to afford to buy his wife and children: "If all my labor is Sweet Home, including the extra, what I got left to sell?" (241). Immediately following Halle's realization that his masters own his labor and he has no surplus to sell, Sethe understands that the threat to her children is economic. "Say it don't pay to have my labor somewhere else while the boys is small," Halle explains, leading Sethe to the realization of what is in store. "I couldn't get out of my head the thing that woke me up: 'While the boys is small.' That's what he said and it snapped me awake. . . . That's when we should have begun to plan. But we didn't. I don't know what we thought—but getting away was a money thing to us" (196-97). The "money thing" represents a paradoxical paradigm that Sethe, Halle, and Paul D want to escape both from and to; they are caught in the logic of the system and their attempts at escape are but a reflex of what Baudrillard calls the mirror of production. As Baudrillard argues, utilizing Lacan's concept of the mirror stage, the mirror of production, that is, the political economy, simply reproduces the primacy of production which is itself a product of capitalism and antithetical to a genuinely revolutionary project.

Beloved succeeds so brilliantly precisely because the text's overarching theme of "remembering" at once exposes and critiques this contradiction. From Morrison's dedication to the "Sixty million and more" to the repetition of that number through the character "with a number for a name—Sixo" and whose cry of freedom is "Seven-O! Seven-O!," numbers represent the "values" which African Americans must transform or transpose in order to survive. In a world where the commodification of human beings is taken to its horrifyingly logical conclusion, where Baby Suggs quite literally comes with a price tag, a "sales ticket" (142), a struggle to make the numbers and accounting signify something other than the primacy of production becomes paramount. As Denver says of her father, "But my daddy said, If you can't count they can cheat you. If you can't read they can beat you" (256). Making the numbers mean something else becomes a form of emancipation. The number 124 Bluestone suggests a missing link, a lack of continuity or history that Sethe's family must create, find, and restore. Similarly, the natural cycle of fertility and reproduction stands in stark contrast to the use-value of reproduction under slavery. Sethe spends "twenty-eight days of having women friends, a mother-in-law, and all her children" (212) before the death of Beloved. She is haunted for eighteen years culminating in Beloved's rebirth, representing the doubling of number nine and suggesting Beloved's double gestation. Baby Suggs makes a feast for ninety people, "three (maybe four) pies grew to ten (maybe twelve). Sethe's two hens became five turkeys" (137). Denver struggles with the story of her birth, more specifically about how the event was attended to by the white girl, Amy Denver, after whom she is named. The young woman's kindness, her taking the personal risk to help a slave escape, and her refusal to turn in Sethe for money, is a source both of wonder and pain for Denver: "it made her feel like a bill was owing somewhere and she, Denver had to pay it. But who she owed or what to pay it with eluded her" (77). In each of these instances, the purpose of accounting has changed, no longer used to classify, categorize, and commodify, but to connect and reveal radical possibilities for genuine emancipation.

The idea of radical possibilities intersects with the concept of transformation or transposition. Just as Morrison's text allows the numbers to mean something else, so too the text appropriates the categories that are intended to establish slaves as commodities. Schoolteacher sets about running Sweet Home as though he were setting up a profit and loss statement, his slaves' assets on one side and their liabilities on the other:

He would have to trade this here one for $900 if he could get it, and set out to secure the breeding one, if he found him. With the money from "this here one" he could get two young ones, twelve or fifteen years old. And maybe with the breeding one, her three pickaninnies and whatever the foal might be, he and his nephews would have seven niggers and Sweet Home would be worth the trouble it was causing him. (227)

The question of "value" here is something that the text seeks to unsettle and displace. The schoolteacher's insistence on cataloguing Sethe's animal characteristics as befitting chattel slaves is undone by Sethe's indirect correlation with cows, drawing upon the ancient Egyptian mythologies and religions that Sethe's name suggests. Seth, one of the major gods of ancient Egypt, assumed part man and part animal form and was often associated with purification rituals. The men of Sweet Home wasted themselves on cows and, as Paul D thinks, "the jump . . . from a calf to a girl wasn't all that mighty" (26). He later reminds Sethe that "you got two feet, Sethe, not four" (165). Again in Egyptian mythology, the cow is representative of mother earth, the nurturer, and provider of food. Alternatively, Sethe is also associated with the serpent as she struggles with Amy's help to deliver Denver: "Down in the grass, like the snake she believed she was, Sethe opened her mouth, and instead of fangs and a split tongue, out shot the truth" (32). As a symbol both of the sublime and of evil, the serpent combines reptile and bird, animal and fish: "It is close to the origin of life, the underlying unity of all life forms . . . demanding to be transformed" (Biedermann 363). It is this impetus toward transformation that haunts Paul D's journey to selfhood as well. His own comparison with Mister, the rooster of Sweet Home, underscores his commodification. He is reduced to chattel when his feet are shackled, a three-spoke collar is laced around his neck, a bit placed in his mouth, and he is tethered to, ironically, a buckboard. As he is paraded past the rooster, Paul D's emasculation is complete. "Mister looked so . . . free. Better than me. Mister was allowed to be and stay what he was. But I wasn't . . . I was something else and that something was less than a chicken sittin in the sun on a tub" (72). Paul D's chance for transformation comes with his symbolic resurrection and rebirth from his wooden grave in Alfred, Georgia. Rising from their box in torrential rains that made escape possible, Paul D and his fellow convicts: "like the unshriven dead, zombies on the loose, holding the chains in their hands" (110), come to the surface to take their first tentative steps as free men.

Symbolic of the commodification inherent in slavery is the leitmotif of consumption whose refrain is fixed in the pivotal scene of the rape of Sethe's breasts. That scene can be usefully juxtaposed with an incident in "Benito Cereno," the point at which Delano spies a "slumbering negress" (2519) with her baby. "Sprawling at her lapped breasts," the baby is nestled in the arms of its mother, who remains "not at all concerned at the attitude in which she had been caught" as she "delightedly caught the child up, with maternal transports, covering it with kisses." Unbeknownst to Delano, the mother is free to revel in her affection for her child, liberated as she is, at least momentarily, from slavery on the *San Dominick*. (His reading of this maternal scene leaves out the fact, as we later learn, that this mother has been an eager participant in the bloody insurrection on board the ship.) Symbolically, her milk is now her own and her babe's, as are her affections and her familial bonds. For Sethe, her milk represents a more tenuous attachment, nourishment for and fragile connection to her (already crawling?) baby, Beloved, while for schoolteacher's nephews, her milk signifies something which they can appropriate and consume, not unlike the ink that she produces for them. As Baudrillard has noted, consumption veils the material under-pinnings and labor which produces consumer society and its goods: "One should never forget that these goods are the *product of a human activity* and that they are dominated not by natural ecological laws but by the laws of exchange value" (*Consumer Society* 14). Although Bau-drillard situates his argument within a neocapitalist, postmodern context, the history of slavery foregrounds the emergence of consumer society by throwing into exaggerated relief the "natural" needs of consumption, needs that are founded less in "nature" and more in the naturalized and manufactured system that is rationalized, homogenized, systematized, and, above all, normalized. The evolution toward commodification and a consumer society brings with it a deviation from the responsibilities of morality, ethics, consciences, and other forms of social affiliation. Hence, the subtext of violence that is the hallmark of gothic fiction, vio-lence that in Morrison's reading of slavery is predicated on the opera-tions of subjectivity defined by commodity signs, culminating in Sethe's understanding of the connection between taking control of capital (her children) and self-definition. It is an understanding which is articulated earlier in "Benito Cereno," in the scene with the young mother who also seizes the opportunity to take control of her milk and the fate of her child through the insurrection on board the *San Dominick*.

One aspect of taking control involves subverting the role of con-sumption in a system that benefits from the exploitation of slave labor, where the "products" of human bodies are consumed. That act of con-sumption is transformed in Melville's and Morrison's texts, emerging in both as a defiant reaction or radical negation of productivist society. Bataille and Baudrillard explain this radical negation in terms of objects and exchanges in rituals that value waste and expenditure, thereby trans-gressing production and utilitarian imperatives. Baudrillard presupposes a fundamental dividing line between symbolic societies, organized around symbolic exchange, and productivist societies, organized around production. He states that the former belongs to a precapitalist, "primitive" (my quotation marks) mode and the latter to a capitalist one. Whether these categories are simplistic or naively nostalgic, historically speaking, is not really germane to my argument. Instead, what is of interest is the "process of challenge [défi]" (Baudrillard, For a Critique 43) that symbolic exchange offers, a challenge that surfaces in Morrison's text, threatening the primacy of labor, commodification, and production. "This is the metabolism of exchange, prodigality, festival—and also of destruction (which returns to non-value what production has erected, valorized). In this domain, value isn't even recognized" (Baudrillard, For a Critique 44).

Significantly, this concept of prodigality, waste, and expenditure is a component of the gothic genre. The sacrifice and waste symbolized by Beloved's death and resurrection is yoked to a subversion of consumption. The house on Bluestone is "spiteful," that is, "full of baby's venom" (1). The ghost is consumed with vengefulness and makes her presence known with "two tiny hand prints . . . in the cake" (1), a kettleful of chickpeas smoking in a heap on the floor, and soda crackers crumbled and strewn in a line next to the doorsill. When she arrives in the form of a young woman, she is continuously thirsty (51), first for water and then for her mother, who is "licked, tasted, eaten by Beloved's eyes" (57). As we explored in the previous section, Beloved assumes the role of succubus while Sethe reenacts the image of the victim, a fading figure whose gradual starvation parallels Beloved's increasing strength. That power is symbolized by Beloved's pregnant shape, the ripening womb of a collective identity that undermines the economics of commodification and consumption as experienced in slavery. Having fed from the stories and memories of her race, Beloved gives permission to her community to begin filling in the gaps left by a society intent on feeding from the lives of human beings. This subversion of consumption is no better illustrated than in the scene following Beloved's murder. Sethe is holding her dead baby, who is pried from her by Baby Suggs, so that she can nurse her younger child. Baby Suggs exhorts her daughter-in-law to "clean up" first, but Sethe wins the battle and "so Denver took her mother's milk right along with the blood of her sister" (152). The scene has the ritualistic and sacrificial overtones that Baudrillard alludes to when writing about "the consumption of the 'surplus' and deliberate anti-production" (Mirror of Production 44). In other words, Sethe refuses the commodification of her children, resorting to the wanton destruction of surplus—her baby. Her milk, which was consumed by the nephews, has now been transformed from an object of consumption to sustenance for Denver, who, by consuming her dead sister's blood along with her mother's milk, becomes part of the sacrifice and no longer a potential commodity.

These sacrificial and ritualistic overtones are foregrounded in the text of "Benito Cereno," more specifically in the death of Don Alexandro at the hands of "Yau who by Babo's command, willingly prepared the skeleton of Don Alexandro, in a way the negroes afterwards told the deponent, but which he, so long as reason is left him, can never divulge" (2550). The specter of cannibalism haunts the text, beginning with images of the "pipe-clayed aspect" (2499) of the ship, "her keel like the ribs from Ezekiel's Valley of Dry Bones" (2500), to the "horrified gestures" of Don Benito upon mention of his dead colleague's name and possible whereabouts of his body, "uncertain what fate had befallen the remains of Don Alexandro" (2547). As the bodies and spirits of the African slaves are consumed by their white masters, so too do Babo's men consume the flesh of Don Alexandro, symbolically replacing the ship's figurehead of Christopher Columbus with the dead man's bleached skeleton. The ritualized death of Don Alexandro underscores and undermines the commodified nature of relations between slaves and their masters by positioning the relation of gratuitous, unproductive expenditure (cannibalism) to actual configurations of power. Don Alexandro's demise literally symbolizes the commodification and consumption of human flesh within the slave trade.

Babo and the slaves are using the economic rationale of the slave system to transform and appropriate the definition of human "value," transforming themselves from subjects that are commodified into literal consumers. In this context, it is important to note that, as a freed woman, Sethe also plays both sides of the fence, at once participating in "productive" activity and yet undermining the logic of capitalism by stealing. She cooks "day and night" (14) to earn money. She also pilfers food from Sawyer's to bring home to her family, surplus that she steals, matches, salt, and butter, "even though she could afford to buy them" (189). Her pilfering is reminiscent of Sixo's encounter with schoolteacher, when he justifies—ironically using the economic rationale of the slave system—his theft of a shoat.

> "You stole that shoat, didn't you?"
> "No. Sir." Said Sixo, but he had the decency to keep his eyes on the meat.
> "And you telling me that's not stealing?"
> "No, sir. It ain't."
> "What is it then?"
> "Improving your property, sir."
> "What?"

"Sixo plant rye to give the high piece a better chance. Sixo take and feed the soil, give you more crop. Sixo take and feed Sixo give you more work."

Clever, but schoolteacher beat him anyway to show him that definitions belonged to the definers—not the defined. (190)

In another attempt at transforming the definition of "value," Sixo's logic follows the continuum of capitalist production and accumulation while making a case for his own subversion of the values of exchange inherent in such a system. Food, in *Beloved,* serves as the negative antithesis to productive activity or to any activity that follows the logic of capitalism. It operates within Baudrillard's ideal of symbolic exchange, an alternative to the values and practices of capitalist societies, founded in the concept of gift and countergift, rather than production and utility. Baudrillard suggests that strategies which involve neither use-values nor exchange-values subvert the workings of a system which demands that all activity be utilitarian and assigned specific values. Further, he offers that symbolic exchange, such as gratuitous gift giving, festivities, sacrifice, and waste escape the logic of the capitalist system. This dynamic is well illustrated by Halle's response to watching helplessly as schoolteacher's nephews rob Sethe of her milk. "It broke him, Sethe," Paul D says. "Last time I saw him he was sitting by the churn. He had butter all over his face" (69). Halle loses his mind in the face of the stark truth that he has witnessed, the complete commodification of his wife, her body, and its issue mere products to be used and exchanged. Consequently, Halle escapes into "butter play" (71), transforming the value of mother's milk into a realm where it becomes non-recuperable to any system of value. Sethe imagines longingly such a respite, an escape to gratuitous expenditure embodying loss and waste.

Other people went crazy, why couldn't she? Other people's brains stopped, turned around and went on to something new, which is what must have happened to Halle. And how sweet that would have been: the two of them back by the milk shed, squatting by the churn, smashing cold, lumpy butter into their faces with not a care in the world. Feeling it slippery, sticky—rubbing it in their hair, watching it squeeze through their fingers. What a relief to stop it right there. Close. Shut. Squeeze the butter. (70)

Squandering a valuable product and turning around to go "on to something new" stands in radical opposition to the dominant types of exchange-, use-, and sign-value in productivist societies, and, in the tightly circumscribed world of slavery, this "insanity" remains one of the few options for both play and destruction outside and opposite the logic of capital.

Through textual metaphors, food in Morrison's text is further intricated in the Baudrillardian concept of symbolic exchange, a practice that is nonequivalent, nonreductive, and outside codes that reduce consumption to the level of prices and power positions. Symbolic exchange, suggests Baudrillard, includes gratuitous gift giving, sacrifice, ritual, festive play, and destruction, activities that oppose a system that controls and profits from every aspect of life. According to Baudrillard, marginal groups in particular, such as blacks, women, and homosexuals, stand outside the productivist code by virtue of their marginal status. This orientation is illustrated in Baby Suggs's rituals in the Clearing. A woman who "had nothing left to make a living with but her heart" (87) leads her people through a ritual of celebration and renewal each Saturday, exhorting them to sing, dance, cry, and reclaim their flesh as their own:

in this here place, we flesh; flesh that weeps, laughs; flesh that dances on bare feet in grass. Love it. Love it hard. Yonder they do not love your flesh. They despise it. . . . And O my people they do not love your hands. Those they only use, tie, bind, chop off and leave empty. Love your hands! Love them. Raise them up and kiss them. Touch others with them, pat them together, stroke them on your face 'cause they don't love that either. (88)

Baby Suggs's "preaching" opens the way for the black community to learn to value themselves not as commodities but as flesh that weeps, laughs, and dances, flesh that is not just to be used, bartered, and exploited. The ritual serves as a reclamation, much as the murder of Don Alexandro serves as a symbolic appropriation of the horrors of the commodification and consumption of human beings. These gatherings are a preamble to the feast that Baby Suggs prepares shortly after Sethe's arrival in Ohio, a celebration of symbolic exchange and excessive expenditure. Food has never been as plentiful, appearing seemingly out of nowhere, unconnected to anything within a productivist system. Stamp provides fish that "were jumping into the boat—didn't even have to drop a line" (136). The impossibility of new peas in September, fresh cream but no cow, and a turkey enough for the whole town was "Too much, they thought" (137), a community grown suddenly suspicious once the festivities were ended. "The reckless generosity on display at 124" leads Baby Suggs to believe she had "given too much, offended them by excess" (138).

This excessive expenditure, of course, culminates the next day in Sethe's murder of Beloved, another component of the cycle of symbolic exchange which opposes the rationality and utility of the economic system. As Baudrillard suggests, all value is placed on life, with death serving as a foundation for social exclusion. "To abolish death, this is our fantasy which is ramified in all directions: that of survival and eternity for religion, that of truth for science, that of productivity and accumulation for the economy" (*Symbolic Exchange* 106). Death is social and economic exile, a challenge to the status quo. "Death becomes radical when it is resocialized and stripped of its individual fatality; when it becomes, in other words, a condition of social being" (Genosko 92). Sethe's murder of Beloved can be read precisely as a radical death which resocializes the community, simultaneously robbing the system of yet another potential commodity and thereby providing opportunities for reintegration of a fragile community. Don Alexandro's demise is another such death which radicalizes the slaves of the *San Dominick* and subverts the traditional hierarchy that supports their commodification. Beloved's return from the dead also harks back to societies which Baudrillard claims experienced no real division between life and death. According to Baudrillard, in these societies, symbolic exchange between life and death was the norm, replete with gifts and ceremonies honoring the dead and hauntings of the living. Once the binary opposition is dissolved, and the bar between life and death lifted, individuals no longer need to submit to social authorities such as the church or state for promises of immortality or protection. It is precisely Beloved's return from the dead that allows Sethe and her community to reconnect, not under the auspices of slavery or emancipation but under a sociocultural impetus that takes precedence over the economy and material necessity.

As Rebecca Ferguson has pointed out, Denver reconnects with her community when death threatens the living at 124 Bluestone. She seeks help from Lady Jones who offers her food to take back to her mother and sister, a gesture that grows to include gifts of food from others in the community, left for Denver on the very tree stump where Beloved had first appeared. "Denver's personal connection with the donors begins through her deciphering the names they leave, or alternatively through identifying their plates, pie dishes and so on" (Ferguson 123). In other words, it is through symbolic exchange, through gratuitous gift giving, that Denver proceeds with the social encounters that culminate in Beloved's exorcism and the beginnings of the reintegration of the black community. In essence, the nature of value has been transformed, from the odious categorization and commodification of slavery and from the "mirror of production" that only recognizes and valorizes codes of production to a communal, ritualistic social order tentatively organized around symbolic exchange. The catalyst that drives the story that is not to be passed on finds roots in a rupture between symbolic exchange and capitalism, in effect a radical alternative that offers possibilities for self-definition and community. The beginnings of that rupture are found in "Benito Cereno," in an act equally as monstrous as Beloved's murder by her mother, that is, a genuine if extreme act of decommodification. Melville's and Morrison's texts raise questions as to the extent to which the logic of the economic is able to restrict and constrain the logic of the cultural by interrogating Baudrillard's assumption that the "individual is nothing but the subject thought in economic terms, rethought, simplified and abstracted by the economy."

10

CONSUMING PASSIONS IN *THE VAMPIRE LESTAT*

> Before all distinctions between form and content, between signifier
> and signified, even before the division between enunciation and
> statement, there is the unqualifiable Saying, the glory of a "narrative
> voice" that speaks clearly, without ever being obscured by the opac-
> ity or the enigma or the terrible horror of what it communicates.
> —Maurice Blanchot, *Vicious Circles* 68

The horror inherent in the second installment of Anne Rice's *Vampire Chronicles* circles around the complicity between seduction and
consumption, a collusion that is linked to what Fredric Jameson has
referred to as the cultural logic of late capitalism. Within the contexts of
late capitalism, there exists a mechanism which aligns the erotic with the
seductive, the longing for submission that has been, in turn, institutionalized and co-opted by commodity culture. This co-optation of cata-
strophic, anarchic expenditure has given rise to a reactive recuperation
of heterogeneity. Transgressive forces are effectively pulled into the
process of exchange-value. Consequently, we have two versions of
seduction. First, as we have seen in earlier chapters, there is seduction as
an alternative to production involving extravagant ritual and unrecupera-
ble expenditure; that is, the link yoking eroticism with violence in texts
such as *Bellefleur,* a connection which, in turn, allows for the undermining of the hierarchical and acquisitive. Seduction operates within the
same paradigm in *Beloved* wherein the vampire/succubus trope calls
into question the complex of social networks and material conditions
that help to reproduce relations of race and gender. Conversely, there
exists "cool" seduction, to borrow from Baudrillard, which has formed a
pact with simulation in a conflation of desire and consumption. Simulation which marks postmodern culture exerts a ludic and cool magnetism:
"Seduction/simulacra: communication like the social functions in a
closed circuit, redoubling by signs an undiscoverable reality: And the
social contract has become a pact of simulation, sealed by the media and
information" (*Symbolic Exchange* 221-22). Lost in a world governed by
a commodified system of sign values, Lestat's story belongs to that order
of the hyperreal and of simulation. More concretely, Rice's narrative

reflects an environment shaped by the proliferation of cultural images and signs, forces that cancel meaning in the white noise of undifferentiated information, thereby collapsing the distinction between reality and unreality. What remains is the apotheosis of the gothic genre, enshrined in a system of sign values linked to commodification. Ironically, the gothic genre which begins its career as reflecting the "unreal" emerges in *Lestat* as a close approximation of reality, an interpretation of the real as the simulacrum that pervades postmodernity itself.

Lestat's attempts at Dionysian frenzy, his rock concerts, his melodramatic antics on stage at Renaud's House of Thespians, change exactly nothing because they are inextricably linked with a commodified system of sign values governed by rules, codes, and a social logic. His human audience is immune to the "reality" that he speaks, his message simultaneously heard and lost in the proliferation of codes, signs, and simulacra behind which stands nothing. Rice's vampire world indirectly legitimates the "real" America not unlike Baudrillard's explication of Disney's legitimating relationship to America: "Disneyland is presented as imaginary in order to make us believe that the rest is real, when in fact all of Los Angeles and the America surrounding it are no longer real, but of the order of the hyperreal and of simulation" (*Symbolic Exchange* 25). Similarly, Rice's vampire world is presented as imaginary to make us believe that the rest is real.

Lestat's story begins with his discovery of the novel *Interview with the Vampire,* written by his sometime cohort, Louis. The book has become a runaway best-seller which readers, of course, take as gothic fiction. This situation prompts Lestat to place "a fresh disk into the portable computer word processor . . . to write the story of my life" (16). His narrative opens as he arises from a half-century of "dream state" (4) awakened by the music of a rock band, Satan's Night Out. He begins writing about the eighteenth century, when, as a mortal born into the French aristocracy prior to the French Revolution, he tries to flee his ancestral home to join a troupe of Italian actors. He is returned home only to achieve heroic status by killing a pack of wolves which are preying upon his village, an act which eventually earns him the admiration and attention of Magnus, who makes him a vampire. Before his transformation, Lestat works as an actor in the theater in Paris and his obsession with the arts becomes the only governing principle, religion, or belief system under which he lives. "Actors and actresses make magic . . . they're saints to me" (46). Both Katherine Ramsland and Bette B. Roberts have compared Lestat to Dionysus, who "represents both the eternal spirit of passion and energy worshiped by the Greeks in frenzied ritual" (Ramsland 51).

The rest of Lestat's story, his encounters with other vampires and his search for origins, is punctuated by a hyperreality, simulations in which images, spectacles, and the play of signs erase the boundaries between representation and reality. "We are illusions of what is mortal, and the stage is an illusion of what is real," explains his mother, Gabrielle (273), about the lives of vampires creating "the imitation of life" (274). In this Baudrillardian universe, signs and modes of representation come to constitute reality; signs interact with other signs, referring to and gaining their significance in relation to other commodity signs. In order to survive psychically if not physically, vampires must consume the signs and codes that, in turn, assist them in their imitation of life. This survival necessarily hinges on an acute self-reflexivity which is reflected in the framework of both *Interview with the Vampire* and *The Vampire Lestat;* the first narrative is a "live" interview which is transformed into a book, which in turn serves as the catalyst for the sequel which masquerades as an autobiography. Lestat's postmodern preoccupations, his commitment to relativism and obsession with both popular and high art forms, come packaged in his autobiography with its paradoxical merging of self-consciousness and historical framework. Both vampires, Louis and Lestat, "exist" by virtue of these publications, their allusions to one another's lives and texts inextricable and intertextual. "We write our own fairy tales" (160), explains Lestat with typical and self-reflexive irony, adding later that Louis "looked as if he'd stepped out of the pages of his own story" (465). However, he acknowledges the influence of other gothic texts on the story of his own life which he has documented in his autobiography:

Yet it was strangely reassuring to know that I hadn't been the first aristocratic fiend to move through the ballrooms of the world in search of my victims—the deadly gentleman who would soon surface in stories and poetry and penny dreadful novels as the very epitome of our tribe. (284)

Louis's and Lestat's stories exist both in real and unreal terms; the reader experiences the materiality of the novel, the activity of reading or interpretation. In the novel itself, Lestat wanders "into the elegant double-decker bookstore called de Ville Books, and there stared at the small paperback of *Interview with the Vampire* on the shelf" (14).

And it didn't matter if they didn't believe it. It didn't matter that they thought it was art. . . . But again, I was going farther than Louis. His story, for all its peculiarities had passed for fiction. In the mortal world, it was as safe as the tableaux of the old Theater of the Vampires in the Paris where the fiends had pretended to be actors pretending to be fiends on a remote and gaslighted stage.

I'd step into the solar light before the cameras, I'd reach out and touch with my icy fingers a thousand warm and grasping hands . . . And suppose—just suppose—that when the corpses began to turn up in ever greater numbers, that when those closest to me began to hearken to their inevitable suspicions—just suppose that art ceased to be art and became real!

The real as subordinate to representation invokes the "aesthetic law" (*Lestat* 335) in Rice's text, the only antidote to meaninglessness, to the vampires' own "stunning irrelevance to the mighty scheme of things." Even "pure evil has no real place," Lestat discovers, except as it is represented in the theater, in the "vampire comics, the horror novels, the old gothic tales—or in the roaring chants of the rock stars who dramatize the battles against evil that each mortal fights within himself" (9). Consequently, it is music and acting that "drove back chaos" and the "meaninglessness" and the "absolute absence of any answer" (49), the catalysts that in turn drive a hyperreal society of simulations from which Rice's immortal vampires cannot escape.

It is this immortality that signifies and categorizes the vampire's existence as simulation. They are more real than real, the new and improved version of mere mortals. Their hearing, sight, and strength is more acute and they are impervious to the ravages of time and the defunct moral dictates of God or Satan. The end of the twentieth century is inscribed as the age of simulation, "where the principle of simulation wins out over the reality principle" (*Symbolic Exchange* 152), a new universe which Rice has translated into gothic horror. The transformed vampire Lestat is just one in the proliferation of models and simulations, a counterfeit within a circular system with neither beginning nor end. He looks into a mirror and sees only "some replica" (91) of his former mortal self, a "mere imitation now of a human body" (388), the "imitation of a man" (408). We may be compelled to ask which is the "real" horror, the vampires or their representation of a hyperreal society of simulations? Or more likely, does this gothic text furnish an "imaginary" space which functions not unlike Disneyland in order "to make us believe that the rest is real"? When Lestat declares that "I am the new evil. I am the vampire for these times. . . . Try to see the evil that I am. I stalk the world in mortal dress—the worst of fiends, the monster who looks exactly like everyone else," his words may well address the special horror of simulation as consisting of the residue and effect of neocapitalism.

A feature of this neocapitalism, among the play of images and signs of the counterfeit, is the transformation of Lestat's "law of aesthetics." In the present stage of simulacra, reproduction itself becomes a dominant principle ordered by the laws of the market. The theater of Renaud, in which Lestat begins his mortal career as an actor, is transformed into the Theater of the Vampires, thanks to the now immortal Lestat's infusion of gold coins which allows the entourage to "thrive" (231). Rice's vampires are as resilient as "the immortal Bank of London and the Rothschild Bank" (6), another version of the system of codes which constitutes the "real." "Those banks have lived as long as vampires already. They will always be there" (309), declares the obviousness of how money begets money. Rice's vampires are the first in gothic history to be fabulously wealthy not through labor, production, or even inheritance but simply through an understanding of how wealth operates as a system of signs that replicates itself continually and without referents; the logic of capital accumulation as dependent only on sign-value. (Significantly, Lestat goes "underground" for more than fifty-five years right before the stock market crash in 1929.) It is his access to vast financial resources that allows him to graduate from the theater to finance his video/rock extravaganza at the close of the twentieth century. "The best French directors for the rock video films. . . . You must lure them from New York and Los Angeles. There is ample money for that. . . . It does not matter what we spend on this venture," Lestat informs his lawyer, feeling "her seduction" (13) as she acquiesces to his grandiose plans. Religion and even atheism are merely "fashion" (41), with traditions and superstitions giving way to "a new style" (201). As Lestat explains to the nineteenth-century vampires whose existence is threatened by their unwillingness to consume the codes and signs of the time, "The people of Paris don't want the stench of graveyards around them anymore. The emblems of the dead don't matter to them as they matter to you. Within a few years, markets, streets, and houses will cover this spot. Commerce. Practicality. . . . The old mysteries have given way to a new style" (200-1). As Nina Auerbach has written, "vampires blend into the changing cultures they inhabit" (*Our Vampires* 6), with Rice's Lestat's parodic scrambling of aesthetic codes as he swings from actor and writer to rock star blending better than most.

To survive necessitates understanding and, above all, consuming the new style, and as Lestat travels to the heart of society, he "drank up its entertainments and its gossip, its literature and its music, its architecture and its art" (288). These entertainments are represented in Rice's text as an amalgam of popular and high art forms which, in turn, are subject to the same rules and system of signification as other commodities, following the codes of style determined by the value of the marketplace. This amalgam is predicated on repetition and recycling of the same, a crucial aspect of Baudrillard's postmodern carnival and evoked in a description of the 1980s in *The Vampire Lestat*:

In the art and entertainment worlds all prior centuries were being "recycled." Musicians performed Mozart as well as jazz and rock music; people went to see Shakespeare one night and a new French film the next. . . . In giant fluorescent-lighted emporiums you could buy tapes of medieval madrigals and play them on your car stereo as you drove ninety miles an hour down the freeway. In the bookstores Renaissance poetry sold side by side with the novels of Dickens or Ernest Hemingway. Sex manuals lay on the same tables with the Egyptian Book of the Dead. . . . Sometimes the wealth and the cleanliness everywhere around me became like an hallucination. (8)

The hallucination that is the postmodern carnival extends from the replication of cultural signs to the parodic, signaling the distance between copy and original. Hence, Lestat's antics on the stage of Renaud's, after his transformation, become a burlesque, a vampire pretending to be human pretending to be a vampire. His "dance became a parody, each gesture broader, longer, slower than a human dancer could have sustained" (120). Rice's text is also a polyphonic, heterogeneous paean to M. M. Bakhtin's definition of the novel as "a diversity of social speech types (sometimes even diversity of languages) and a diversity of individual voices" (262), to the extent that the concept itself is all but parodied in Lestat's performance of the English language:

The language I use in my autobiography—I first learned it from the flatboatmen who came down the Mississippi to New Orleans about two hundred years ago. I learned more after that from the English language writers—everybody from Shakespeare through Mark Twain to H. Rider Haggard, whom I read as the decades passed. The final infusion I received from the detective stories of the early twentieth century in the *Black Mask* magazine. The adventures of Sam Spade by Dashiell Hammett. . . . When I write I drift into a vocabulary that would have been natural to me in the eighteenth century, into phrases shaped by authors I've read. But in spite of my French accent, I talk like a cross between a flatboatman and detective Sam Spade, actually. So I hope you'll bear with me when my style is inconsistent. (3-4)

Lestat emerges as the quintessential decontextualized, decentered subject for whom "History had no meaning" (21). He rumbles into the last quarter of the twentieth century either on a black Harley-Davidson motorcycle or behind the wheel of a Porsche in the trappings of the rock star which has become an almost universal code. Similarly, his vampire cohorts emerge not so much as subjects or even characters but as copies, parodies of subjects in paintings or literary figures. He and Gabrielle are like "images painted" by the old masters "in cerulean and carmine and gold" (267), while "Armand might have looked like a god out of Caravaggio, Gabrielle a marble archangel at the threshold of a church" (322). However, as the years pass and the styles change, Armand assumes (consumes) the trappings of the Victorian age, appearing "like a young man out of the novels of Dickens in his somber and sleekly tailored black frock coat, all the Renaissance curls clipped away. His eternally youthful face was stamped with the innocence of a David Copperfield and the pride of a Steerforth" (438).

This pliancy, the result of playful combinations and infinite inter-substitutions, extends to constructions of gender and toward, according to Baudrillard, sexual indifferentiation and erotic polyvalency. The direction points toward bisexuality or omnisexuality which becomes a game, ritualized and ironic (*Seduction* 15). The image of the voracious child-vampire Claudia, reduced to ashes in *Interview with the Vampire,* is supplanted by the figure of Gabrielle in Rice's second installment of her *Chronicles.* Powerful, independent, androgynous, she begins as Lestat's mother but emerges as a force which foregrounds the text's emphasis on the collapse of sexual differentiation and its attendant taboos. Lestat, definitive seducer, embodies a decentered eroticism that propels him to break all the rules, including the greatest prohibition of all:

Old truths and ancient magic, revolution and invention, all conspire to distract us from the passion that in one way or another defeats us all. . . . we dream of that long-ago time when we sat upon our mother's knee and each kiss was the perfect consummation of desire. What can we do but reach for the embrace that must now contain both heaven and hell: our doom again and again and again. (430)

Lestat's merging with Gabrielle in the vampiric act is described in the most erotic of terms: "she was flesh and blood and mother and lover and all things beneath the cruel pressure of my fingers and my lips, everything I had ever desired" (138). After her metamorphosis, Lestat "went to kiss her again and she didn't stop me. We were lovers kissing. . . . She was simply she, the one I had needed all of my life with all of my being. The only woman I had ever loved" (147-48). In the dark, they are "lovers carved out of the same stone who had no memory of a separate life at all" (234). This fusion suggests an oedipal pliancy within the orbit of the forbidden, anarchic, and incestuous, a semiotic space which frees

the boundaries of sexual identity and language. The dissolution of fixed
categories reflects the postmodern carnival, of masquerade and simulation. Gabrielle, itself a gender-neutral name, metamorphoses into more
than just a vampire. As a mortal woman trapped by the exigencies of a
repressive historical period, she finds escape in the books and fantasies
of murder of her husband and sons (34), a desire she shares with Lestat.
She "hated to be called mother" (36) and, once a vampire, quickly leaves
the role behind entirely, the oppressive husband, the children who
devoured and abandoned her, to become instead "no mother anymore"
(139). She leaves behind her constricting skirts and long hair and dons
loose trousers and a dusty hat to become a world wanderer. Her masquerade is complete when Lestat glimpses the "figure of an unearthly
young boy, an exquisite young boy, pacing the floor of the chamber. Of
course it was only Gabrielle" (164). Lestat's own walks on the wild side
include vampiric relations with members of either sex and an effeminate,
flamboyant persona complete with lavender velvet *roquelaure* (French
for disguise) (115) tossed over his shoulders. The boundaries separating
constructions of male and female are blurred: "she (Gabrielle) was not
really a woman now, was she? Any more than I was a man. For one
silent second the horror of it all bled through" (151).

Once again, the "horror" may refer to vampiric transformation or it
may also refer to the terror of a radically relativistic universe, and in the
words of Baudrillard, "a brothel of substitution and commutation":

Determinism is dead, indeterminism reigns. We have witnessed the ex-termina-
tion (in the literal sense of the world) of the real of production and of the real of
signification. . . . This historical and social transmutation is readable at every
level. . . . All the grand humanist criteria of value, those of an entire civilization
of moral, aesthetic and practical judgement, are wiped out in our system of
images and signs. Everything becomes undecidable. (*Symbolic Exchange* 27-
28)

It is a universe of nihilism, according to Baudrillard, one which lacks the
depth and fixed foundation required for meaning. It would seem that
Lestat's role is to communicate and exemplify the postulates of nihilism,
and in doing so, he unleashes the wrath of fellow fiends who cling to old
beliefs and reference points. He shatters mysteries "like so much glass.
. . . You break and that is all" (197), he's told, leaving nothing to fill the
void. Lestat exemplifies the "deserted metaphors" (313) of the postmodern age he parodies so well, acutely aware of "that din, that dissonance,
that never ending shrill articulation of the meaninglessness" (313) and of
the "time when man was the center of this great world in which we

roam, a time when for every question there had been an answer" (198). Even the dark gift, the ritual and sacrifice of human blood, is transformed into an empty metaphor, a sign robbed of a representative equivalent. At one point in history, in the dimly envisioned groves of the mythical lands of Dionysus and in the transubstantiating creed of Christianity, the sacrifice had meaning. "If there was not meaning, at least there was the luster of congruence, the stunning repetition of the *same old theme*. And the god dies. And the god rises. But this time no one is redeemed" (437).

A variation on that same old theme is resuscitated, however, in the empty frenzy of Lestat's rock concert, the climax of the novel. The pagan ritual or Christian mass, with its promise of transcendence, gives way to the mass (as in Lestat's concert audience), a ritual diverted into the spectacular and divested of meaning. At the rock concert, Lestat and his musicians are not pagan gods worshiped by thousands waiting to be consumed in a Dionysian frenzy but simply a counterfeit, a simulation, "an impossible hallucination on the giant screens" (469):

Twilight, and everywhere light hit, the crowd went into convulsions. What was it about this sound? It signaled man turned into mob—the crowds surrounding the guillotine, the ancient Romans screaming for Christian blood. But there was no violence here; there was no death—only this childish exuberance pouring forth from young mouths and young bodies, an energy focused and contained as naturally as it was cut loose. (467-68)

In the mode of ultimate irony, the rock concert is a simulation of the social and the transcendent, emptied of the promise of death, ecstasy, or salvation. The masses are trapped within a universe of simulacra in which it is impossible to distinguish between the spectacle and the real. Interiority, subjectivity, and meaning are replaced with obscenity, fascination, and relativity in a seductive play of consumption. This is not a spectacle governed by gratuitous expenditure, but rather an entertainment emblemmatic of economic co-optation, in which a potentially transgressive force is neutered and effectively pulled into the process of exchange value and commodification. It is cool seduction that allows for the co-optation of anarchic expenditure, the "new evil" (464) which Lestat represents and screams to the oblivious masses attending his concert: "All your Demons are visible/All your Demons are material" (472). The horror is that the unreal—the simulacra, the counterfeit, the impossible hallucination on giant screens—has become real.

CONCLUSION

Throughout this book it has been my intention to suggest that a gothic pall hangs over the texts that comprise America's literary history, and to propose that same shadow extends to contemporary novels in a continuum which persists in shaping and reflecting a cultural milieu driven by socio-economic contexts. However, this supposition, predicated on the subversion, seduction, consumption equation, gives rise to further questioning and, ideally, to reconsiderations of the whole of the American canon which has long been divided into the separate camps of realism and romance, marginal and mainstream. Undeniably, it is paradoxical that the romance genre, a subset of which is the gothic novel, provides the outline upon which materialization as social sign is drawn. This paradox is at once accentuated and deciphered by Morrison's, Oates's, and Rice's rewriting and subversion of canonical texts, a type of revisioning that gothicizes the American romance by blurring the boundaries between the marginal and the mainstream and, in doing so, proposes a "realist" impetus lurking beneath the cobwebs and dark passageways of the gothic genre. In effect, it is subversive to suggest that first, the romance may be read or rewritten as gothic and, second, that neither legacy, romance or gothic, can be defined simply as out of place or out of time, disengaged from ideology or economics. However, it is also subversive to assign the seductive with the project both of reinforcing and undermining the ostensible gothic formula which the majority of critics has interpreted as psychological or theological in scope. The erotic, albeit repressed and then reformulated in later contemporary gothic texts, can be read several ways, as mirroring religious and psychological states or as expressing a desire that must be directed away from the excessive and nonproductive and reconfigured to find recompense in a culture of consumption. The alignment of the seductive with consumption conjures the true horror of an existence defined by the touchstones of commodification, a bogeyman who is really just a salesman in disguise.

There are those who might argue that "reality" is frightening enough without the special effects provided by the gothic and, indeed, there follows a venerable tradition of realist fiction and a body of criticism that links realistic novels to the socio-economic system. Claude Rehered Flory's *Economic Criticism in American Fiction: 1792-1900*

(1936) and Walter F. Taylor's *The Economic Novel in America* (1942) trace American novelists' critical responses to social, political, and economic challenges. In *The Image of Money* (1969), Jan Dietrichson offers a comprehensive discussion of the image and function of money in Henry James and William Dean Howells, a historical examination of wealth and the Gilded Age. The late seventies and eighties brought focused analyses on the relation between literary and economic exchange. In Marc Shell's *The Economy of Literature* (1978) and *Money, Language, and Thought* (1982), similarities are drawn between metaphorization and economic representation and exchange, positing that all literary works can be studied in terms of economic form rather than just in terms of economic content (Economy 154). Continuing in this vein, Michael T. Gilmore, Walter Benn Michaels, and Wai-Chee Dimock regard literary products as commodities and literary creation as an aspect of industrialization and production. In *American Romanticism and the Marketplace,* Gilmore analyzes the connections between writers and the market through their reactions and responses to the socio-economic challenges of the nineteenth century. How, when, and why they published their texts becomes his focus. Walter Benn Michaels offers a New Historicist approach predicated on two assumptions, the first of which posits that literary works should be studied in relation to the economic conditions and cultural values of their particular period and, second, that all social activities are essentially economic, involving evaluation and exchange.

At their foundation, these perspectives share a common belief in the realistic novel's role of social reconstruction. As Da Zheng asserts in *Moral Economy and American Realistic Novels*:

Ever since its emergence as a new genre, the novel has been carrying an ideological function of problem solving, and much of this function is performed with its formal designs. By selecting, omitting, and arranging social facts, the novel exercises its explanatory and problem-solving capacities which no other cultural medium could adequately substitute for. (10)

Analogously, Albert Habegger argues that novel-reading always was and has become a type of prescriptive exercise, dealing with "potential life-consequences" and "life-processes" (ix) with which readers must grapple. Consequently, he makes a case for realism as "the central and preeminent literary type in democratic society" (vii). This alignment of realism with ideological function is problematic, losing currency in its reluctance to engage the tropic, that is, to yoke the economic with the discursive. In its essence, the novel, whether falling within the category of realism or romance, is not a system of ideas braced by a cogent set of arguments. Instead, the "literal" component of realism, romance, or gothic is simultaneously supported or undermined by the inescapably rhetorical nature of language, a process which allows texts to be read against themselves through their tropological structures. So to come full circle and return to the contention that "reality," as represented through realism, is frightening enough—that supposition does not prevent the gothic genre, with its antimimetic, allegorical, and symbolic structure, from exerting its subversive influence not only as an expression of social experience conducted at the level of commodity-form but also as an important component of the American literary canon as a whole.

The question of canon is, typically, a contentious one and pivotal to a discussion of the place of realism, romance, and gothic in the traditional hierarchy of literary production. Habegger is most direct in his claim that he regards "the realistic novel as a principal type of American fiction . . . the central and preeminent literary type in democratic society" (vii). However, the genre did not make an appearance until the last third of the nineteenth century, a response to the "bewildering and sometimes sudden change in social conditions and living patterns, . . . the explosion of violent class conflict, and the emergent features of a mass society" (Borus 12). Conversely, the romance clearly predates realism both chronologically and in its professed subject matter. According to Daniel H. Borus, Hawthorne considered his craft as a "triumph of the primacy of the nonvisible world over the visible one" (37), a way of transcending social determinants and as a protest against material forces. Yet, paradoxically, writers such as Hawthorne, Melville, and Poe wrestled with an acute ambivalence towards the marketplace and literary commodification (Charvat, *Literary Publishing and Profession*). While not a subject of consideration in this discussion, that ambivalence gestures toward the latent materialist impulses inherent in the gothic genre, a willingness to struggle with social and ethical implications while moving away from the plots of progress (Kilgour, *From Communion*) suggested by realist texts.

The question of commodification extends to the book itself as an item of consumption while recognizing more directly the role of the consumer or reader, in other words, the chain of receptions from one generation to the next. This issue emerges from my discussion of the gothic as a topic that requires further exploration in terms of how texts work both within and outside the canon and, more specifically, within the dialectic of production, reception, and the complexities of literary historiography. What is the difference, in the context of reception theory, between a novel by Hawthorne or Morrison? What makes the same text a best-seller by nineteenth-century standards and a canonical work outside the popular culture orbit one hundred years later? How is the commodification of culture represented in literary texts and, in turn, how has the commodification of literature itself evolved? The boundaries between realism and romance/gothic are not as fixed as once supposed, a matter more of "reception" than established definitions. A text by Hawthorne or Poe is as "real" as a text by Howells or Dreiser, as much a response to and a part of discursive and cultural practices. In other words, just as the romance can be read as gothic, the gothic can be read as realism, not in terms of mimetic accuracy but in terms of social and economic implications that trace both thematically and historically conditioned changes and variations in reader response.

Untangling the strands of the semiological code of capitalism requires focusing on the principles of production and consumption as they relate to desire within a culture firmly situated within the marketplace. Such a reconsideration can reopen certain canonical texts and reposition them in a context that questions traditional ways of reading them, simultaneously enriching the response to texts that might otherwise be regarded as one-dimensional within a contemporary and more popular context. Certainly, the result of such an inquiry will be a return to an engagement with the subversive, seductive, and most certainly, a culture of consumption from which, in true American gothic fashion, there is no escape.

WORKS CONSULTED

Adamson, Joseph. *Melville, Shame, and the Evil Eye: A Psychoanalytic Reading*. Albany: U of New York P, 1997.

Anderson, Linda. "The Re-imagining of History in Contemporary Women's Fiction." *Plotting Change: Contemporary Women's Fiction*. Ed. Linda Anderson. New York: Routledge, 1990. 129-41.

Auerbach, Nina. *Our Vampires, Ourselves*. Chicago: U of Chicago P, 1995.

——. *Woman and Demon*. Cambridge, CT: Harvard UP, 1982.

Badley, Linda. *Writing Horror and the Body: The Fiction of Stephen King, Clive Barker, and Anne Rice*. Westport, CT: Greenwood, 1996.

Bailey, J. O. "What Happens in 'The Fall of the House of Usher'?" *American Literature* 35 (1964): 445-66.

Bakhtin, M. M. *The Dialogic Imagination*. Ed. Michael Holquist. Austin: U of Texas P, 1981.

Barnett, Pamela E. "Figurations of Rape and the Supernatural in *Beloved*." *PMLA* 112 (1997): 418-27.

Barthes, Roland. *Image-Music-Text*. Trans. Stephen Heath. London: Fontana, 1977.

Bataille, Georges. *Eroticism: Death and Sensuality*. Trans. Mary Dalwood. San Francisco: City Lights, 1986.

——. *Visions of Excess: Selected Writings: 1927-1939*. Trans. Alan Stoekl. Minneapolis: U of Minnesota P, 1985.

Baudrillard, Jean. *The Consumer Society: Myths and Structures*. Trans. Brian Singer. London: Sage, 1998.

——. *For a Critique of the Political Economy of the Sign*. Trans. Charles Levin. St. Louis: Telos, 1981.

——. *Mirror of Production*. Trans. Mark Poster. St. Louis: Telos, 1975.

——. *Seduction*. Trans. Brian Singer. New York: St. Martin's, 1990.

——. *Simulacra and Simulation*. Trans. Sheila Faria Glaser. Ann Arbor: U of Michigan P, 1994.

——. *Symbolic Exchange and Death*. Trans. Iain Hamilton Grant. London: Sage, 1993.

Baym, Nina. "Concepts of the Romance in Hawthorne's America." *Nineteenth-Century Fiction* 38 (1984): 426-48.

Behrendt, Stephen C. "Language and Style in Frankenstein." *Approaches to Teaching Shelley's Frankenstein*. Ed. Stephen C. Behrendt. New York: MLA, 1990. 78-84.

Bell, Millicent. "Woman in the Jamesian Eye." *The Book Page.* New York: Mercantile Library of New York, 1995. 1-8.

Benvenuto, Bice. *The Works of Jacques Lacan: An Introduction.* London: Free Association, 1986.

Bercovitch, Sacvan. "The Rites of Assent: Rhetoric, Ritual, and the Ideology of American Consensus." *The American Self: Myth, Ideology, and Popular Culture.* Ed. Sam B. Girgus. Albuquerque: U of New Mexico P, 1981. 5-43.

Biedermann, Hans. *The Wordsworth Dictionary of Symbolism.* New York: Facts on File, 1992.

Blanchot, Maurice. *Vicious Circles.* Barrytown, NY: Station Hill, 1985.

Bodziock, Joseph. "Richard Wright and the Afro-American Gothic." *Richard Wright: Myths and Realities.* Ed. C. James Trotman. New York: Garland, 1988. 27-42.

Borus, Daniel H. *Writing Realism: Howells, James, and Norris in the Mass Market.* Chapel Hill: U of North Carolina P, 1989.

Brooks, Peter. *Psychoanalysis and Storytelling.* Cambridge, MA: Blackwell, 1994.

Brown, Charles Brockden. *Edgar Huntley, or, Memoirs of a Sleep-Walker.* New York: Penguin, 1988.

——. *Wieland, or, The Transformation, an American Tale.* Garden City, New York: Doubleday, 1962.

Bryant, Jerry H. *The Open Decision: The Contemporary American Novel and Its Intellectual Background.* New York: Free, 1970.

Carroll, Noel. *The Philosophy of Horror, or Paradoxes of the Heart.* New York: Routledge, 1990.

Castronovo, Russ. *Fathering the Nation: American Genealogies of Slavery and Freedom.* Berkeley: U of California P, 1995.

Charvat, William. *Literary Publishing in America, 1790-1850.* Philadelphia: U of Pennsylvania P, 1959.

——. *The Profession of Authorship in America, 1800-1870.* Ed. Matthew J. Bruccoli. Columbus: Ohio State UP, 1968.

Chase, Richard. *The American Novel and Its Tradition.* New York: Doubleday, 1957.

Clair, John. *The Ironic Dimension in the Fiction of Henry James.* Pittsburgh: Duquesne UP, 1965.

Clover, Carol J. "Her Body, Himself: Gender in the Slasher Film." *Fantasy and the Cinema.* Ed. James Donald. London: British Film Institute, 1989. 91-133.

Creighton, Joanne V. *Joyce Carol Oates.* New York: Twayne, 1992.

Davidson. Cathy. *Revolution and the Word: The Rise of the Novel in America.* New York: Oxford UP, 1986.

Day, William Patrick. *In the Circles of Fear and Desire: A Study of Gothic Fantasy*. Chicago: U of Chicago P, 1985.

Dayan, Joan. "Amorous Bondage: Poe, Ladies, and Slaves." *American Literature* 66 (1994): 239-73.

——. "Romance and Race." *Columbia History of the American Novel*. Ed. Emory Elliott. New York: Columbia UP, 1991. 89-109.

D'haen, Theo. "Postmodern Gothic." *Exhibited by Candlelight: Sources and Developments in the Gothic Tradition*. Ed. Valeria Tinkler-Villani, Peter Davidson, Jane Stevenson. Amsterdam-Atlanta, GA: Rodopi, 1995. 283-94.

Dickstein, Morris. *Double Agent: The Critic and Society*. New York: Oxford UP, 1992.

Dietrichson, Jan W. *The Image of Money*. New York: Humanities, 1969.

Dimock, Wai-Chee. "Degrading Exchange: Edith Wharton's House of Mirth." *PMLA* 100 (1985): 783-92.

Doane, Joan. "In Love with Consumption: From Anne Rice's Novels to Neil Jordan's Interview with the Vampire." *Vision/Revision: Adapting Contemporary American Fiction by Women to Film*. Bowling Green, OH: Bowling Green State U Popular P, 1996. 227-47.

Druce, Robert. "Pulex Defixus, or, the Spellbound Flea: An Excursion into Porno-Gothic." *Exhibited by Candlelight: Sources and Developments in the Gothic Tradition*. Ed. Valeria Tinkler-Villani, Peter Davidson, Jane Stevenson. Amsterdam-Atlanta, GA: Rodopi, 1995. 221-42.

Eco, Umberto. *A Theory of Semiotics*. Bloomington: Indiana UP, 1976.

Ellis, Kate. "Monsters in the Garden: Mary Shelley and the Bourgeois Family." *The Endurance of Frankenstein: Essays on Mary Shelley's Novel*. Ed. George Levine, and U. C. Knoepflmacher, Berkeley: U of California P, 1979. 123-42.

Evans, Martha Noel. "Hysteria and the Seduction of Theory." *Seduction and Theory: Readings of Gender, Representation, and Rhetoric*. Ed. Dianne Hunter. Urbana: U of Illinois P, 1989. 73-85.

Faulkner, William. *Absalom, Absalom!* New York: Random House, 1986.

Ferguson, Rebecca. "History, Memory, and Language in Toni Morrison's *Beloved*." *Feminist Criticism: Theory and Practice*. Ed. Susan Sellers, Linda Hutcheon, and Paul Perron. Toronto: U of Toronto P, 1991. 109 27.

Fiedler, Leslie A. *Love and Death in the American Novel*. New York: Stein & Day, 1966.

Fishburn, Katherine. *Women in Popular Culture: A Reference Guide*. Westport, CT: Greenwood, 1979.

Fleenor, Juliann E. *The Female Gothic*. Montreal: Eden, 1983.

Flory, Claude Rehered. *Economic Criticism in American Fiction, 1792 to 1900*. Philadelphia: Quadrangle, 1936.

Frow, John. *Time and Commodity Culture: Essays in Cultural Theory and Post-modernity*. Oxford: Clarendon, 1997.

Gardner, John. "The Strange Real World." *Joyce Carol Oates: Modern Critical Views*. Ed. Harold Bloom. New York: Chelsea House, 1987. 99-104.

Gates, Henry Louis, Jr. "The Blackness of Blackness: A Critique of the Sign and the Signifying Monkey." *Studies in Black American Literature Volume 1: Black American Prose Theory*. Ed. Joe Wexlmann and Chester J. Fontenot. New York: Methuen, 1984. 129-81.

Genette, Gérard. *Narrative Discourse: An Essay in Method*. Trans. Jane E. Lewin. Ithaca: Cornell UP, 1980.

Genosko, Gary. *Baudrillard and Signs: Signification Ablaze*. London: Routledge, 1994.

Gilbert, Sandra M., and Susan Gubar. *The Madwoman in the Attic*. New Haven: Yale UP, 1979.

Gilmore, Michael T. *American Romanticism and the Marketplace*. Chicago: U of Chicago P, 1985.

Goddu, Teresa A. *Gothic America: Narrative, History, and Nation*. New York: Columbia UP, 1997.

Goode, John. "Women and the Literary Text." *The Rights and Wrongs of Women*. Ed. Juliet Mitchell, Anne Oakley. Harmondsworth: Penguin, 1976. 217-55.

Grixti, Joseph. *Terrors of Uncertainty: The Cultural Contexts of Horror Fiction*. New York: Routledge, 1989.

Gross, Louis. *Redefining the American Gothic: From Wieland to The Day of the Dead*. Ann Arbor: UMI Research, 1989.

Guiley, Rosemary. *The Encyclopedia of Ghosts and Spirits*. New York: Facts on File, 1992.

Gwin, Minrose C. "Green-eyed Monsters of the Slavocracy: Jealous Mistresses in Two Slave Narratives." *Conjuring: Black Women, Fiction, and Literary Tradition*. Ed. Marjorie Pryse and Hortense J. Spillers. Bloomington: Indiana UP, 1985. 39-52.

——. "(Re)Reading Faulkner as Father and Daughter." *Refiguring the Father: New Feminist Readings of Patriarchy*. Ed. Patricia Yaeger and Beth Wallace-Kowaleski. Carbondale: U of Illinois P, 1989. 238-58.

Habegger, Alfred. *Gender, Fantasy, and Realism in American Literature*. New York: Columbia UP, 1982.

Harris, Trudier. *Fiction and Folklore: The Novels of Toni Morrison*. Knoxville: U of Tennessee P, 1991.

Haug, Wolfgang. *Critique of Commodity Aesthetics: Appearance, Sexuality, and Advertising in Capitalist Society*. Trans. Robert Bock. Cambridge: Polity, 1986.

Hawthorne, Nathaniel. *The House of the Seven Gables.* New York: Penguin, 1986.

——. *The Scarlet Letter. Heath Anthology of American Literature.* Ed. Paul Lauter. Lexington, MA: Heath, 1994. 2178-2315.

Hill, Robert W. "A Counterclockwise Turn in James's 'Turn of the Screw'." *Twentieth-Century Literature* 27 (1981): 53-71.

Hutcheon, Linda. "Introduction." *Double-Talking: Essays on Verbal and Visual Ironies in Canadian Contemporary Art and Literature.* Ed. Linda Hutcheon. Toronto: ECW, 1992. 11-38.

——. *Poetics of Postmodernism: History, Theory, Fiction.* New York: Routledge, 1988.

——. *A Theory of Parody: The Teachings of Twentieth-Century Art Forms.* New York: Methuen, 1985.

Ingebretsen, Edward J. "Anne Rice: Raising Holy Hell, Harlequin Style." *The Gothic World of Anne Rice.* Ed. Gary Hoppenstand and Ray B. Browne. Bowling Green, OH: Bowling Green State U Popular P, 1996. 91-110.

——. *Maps of Heaven, Maps of Hell: Religious Terror as Memory from the Puritans to Stephen King.* Armonk, NY: Sharpe, 1996.

Jackson, Rosemary. *Fantasy: The Literature of Subversion.* London: Methuen, 1981.

James, Henry. *Henry James: The Stories of the Supernatural.* Ed. Leon Edel. New York: Taplinger, 1970.

——. "The Jolly Corner." *American Poetry and Prose.* Ed. Norman Foerster and Norman Grabo. Boston: Houghton Mifflin, 1971. 712-26.

——. *Selected Letters.* Ed. Leon Edel. Cambridge: Harvard UP, 1987.

——. "The Turn of the Screw." *The Turn of the Screw and Other Stories.* Oxford: Oxford UP, 1992.

Jameson, Fredric. *The Political Unconscious: Narrative as a Socially Symbolic Act.* Ithaca: Cornell UP, 1981.

Janeway, Elizabeth. "'But Why Do They Read Those Things?' The Female Audience and the Gothic Novel." *The Female Gothic.* Ed. Julian E. Fleenor. Montreal: Eden, 1983. 57-68.

Johnson, Barbara. "My Monster, Myself." *Diacritics* 12 (1982): 2-10.

Jordan, Cynthia S. *Second Stories: The Politics of Language, Form, and Gender in Early American Fictions.* Chapel Hill: U of North Carolina P, 1989.

Kazin, Alfred. *Bright Book of Life: American Novelists and Storytellers from Hemingway to Mailer.* Boston: Little, Brown, 1973.

Kendall, Lyle H., Jr. "The Vampire Motif in 'The Fall of the House of Usher.'" *College English* 24 (1963): 450-53.

Kerr, Elizabeth. *William Faulkner's Gothic Domain.* Port Washington, NY: Kennikat, 1979.

Kilgour, Maggie. *From Communion to Cannibalism: An Anatomy of Metaphors of Incorporation*. Princeton: Princeton UP, 1990.

——. *The Rise of the Gothic Novel*. New York: Routledge, 1995.

Knoepflmacher, U. C. "Thoughts on the Aggression of Daughters." *The Endurance of Frankenstein: Essays on Mary Shelley's Novel*. Ed. George Levine and U. C. Knoepflmacher. Berkeley: U of California P, 1979. 89-119.

Kowalewski, Michael. *Deadly Musings: Violence and Verbal Form in American Fiction*. Princeton: Princeton UP, 1993.

Kristeva, Julia. *Language and the Unknown: An Initiation into Linguistics*. Trans. Anne Menke. London: Harvester Wheatsheaf, 1989.

Lacan, Jacques. "Desire and the Interpretation of Desire in Hamlet." *French Yale Studies* 55-56 (1977): 11-52.

——. *Ecrits: A Selection*. Trans. Alan Sheridan. New York: Norton, 1977.

——. *Ego in Freud's Theory and in the Technique of Psychoanalysis, Seminar II, 1954-55*. Ed. Jacques-Alain Miller. Trans. Sylvana Tomaselli. New York: Norton, 1988.

——. *Feminine Sexuality*. Ed. Juliet Mitchell, Jacqueline Rose. Trans. Jacqueline Rose. New York: Norton, 1985.

——. *Four Fundamental Concepts of Psychoanalysis*. Ed. Jacques-Alain Miller. Trans. Alan Sheridan. New York: Norton, 1978.

——. *Freud's Papers on Technique, Seminar I, 1953-54*. Ed. Jacques-Alain Miller. Trans. John Forrester. New York: Norton, 1988.

——. "Seminar on the Purloined Letter." *Yale French Studies* 48 (1972): 38-72.

Lanser, Susan Sniader. *The Narrative Act: Point of View in Prose Fiction*. Princeton: Princeton UP, 1981.

Leverenz, David. "Mrs. Hawthorne's Headache: Reading *The Scarlet Letter*." *The Mother Tongue: Essays in Feminist Psychoanalytic Interpretation*. Ed. S. N. Garner, C. Kahane, and M. Sprengnether. Ithaca: Cornell UP, 1985. 194-216.

Levin, Harry. *The Power of Blackness: Hawthorne, Poe, Melville*. New York: Knopf, 1958.

Liberman, Terri R. "Eroticism As Moral Fulcrum in Rice's *Vampire Chronicles*." *The Gothic World of Anne Rice*. Ed. Robert Hoppenstand and Ray B. Browne. Bowling Green, OH: Bowling Green State U Popular P, 1996. 109-21.

Lukacher, Ned. "'Hanging Fire': The Primal Scene of the 'Turn of the Screw.'" *Henry James's Daisy Miller, The Turn of the Screw, and Other Tales*. Ed. Harold Bloom. New York: Chelsea House, 1987. 117-32.

Lustig, T. J. *Henry James and the Ghostly*. Cambridge: Cambridge UP, 1994.

Malin, Irving. *New American Gothic*. Carbondale: Southern Illinois UP, 1962.

Marigny, Jean. *Le Vampire dans la Littérature Anglo-Saxonne.* Paris: Diffusion Didier Erudition, 1985.

Martin, Robert K. "Haunted by Jim Crow: Gothic Fictions by Hawthorne and Faulkner." *American Gothic: New Interventions in a National Narrative.* Ed. Robert K. Martin and Eric Savoy. Iowa City: U of Iowa P, 1998. 129-42.

McKinstry, Susan Jaret. "A Ghost of An/Other Chance: The Spinster-Mother in Toni Morrison's Beloved." *Old Maids to Radical Spinsters.* Ed. Laura L. Doan. Urbana: U of Illinois, 1990. 258-74.

Melville, Herman. "Benito Cereno." *Heath Anthology of American Literature, Vol. 1.* Lexington, MA: Heath, 1994. 2597-2654.

——. "Hawthorne and His Mosses." *The Piazza Tales and Other Prose Pieces 1839-1860.* Ed. Harrison Hayford et al. Evanston: Northwestern UP and the Newberry Library, 1987. 239-53.

Michaels, Walter Benn. *The Gold Standard and the Logic of Naturalism.* Berkeley: U of California P, 1987.

Mitchell, Juliet. *Feminine Sexuality: Jacques Lacan and the "École Freudienne."* Ed. and trans. Jacqueline Rose. New York: Norton, 1982.

Moers, Ellen. "Female Gothic." *The Endurance of Frankenstein: Essays on Mary Shelley's Novel.* Ed. George Levine and U.C. Knoepflmacher. Berkeley: U of California P, 1979. 77-87.

——. *Literary Women.* Garden City, NY: Doubleday 1977.

Morrison, Toni. *Beloved.* New York: Knopf, 1987.

——. *Playing in the Dark: Whiteness and the Literary Imagination.* Cambridge: Harvard UP, 1992.

Mulvey, Laura. "Visual Pleasure and Narrative Cinema." *Feminisms: An Anthology of Literary Theory and Criticism.* New Brunswick, NJ: Rutgers UP, 1991. 432-42.

Mussel, Kay. *Women's Gothic and Romantic Fiction· A Reference Guide.* Westport, CT: Greenwood, 1981.

Myers, F. W. H. *Human Personality and Its Survival of Bodily Death.* London: Longmans, 1903.

Oates, Joyce Carol. *Bellefleur.* New York: Dutton, 1980.

Orians, George. *A Short History of American Literature.* New York: Crofts, 1940.

Oxford English Dictionary. 2nd ed. Oxford: Oxford UP, 1979.

Poe, Edgar Allan. *Collected Works of Edgar Allan Poe.* New York: Greyston, 1952.

——. "The Philosophy of Composition." *The Complete Works of Edgar Allan Poe.* Vol. 14. Ed. James A. Harrison. New York: AMS, 1965. 193-208.

Poovey, Mary. "The Anathematized Race: The Governess and Jane Eyre."

   Uneven Developments: The Ideological Work of Gender in Mid-Victorian England. Chicago: U of Chicago P, 1989. 126-63.

Porte, Joel. *The Romance in America: Studies in Cooper, Poe, Hawthorne, Melville, and James.* Middletown, CT: Wesleyan UP, 1969.

Puckett, Newbell Niles. *Folk Beliefs of the Southern Negro.* Chapel Hill: U of North Carolina P, 1926.

Ragland-Sullivan, Ellie. *Jacques Lacan and the Philosophy of Psychoanalysis.* Kent: Croom Helm, 1986.

Ramsland, Katherine. *Prism of the Night: A Biography of Anne Rice.* New York: Dutton, 1991.

Reynolds, David. *Beneath the American Renaissance: The Subversive Imagination in the Age of Emerson and Melville.* Cambridge: Harvard UP, 1989.

Rice, Anne. *Interview with the Vampire.* New York: Knopf, 1976.

——. *The Vampire Lestat.* New York: Knopf, 1985.

——. *The Witching Hour.* New York: Knopf, 1990.

Rich, Adrienne. "When We Dead Awaken: Writing as Re-Vision." *Adrienne Rich's Poetry.* Ed. B. C. Gelpi and A. Gelpi. New York: Norton, 1975. 90-98.

Ringe, Donald A. *Charles Brockden Brown.* Boston: Twayne, 1991.

Roberts, Bette B. *Anne Rice.* New York: Twayne, 1994.

Savoy, Eric. "A Theory of American Gothic." *American Gothic: New Interventions in a National Narrative.* Ed. Robert K. Martin and Eric Savoy. Iowa City: U of Iowa P, 1998. 3-19.

Schwab, Gabriele. "Seduced by Witches: Nathaniel Hawthorne's The Scarlet Letter in the Context of New England Witchcraft Fictions." *Seduction and Theory: Readings of Gender, Representation, and Rhetoric.* Ed. Dianne Hunter. Urbana: U of Illinois P, 1989. 170-94.

See, Fred G. *Desire and the Sign: Nineteenth-Century American Fiction.* Baton Rouge: Louisiana State UP, 1987.

Shaviro, Steven. *Passion and Excess: Blanchot, Bataille, and Literary Theory.* Tallahassee: Florida State UP, 1990.

Shell, Marc. *The Economy of Literature.* Baltimore: Johns Hopkins, 1978.

——. *Money, Language, and Thought: Literary and Philosophical Economies from the Medieval to the Modern Era.* Berkeley: U of California P, 1982.

Shelley, Mary. *Frankenstein.* Philadelphia: Running, 1990.

Showalter, Elaine. "A Criticism of Our Own: Autonomy and Assimilation in Afro-American and Feminist Literary Theory." *Feminisms: An Anthology of Literary Theory and Criticism.* Ed. Robyn R. Warhol and Diane Price Herndl. New Brunswick, NJ: Rutgers UP, 1991. 168-88.

Sjoberg, Leif. "An Interview with Joyce Carol Oates." *Contemporary Literature* 23 (1982): 267-84.

Spillers, Hortense. "Introduction." *Conjuring: Black Women, Fiction and Literary Tradition.* Ed. Marjorie Pryse and Hortense Spillers. Bloomington: Indiana UP, 1985. 1-24.

Spivak, Gayatri Chakravorty. "Three Women's Texts and a Critique of Imperialism." *Feminisms: An Anthology of Literary Theory and Criticism.* Ed. Robyn R. Warhol and Diane Price Herndl. New Brunswick, NJ: Rutgers UP, 1991. 798-814.

Sprengnether, Madelon. "Enforcing Oedipus: Freud and Dora." *In Dora's Case: Freud, Hysteria, Feminism.* Ed. Charles Bernheimer and Claire Kahane. New York: Columbia UP, 1985. 51-71.

Tanner, Tony. *City of Words: American Fiction, 1950-1970.* New York: Harper & Row, 1971.

Tate, Allen, Katherine Anne Porter, and Mark Van Doren. "James: 'The Turn of the Screw' Radio Transcript." *A Casebook on Henry James* The Turn of the Screw. Ed. Gerald Willen. New York: n.p., 1960.

Taylor, Walter F. *The Economic Novel in America.* Chapel Hill: U of North Carolina P, 1942.

Todorov, Tzvetan. *Poétique.* Paris: Seuil, 1973.

Twitchell, James. *Dreadful Pleasures: An Anatomy of Modern Horror.* New York: Oxford UP, 1985.

——. *The Living Dead: A Study of the Vampire in Romantic Literature.* Durham, NC: Duke UP, 1981.

Wald, Patricia. *Constituting Americans: Cultural Anxiety and Narrative Form.* Durham, NC: Duke UP, 1995.

Waller, G. F. *Dreaming America: Obsession and Transcendence in the Fiction of Joyce Carol Oates.* Baton Rouge: Louisiana State UP, 1979.

Wallerstein, Immanuel. "Household Structures and Labour-Force Formation in the Capitalist World-Economy." *Race, Nation, Class: Ambiguous Identities.* London: Verso, 1991. 105-17.

Waxman, Barbara Frey. "Changing History through a Gendered Perspective: A Postmodern Feminist Reading of Morrison's *Beloved.*" *Multicultural Literatures through Feminist/Poststructuralist Lenses.* Ed. Barbara Frey Waxman. Knoxville: U of Tennessee P, 1993. 57-83.

Wesley, Marilyn C. *Refusal and Transgression in Joyce Carol Oates's Fiction.* Westport, CT: Greenwood, 1993.

Wolstenholme, Susan. *Gothic (Re)Visions: Writing Women as Readers.* Albany: SUNY P, 1993.

Zheng, Da. *Moral Economy and American Realistic Novels.* New York: Peter Lang, 1996.

Zizek, Slavoj. *Looking Awry: An Introduction to Jacques Lacan through Popular Culture.* Cambridge: MIT, 1991.

INDEX